INFINITE: RISE OF A REBEL

DIANA PRIYANKA CHOWDHURY

LEGENDARY MYSTICS

CONTENTS

PROLOGUE

"In the beginning, there was no one but Anorea: the supreme, omnipresent, and the most magnificently beautiful being. This dark-skinned, cat-eyed beauty with heavy, long, black, flowing wavy hair existed everywhere as restful darkness—like a warm blanket that wraps you in love and comfort. However, she was very lonely. As forever is a long time to live alone, she decided to invent Creation. Anorea, the one who always existed, darkness incarnate, the one who is present in everyone and everything—that ultimate power gave birth to Areliam, the universe we now reside in

"One moment there was nothing but a blank state of blackness, and then out came creation like an erupting volcano.

"The great eternal mother Anorea tore through her own self to create new existences. She broke herself into four pieces, each piece becoming a planet. Thus, the four everlasting planets Solem, Yonder, Ragonia, and Harbor came to be in the newly formed cosmos. Then, she created the three primordial races through the Mother's Womb present in Solem.

"The Elementals who had the power to create elements, the Anons who had the power to shape those elements, and the Veiled Ones who taught them how to use their powers. Together they created things like the stars, other planets, asteroids, and such. Lastly, it was the Veiled Ones clan of Paradigm that harnessed Anorea's powers and breathed life into all the living beings of this universe. Imagine the

Elementals, under the guidance of Veiled Ones, releasing an endless stream of fire out into the void, and the Anons shaping stars out of that. Then envision the Elementals and Anons building planets around those stars, that the Paradigms populated with intelligent life forms.

"The Anons were one of the most powerful creations of Anorea. However, very soon after the beginning of the universe, they were no longer happy to just remain as one of the best. They wanted to control all. So, they started a war. This war went on for thousands of years, where Elementals would create destructive elements like lightning to weaken the Anon, till they figured out how to shape the newly created element in a way that could be harmful to the Elementals.

"The Veiled Ones tried their best to keep out of the conflict. However, we Veiled Ones are the keepers of knowledge. As such, we knew how disastrous the continuous clashing of the two primordial races would prove for the freshly born universe. So finally, we mediated between the Elementals and the Anons and convinced them to take turns in ruling the universe. The Veiled Ones created a tournament, the winners of which would go on to rule the universe until the winners of the next tournament were declared. The Anons pretended to accept this but worked behind the scenes to destroy the Elementals and subjugate the Veiled Ones with a power-binding curse.

"When all-out war finally broke, most Veiled Ones sided with the Elementals. However, then the Anons activated their power-binding curse and destroyed the strongest clans of the Veiled Ones. The Veiled Ones were given an ultimatum by the Anons: either help the Anons defeat the Elementals or lose their powers forever. This left the Veiled Ones with no choice but to turn on the Elementals. So, on the eve of the Battle of the Behemoths, the Veiled Ones betrayed the Elementals. With their help, the Anons gained victory over the Elementals. Once they won, though, the Anons enslaved the Veiled Ones to make sure they could never rise up against the Anon rule."

"Pa, were we Veiled Ones really very powerful before?" asked a beautiful five-year-old black boy getting a haircut, sitting on his father's lap. The boy was named Leon

Hearth-Bringer, lovingly called Leo by most. His father was telling him this story to keep him still while cutting his hair.

"Yes, Leo, we were. Now, stay still so I can properly cut your hair," replied his father Calaren Hearth-Bringer.

They were sitting somewhere in Solem's countryside under a beautiful light pink sky. The weather was nice. The rays of Eloth, the red giant star Solem was currently orbiting around, made the day shine brighter. There were people nearby but not too many. The black Veiled Ones were mostly dressed in rags while the white Anons wore fancy clothes. Most were minding their business. Nonetheless, a few men more interested in controlling others' lives than their own were still present.

"Hey, you! How dare you impart that information. Don't you know Veiled Ones are forbidden from holding knowledge! You must be punished," said a white man clad in garbs pricier than his character.

Calaren couldn't even say anything back before the man called more people like him who together started to beat him. Leo's father had no option but to take the beating quietly so that Leo could remain unharmed. The men used sticks, rocks, and clubs to beat Calaren until he was heavily bleeding and senseless.

"Stop! Please stop. Please don't hurt my father. He didn't do anything wrong," pleaded Leo, but the men didn't stop. Leo tried to pull Calaren out, but his small hands couldn't reach his father. So, Leo went around asking for help from others at the scene. No one helped him. People chose to stay silent, averting their eyes rather than stepping in to stop the violence.

Until a miracle happened. A black man stepped up to interfere. A ball of fire engulfed the men beating up Leo's father. The men screamed and rolled on the ground to put out the flames. After the fires were dowsed, they got up on their feet, ready to bring down the man who had attacked them. Except, they stood frozen in fear after seeing who it was.

"I'll personally kill anyone who lays a finger on Calaren Hearth-Bringer or his family," said the man before signaling the men behind him to treat Leo's father. Once Calaren was treated, the man instructed his guards to take Leo and his father back to their home.

Before leaving, Leo went up to the man and said, "Thank you!" The man looked down at Leo and nodded his head.

Leo was so traumatized by this event that he forgot to ask the man's name. The only thing he noticed to remember him by was a cat face on his wrist. However, Leo did learn an important lesson that day: No one can stand alone against injustice.

Chapter One

G old-plated.

    Gold plating is a process through which cheap objects are made to seem valuable. Shiny outside but hollow inside. Leon Hearth-Bringer remembered his mother's explanation of it while he witnessed his people being devalued by their unqualified and overrated masters.

Leo looked at the two separate lines in front of the majestic gates of Shalom. One of the Veiled Ones and the other of the Anons. He couldn't help but notice the differences in treatment. Shalom is the shining city of Solem. Built on top of the magical catacombs of caves known as the Mother's Womb. It is the only remnant from the birthing days of the universe of Areliam. From its immaculately clean streets to its beautiful residential and work buildings, to its tranquil parks and lakes, everything is maintained through the labor of the enslaved Veiled Ones. However, the only ones allowed to enjoy all these services are the Anons, and a few chosen token Veiled Ones on their side.

It was an extremely rare and joyous day. Today, the Mother's Womb would give life to another being, an event that hasn't happened since the birth of the three primordial races. However, the Anons restricted the number of Veiled Ones who can enter the city. Not only that, the small number of Veiled Ones with entry permits were still made to wait at the gate.

The line with the Anons had but only one guard, who served more as an informant to the travelling Anons from outside of Shalom—that line was moving rapidly. However, there was a mile-long line of Veiled Ones, all being questioned and searched thoroughly before entering the city. *It's so pathetically funny that the Veiled Ones waiting to get in today, looked upon with so much suspicion and distrust, are the same Veiled Ones without whom the city of Shalom would stop functioning.*

Leo stood impatiently with his parents in the line for Veiled Ones to enter Shalom. Today, all the Veiled Ones going inside Shalom wore their best clothes. It still wasn't much compared to the elaborate clothing of the Anons, though. *What is the point of all this? Why did the Anons eradicate the Elementals and enslave us Veiled Ones?* He took another look at the gleaming entrance to Shalom and then at the mistreatment of the Veiled Ones waiting in line.

It's a trick! The Anons can't possibly run everything by themselves. We Veiled Ones are keepers of knowledge and magic. We were the ones who taught both the Anons and the Elementals how to use their powers in the first place! They need us! However, the Anons don't want us to know that, lest we claim our rightful place as their equals! So, the reason they enslaved us was to make us do all the hard work of keeping Areliam prosperous, without paying us any compensation. That way, they can hog all the good things only for themselves. I can't be the only one seeing this through. It's so obvious that others must see this too! So, why isn't anyone else speaking out against it?

Seeing his son becoming restless, Calaren Hearth-Bringer reached out and touched Leo's shoulders. "Remember what we talked about, Leo."

"Don't worry, I'll remember not to raise any questions," Leo replied, shaking off his father's hand.

June Heath-Bringer reached out to hold Leo's hand, smiled, and said, "It's for our own good, sweetheart." Leo looked hard at both of his parents. Calaren was a handsome, lean, tall, middle-aged black man with a shaved head who looked much younger than his age. June was around the same age as Calaren, who also looked much younger. She had light brown skin, was plump and possessed very short but thickly lustrous hair. However, now both of their beautiful faces were covered in fear. Before Leo could say something to calm them, one of the Anon guards signaled the person in front of them to step forward.

"What is your name, and what are you doing here?" asked the guard suspiciously.

"My name is Jeriah Gourmetdine, and I work at the Snack Stop in Shalom Square," answered Jeriah.

"Really? That shop is incredibly famous and they have high-quality standards. I have never seen you around here before, though. Now, you aren't lying just to get in town for the festivities, are you?" asked the guard in a tone that said *you do not belong here*.

"No, sir, I am telling the truth. I'm a regular employee of Snack Stop. I have been..."

"Stop," said the guard, holding up his right hand and snorting in disgust as if he smelled something awful. "Look, do you have any proof of working there? If not, just get out of here so I can inspect the others in your lot."

"Ah, yes, sir. See, I'm wearing the uniform of Snack Stop," said Jeriah while pointing towards the Snack Stop logo on his uniform.

"Ehh, anyone can get one of those. Now, do you have any substantive proof or not?" asked the irritated guard.

"Well, I already gave my ID to the guard before you. He didn't give it back before going on break, but you can ask anyone around here, sir. They all know I work there," said Jeriah with panic in his voice.

"That's enough," said the guard, getting angry for no reason. "All you cockroaches stick together; so, of course, they'll lie for you. I'd sooner believe a snake before believing any one of you!" yelled the guard as he reached for his weapon.

"Uncle Jeriah, since you won't be going to the Snack Stop today, I'm taking the premade snacks you brought. Better we eat it than it go to waste" said Leo loudly while looking around at everyone he had already passed out the snacks to. While the confrontation between Jeriah and the guard was going on, Leo had slipped out one of the premade snack containers from Jeriah's bag. Then he shared the snack inside with a few of the Anon children and their families going inside Shalom.

Leo looked back at the Anons he had shared the snacks with. "Hey, you guys want some more of this multi-world famous spicy puffed rice salad? The man who usually makes them won't be there today because this guard won't let him into the city. So, consider yourselves lucky that you are the only ones who'll be able to taste this today," said Leo loudly, pointing towards Jeriah.

Hearing Leo say all this, many of the Anons started to direct their attention to the guard in question. Finally, an Anon stepped up to tackle the guard. "Listen here, Guard Boyle, was it? I have been to Shalom before and have seen this man working at the Snack Stop. So, he is speaking the truth. The Snack Stop is one of the major attractions of Shalom, and even though they are going to open later today, I guarantee there is already a big line forming outside its door as we speak. My family and I are planning to stop by there as well. So, let this man go now to serve us all, or I'll report you to Guard Commander Randor," the man spoke angrily.

Seeing his people turn against him, the guard had no choice but to let Jeriah go. "Fine," said Guard Boyle while removing his hand from his weapon. "But I'll be watching you—closely. You got that?" said a fuming Guard Boyle.

"Wait!" yelled Leo while running towards another guard. He stopped right in front of a guard just returning from break. "Hey, are you the one who took all our IDs before going on your looooong break? Well, the other guards are asking for them; so, I'm returning them now." Before that guard could react, Leo snatched the bag full of the mirror IDs hanging from his shoulder and ran back to the Veiled Ones. "Here everyone, grab on to your IDs. Also, to save time, just show them right before entering the city and don't hand them to anyone else again." All the Veiled Ones quickly took back their IDs, but this did not go down well with the guard of the year, the Anon Boyle.

Yet, before Boyle could do anything, Leo grabbed his parents' and Jeriah's mirror IDs and ran towards the kind Anon who had helped him. Once Leo reached him, he immediately pulled out Jeriah's handheld mirror ID, which showed the reflection of its owner, and flashed all of the relevant information about that person. "Hello, sir. Look, you were absolutely right about Uncle Jeriah! Also, since you have been so kind here, you can have the rest of the snack." Leo handed the man the container with the snack, then he ran towards Jeriah to hand off his ID. "I'd say you are late enough getting to work as it is, Uncle Jeriah. You should go now before it gets even later," said Leo.

Jeriah said, "Thank you, my lad. I promise I'll never forget this," while quickly taking his ID. Then he ran past all the guards with his full might.

Leo saw Jeriah safely pass the gates, then he returned to his parents and quickly handed them their mirror IDs as well. "Here you go, Pa and Ma. We should get going as well. We have a long day ahead of us too, no?" Leo asked, grinning from ear to ear.

Before the fuming Guard Boyle or Leo's dumbstruck parents could say anything, the kind Anon walked up to them to introduce himself. "Hi, I'm Mathew. Over there is my wife Penelope and our son Mason. We live in Harbor, but usually make at least one trip to Shalom a year. You are Calaren Hearth-Bringer, the famous singer and traveling performer, right? You are so famous, but are really hard to find outside of your events. Who knew it was because you were hiding away here? By the way, you have a bright son, you know. He is like a beautiful and smart baby black panther. It's very rare for your kind to show such intelligence. You should enroll him in the Anon Academy for Veiled Ones back at Harbor."

Leo was getting irritated hearing all this, but before he could set Mathew right, June stepped in.

"Oh no, no, really he doesn't have any powers, so what'll he even do there? It's just he is a bit quick on his feet and likes to help people here and there, but that's all. Right, Leo?" asked June through gritted teeth. Leo knew nothing good ever came out of angering his mother. So, he quietly nodded his head.

"Thank you so much for all the help, Mathew. Also, thank you for the suggestion of enrolling my boy into the Academy as well. But really, he is not worthy. We know because we are his parents. Now we have to get going because I am performing at the Mother's Womb opening ceremony today and need to do some last-minute rehearsals. Well, that's it then. Bye for now and hope to see you guys at the ceremony. Thanks for everything, once again," Calaren said loudly while walking fast towards the city gates, holding on to the IDs in one hand and Leo's hand tightly in the other. June bowed to Mathew and then hurriedly followed behind her husband and son.

"Right, see you there then," said Mathew self-importantly with a proud smile on his face as if he has just righted all that was wrong in the universe.

Leo looked back to catch Mathew's smug smile. *What an idiot! He does know we Veiled Ones go through this torture every single day of our lives, right? One day's survival is no guarantee for the next. Now both Uncle Jeriah and my family are targets. From now on, we have to make sure to avoid Guard Boyle at all costs, because there won't always be someone to stop him.*

***

As soon as they entered the city gates, Calaren and June took Leo to a secluded corner a little bit off the main path and stared down at him angrily for a long while. Finally, Cal spoke up in a stern voice, "What was all that about?"

"What? At no point during what just happened did I ask a question... I think," said Leo while shrugging and smiling mischievously.

"Do not anger me more than you already have, boy," June said in a hushed but firm voice as she put her hands on her hips.

"Ok, then what would you guys have me do? Just stand by while someone we know gets beaten to death for no fault of his own?" Leo retorted crossly.

"You don't know that Jeriah would have been killed or hurt for sure," Cal said in a limp tone.

"Who are you kidding, Pa? You know they have killed people for far less than that. Don't you remember your beating at the countryside! How can you, of all people, let it happen to someone else?" asked an exasperated Leo.

"We keep quiet because that is the only way for us to survive in this world, and you will do so as well if you want to live, child," June answered coldly.

Before Leo could ask how he was supposed to do so or shoot off any of the other questions he had, the sky darkened. The sounds of thousands of wind chimes started tolling from above. The Anons' flying city of Ascendance, currently stationed above the skies of Solem, was getting ready to broadcast. "A message is about to be beamed down," said Calaren. As soon as he finished speaking, a holographic message materialized, where the King and Queen appeared together.

King Ran, a handsome white man with brown eyes and hair, stared down at everyone with a smile. "Great people of the Anon Empire! I hope I find you all in good health and happiness. To all those who have gathered here in Solem and all those who are currently watching us from Harbor and Yonder, from our Anon citizens to all the loyal Veiled Ones in our care, everyone rejoice! Today is a historic day..."

"Loyal Veiled Ones in our care, my ass. Just say slaves, because that is what you have made of us," said Leo, grimacing.

"Language, young one! No child of mine is going to use inappropriate words in front of me," said June, while looking appalled at Leo's utterance of the word *ass*.

Leo looked up at his mother, then looked at his father, trying to hide a snicker, and muttered under his breath. "Fine then. I'll just use these words when you are not around."

"What was that?" asked June while squinting her eyes.

Leo quickly responded, "I was just saying that, oh Anorea, can't they bore someone else with their fake smiles and regular patronizing chats?"

Calaren smirked and replied, "Then how are they going to keep reminding us of who is superior? Anyways, don't pay attention to what they say. Pay attention to who they are surrounded by instead. It will help you identify who you need to watch out for at today's event. See that pale, bald, fat, ugly man with dark eyes standing right behind the King and Queen trying to be seen as much as he can? That man is Emanuel Cursebinder. He is the main one behind the curse that is put on us. Be very careful of him; he can use his words as curses, and his Elemental half gives him the power to create different metals as well. It is best to avoid him at all costs. But by chance, if you have to deal with him, try to be as nice as possible. He won't differentiate between friend or foe when cursing someone."

Leo raised his hand and pointed towards the hologram and asked in a grim voice, "Ok, so who is that shadowy figure whose glimpses keep moving in and out of the frame?"

"Good eye, son," said a pleasantly surprised Calaren. "That mystery black man would be Edwin Gainsworth.

Leo looked at his father in shock and asked, "The same Gainsworth that betrayed us first?"

"Yes," replied Calaren. "The Gainsworth family has always been enormously powerful. The Cursebinders and Spellcasters are branch families of the Gainsworths. However, while Cursebinders focus specifically on curses, the Spellcasters use magic to cast spells. The main family of Gainsworths usually have both spell casting and cursing abilities. Also, they use magic to attract luck and success in whatever they do. They specialize in preventive, protective, attraction, and accumulative spells. You want to prevent an accident or protect yourself from harm, there is a Gainsworth spell for that. You want to attract good health or accumulate wealth, then there is a Gainsworth spell for that. You want to find love, guess what—there is a Gainsworth spell for that as well," said Calaren jokingly.

"Cal, honey, we gotta do something about your sense of humor deteriorating day by day. Not that you had a good amount of it to begin with," said June, while heaving a sigh.

"Well, you are welcome to chime in and show me how it's done, honey," said Calaren in a slightly irritated voice.

June ignored Calaren and said, "Leo, look. See that statuesque man standing by the King, the one with light blue eyes and blond hair. That is Orias the Great. He is the Anon of Fire and the only man of honor among those scoundrels. Also, another key henchman is missing here, Kaint Swordsbane. He is extremely dangerous as well. His Elemental half can create lightning, while his Anon half can control air. You'll recognize him instantly if you are unlucky enough to be in his presence. A tall, fat white man with tanned skin, brown eyes, and long brown hair. He is a boisterous loudmouth who thinks he can do anything he so damn well chooses. Am I missing anything, husband?"

Calaren let his annoyance go and said, "No, nothing, my love," with a smile and softened eyes that only had June in them.

"Umm, Ma. You said the cuss word damn," said Leo, pouting.

"No, I didn't," June denied right away while folding her arms. "Anyways, that's not important right now."

"Okay!" said Leo as he rolled his eyes.

"Just look at them conning the general public! They are handing out entrance permits to the Mother's Womb only to their pre-selected favored ones. None of the Veiled Ones getting those permits, supposedly by chance, ever interact with us regular enslaved Veiled Ones. I haven't even seen any one of them ever step off of Ascendance. They are privileged enough to have been brainwashed by the Anons in thinking enslavement is a blissful thing," said June, while digging her nails in hard on her arms the whole time.

"Careful of what you both say now. We will soon have some unfriendly company," said Calaren as he pointed towards an entourage of armed guards being led by a young Veiled One boy heading straight for them.

CHAPTER TWO

A s the group headed by the boy came closer, he looked to be about thirteen. He seemed healthy and was well dressed. Smooth black skin with bright dark brown eyes and short, black, curly hair. With the confidence and attitude the boy carried as he walked, it didn't look like he had suffered any of the hardships that Leo or most of the other children of Veiled Ones suffer.

The propaganda-filled patronizing speech and giving out of Mother's Womb entrance tickets finished broadcasting just as the boy and the people following him stopped in front of Calaren. The boy started speaking in an authoritative tone and said, "Hello, Mr. Hearth-Bringer. I'm Ethan Gainsworth, son of Edwin Gainsworth. My father and the finance minister Emanuel Cursebinder would like an audience with you and your son before the start of the main event today. So, if you two could please just follow me..."

"I'm not going anywhere without my mother," Leo interjected loudly, cutting off Ethan.

"It'll only be for a short while that you will meet with my father, and Mr. Cursebinder. Your mother can stay with me for that time. Afterward, you will be free to hide behind her again," said Ethan as he eyed Leo holding his mother's hand.

Leo snapped back. "At least my parents don't use me as an errand boy. Oh sorry, it takes two people to make a team of parents. Where is your mother again? Do you even have one? If you do, then can I meet her, cause you know I'm curious to see what kind of mother approves of sending her kid around to harass people."

Even though the whole atmosphere around them was one of cheer and celebration, for a few moments after Leo said those words, it seemed like the immediate area surrounding them had frozen in terror. Then suddenly Ethan lurched at Leo and started to beat him. The Anon guards who were accompanying Ethan all just stood still, doing nothing. Some of them were enjoying seeing one Veiled One beating up another.

June and Calaren both sprang into action to help their son, though. "We are sorry, Leo doesn't know your mother died while protecting Harbor from an Elemental invasion. As you know, knowledge of the past is forbidden to be learned by Veiled Ones. That is why we couldn't tell him all this; that is why he said those words without knowing. So, please, please, please just let him go," June said through her tears as she tried to separate the boys.

Calaren, however, took a more indirect approach. "Your father wanted to speak to both my son and me. So, you need to leave him well enough to do that. Now let him go before it's too late," said Calaren while frantically trying to protect Leo from all of Ethan's punches. Hearing this, Ethan finally relented, but not before sticking a sleeping dart into Leo's arm, causing Leo to pass out while bleeding from his mouth and nose.

"There. That'll keep his mouth shut till we reach my father. Guards, make sure to knock him out again if by chance he does wake up before we get to see my father. Mr. and Mrs. Hearth-Bringer, now bring your useless son and follow me," said Ethan while wiping blood from his face, a result of Leo getting in some counter punches. Calaren picked Leo up in his arms and started following Ethan while a silent rage burned him from within. June, on the other hand, kept wiping away Leo's blood while walking beside her husband as uncontrolled tears flowed down her cheeks. All around them, people were staring in pity and fear, but no one from the crowds of people watching were courageous enough to speak up against what just happened.

It took quite some time to reach their destination: the entrance to the Mother's Womb located, at the center of Shalom. Due to the festivities, the entrance was surrounded by various stalls, shops, and other make-shift arrangements. Ethan and the group entered one such make-shift holding area designated exclusively for the Anons. Then, they went up to a specific tent where Calaren and Leo were supposed to meet with Emanuel Cursebinder and Edwin Gainsworth.

"Mr. Hearth-Bringer, you and your son will wait inside the tent for my father and Mr. Cursebinder while your wife waits outside with me. Hope you are smarter than your son and will comply with us willingly," said Ethan angrily.

"Oh, it's ok. June can join us too, Ethan," said a cheerful voice.

Everyone looked around in shock to see Emanuel Cursebinder peek out of the tent with Edwin Gainsworth standing right behind him.

Emanuel looked at an unconscious, beaten-up Leo in Calaren's arms and said sympathetically, "You guys were so late! Now, I can see why. I'm sorry for your child being hurt, Cal, but now that you are finally here, let us all just talk things out peacefully. Please step in with your child. You come in as well, June."

"But..." Ethan started to speak out in protest.

"No buts, we will take things from here. You go to the infirmary and get yourself treated. So, leave. Now," said Edwin in a *no resistance will be tolerated against my order* voice.

"Yes, Father," said Ethan in a defeated tone while already turning to go towards the infirmary.

"Follow him and make sure he gets treated well and swiftly," Emanuel ordered the guards that had followed Ethan up till now.

"Yes, sir!" said the guards with Ethan before following behind him.

Calaren looked at June, who looked back with fearful eyes. Then he looked down at Leo still unconscious in his arms and noticed that the bleeding had stopped. As Cal looked up from his son, he saw the inside of the tent being equipped with fancy, comfortable chairs, and great food and drinks. *Ok, with this opulent atmosphere, maybe they really just want to talk; even if they wanted to do more, it's not like I can stop them*, thought Calaren. So, he took a deep breath, held it in for a second longer than it should have been held. Then he let it go and signaled with his eyes for June to enter the tent before he stepped in.

"Just set Leon down anywhere. We'll call for a medic right away so you won't have to go anywhere. I'm really sorry that this happened. We just got here a few moments ago, being busy with the broadcast and all. That is why we couldn't attend to you ourselves. However, let's talk now." Emanuel said all this while pestering around Calaren and June, but there was genuine concern in his voice.

Calaren set Leo down on one of the chairs, then turned around and grabbed Emanuel by the collar. "Haven't you had enough!" yelled Calaren. "Now you are back again to take whatever little happiness I have left! What do you want? Spit it out. WHAT DO YOU WANT?" Calaren continued to yell while still holding Emanuel by the collar.

"Our arrangement was for you and your wife only. Your child was not included in the agreement terms," said Edwin in a steely voice while standing with his arms crossed, blocking the exit to the tent.

"Oh yeah, we remember! You tried your best to make sure that I couldn't become a mother. But there is a Goddess Edwin, and she gave us Leon. All your spells, curses and poisons failed; now you have no right on our Leo," said June heatedly while holding Leo tightly.

"It really wasn't like that, June. We had to do what we did to keep you both safe. There was no other way," said Emanuel while gasping for breath as Calaren was still choking him by holding on to his collar too strongly.

"Oh, yes! It had to be done so you can emotionally blackmail us into taking charge of the orphaned Hearth-Bringer children. It had to be done so you can use us as your star puppets. So, because of being childless, we would be attached to those kids just enough to make sure they grow up well, and once that is done, you can use them to your liking. We refused your offer and chose to walk away from everything in exchange for making June incapable of bearing children. You even killed our first child in her mother's womb. So, why are you back now? We have nothing more to give you. Leave us alone once and for all," said Calaren loudly and breathlessly before finally letting go of Emanuel's collar and chucking him across the tent.

Edwin saw Emanuel land on the other side of the tent, yet didn't lift a finger to help. He just kept staring at Calaren. Finally, after moments of painful silence, Edwin said coldly, "We did leave you alone. Even though our agreement was only to let you and your wife have a life of your choosing, we turned a blind eye to your son's existence as well. However, now that your son has activated his powers, we can no longer do that."

"The deal was that after we agree to your orders my family and I will get to choose what we do with our lives. Leon, my son is part of my family, and as such, he too has that right," said Calaren angrily.

"You know us talking to you is just a formality, right? It was Emanuel's idea. He thought you might finally listen to reason. Look where that got him though." Edwin pointed at Emanuel, who had finally gotten off the ground and was trying unsuccessfully to get a word in between Edwin and Calaren. "So, let me be clear. We can do whatever we want to anyone and whenever we want to. You have no power to stop us," said Edwin while walking menacingly till he got right in front of Calaren's face.

"Wrong. It's you who needs us and not the other way around. So, we hold all the power in this scenario. You will either respect this fact or suffer the consequences of not understanding it," said a now awakened Leo—calmly and boldly.

CHAPTER THREE

T he atmosphere inside the tent had turned tense. Edwin shifted his gaze from Calaren to Leo, who by this time had recovered extremely well from Ethan's beating and was standing on his feet. Finally, Edwin the grim, who didn't usually smile much, smirked and said, "You will make me suffer the consequences of my actions?"

"Only if you don't respect our decision," said Leo, standing proud.

"Oh, and exactly how you are going to do that, child?" asked Edwin amusingly.

"By using your secret against you," said a confident Leo.

"Great! However, will you please let me know what secret of ours would that be?" asked Edwin mockingly, his eyebrows raised.

"The secret that you are losing your powers and you need the Hearth-Bringers to help you regain them," said Leo with a mysterious smile.

Suddenly all signs of amusement on Edwin's face disappeared. "Exactly what makes you say this?" he asked menacingly.

"Your Veiled One mark. It is fading, which is a direct sign of you losing your powers," said Leo.

"I have my mark covered. So, how do you know it is fading?" asked Edwin suspiciously as he walked towards Leo.

"I just got beaten to a bloody mess by your son. During that time, I noticed the fading cat face mark on his wrist. Since the strength of our powers is symbolized by the brightness of our marks, and because our powers are linked to our lineage, I knew that if your son's mark is fading yours will be too. Also, as a Gainsworth you should have preventive spells in place that protect you from heavy bodily harm. Yet, I was still able to damage your son a lot. This means your powers are diminishing." Leo said all this while smiling haughtily at his deductive skills.

Edwin stopped well before reaching Leo, turned to look at Emanuel, and said definitely, "This decides it. The boy is too dangerous to be left alone. We must take him into custody right now!"

"Yes, just imagine how much of a benefit he'll be to us in the future. To all of us," said Emanuel while looking at Calaren. "Don't worry. I'll personally take him in under my wing. From education to wealth, he won't be lacking in anything. Also, we'll make sure you and June will be provided for as well. It will be a win-win situation for all!"

"You have to do better than that if you want us, especially me, to cooperate with you," said Leo sharply.

"Enough! Listen, kid! From this point on, you will only speak when spoken to. You have pushed your limits far enough. Any more and I'll put all of you in chains and make you do our bidding forcefully," Edwin spat.

"You can surely do that, but doing so won't serve anyone. I believe the Hearth-Bringers are extremely special amongst all the Veiled Ones. A lot of us can use our powers subconsciously, so the power draining curse doesn't affect us much. Coupled with the fact that our ancestral protections are on par and might even be greater than you Gainsworths ensures our power grows while the power of other Veiled Ones like you diminishes." Leo paused for a brief moment to let the weight of his words sink in.

"However, I'm the most special among all of the current Hearth-Bringers, as I have awakened the healing powers that have remained dormant for generations in our family. As you can see, I'm almost completely healed from your son's attack while he is still getting treated at the infirmary. However, the bad news here is that I don't know how all this works. Now, I bet even you don't know how all this is working. You must have exhausted all resources before reaching out to us. For if there were any other way, then we wouldn't still be talking about all this right now. Under these circumstances, forcing me to use my powers will only damage me and your chances to rectify your weakened powers. The better thing would be to give me the time and space. Then, I can organically discover and use my abilities to help you," said Leo.

"Ok, so what do you want in return?" asked Emanuel hurriedly before Edwin had a chance to do something violent to Leo in his anger.

"Thank you for asking! You must be as smart as people say. I can see that you recognize and act on opportunities fast! So, I don't only want wealth for our family. I also want protection, rank in society, and power. No more of this being bullied by the Anons, or by any of you for that matter," said Leo while looking directly at Edwin.

Emanuel started saying, "I think that is a fair trade..."

"Of course, it is! I am going to be saving all of the Veiled Ones after all! Anyways, I want a high-ranking position for my father and wealthy accommodations and protection provided to us as soon as possible. You can also take this opportunity to assign your people to openly spy on us this time. You know, to make sure we will be doing all your biddings as faithfully as possible," said Leo, still smiling.

"Wait, we do not agree to this!" said June in a panic. Calaren immediately sprinted over to June and held her in his arms to calm her down.

"I agree with June. You guys deserve to lose your powers. We have never helped you before, and we will never help you now or in the future—ever," said Calaren while looking at both Emanuel and Edwin with righteous contempt.

"This is not a negotiation! None of you have any power to accept or deny our orders. We will not allow any resistance!" yelled a fuming Edwin.

"I see we both need time to make our uncooperative parties understand what is at stake. So, I suggest you stay here and reason with this angry old man of a partner while I go backstage to talk some sense into my parents privately," Leo said to Emanuel in a tired voice.

"Yes, I believe that would be for the best," said Emanuel, nodding his head.

"Ok, then we'll meet here again after the end of the event today to discuss more details about our arrangements," said Leo as he walked over to grab some fruits off of the array of platters filled with fancy food items in the corner of the tent.

"Agreed," said Emanuel.

"Ma, Pa, let's go. Pa, don't you have to get ready for your performance as well?" asked Leo while rushing his parents out of the tent. Just before he left, though, Leo couldn't help but grin as he heard Edwin say furiously, "No one talks to us like that, least of all a ten-year-old!"

To this statement, Emanuel just stated matter of factly, "But he is an extremely useful ten-year-old!"

CHAPTER FOUR

T he Hearth-Bringers walked silently towards the staging area. While June was genuinely afraid of what just happened, Calaren was burning with fury, but both of them kept quiet on Leo's signal. Looking around, Leo gulped down the fruits he had taken from the tent. From every corner, he could feel eyes on them. Some were watching them while pretending to do work, and others were just plain staring openly.

It will be really hard to explain everything to Ma and Pa with everyone's attention on us. But we'll have some privacy once we reach backstage. That'll be the time I can tell them why I said all that, thought Leo.

"There you are, Calaren!" shouted the Anon Rosen, a middle-aged balding white man with black eyes and a considerable amount of belly fat, his father's boss. "What took you so long? We have been waiting for a long while, and now there isn't much time before the event starts. You know yours is the first act, right? So, you need to be well prepared," Rosen continued as he jogged over to Cal. However, he took one look at June and stopped abruptly. "Your wife doesn't look so good. Is everything ok?" Rosen asked with genuine concern, while being out of breath.

"Everything is fine! We just need a few minutes to ourselves before the event. I know that'll leave us no room for any last-minute practice runs, but trust me, I will still give a stellar performance, as we've practiced a lot beforehand," said Calaren pleadingly.

"Fine. Just sit your wife down in my office. It should be private, as everyone knows to find me out here looking over the final touches before the event," said Rosen, pointing towards his office.

"Thanks a lot, Rosen. I appreciate it," Calaren said gratefully.

"Don't mention it. I'll come to get you when it's time for your performance. Just try to relax a little before then," said Rosen.

"Will do, boss," replied Calaren, forcing a smile.

The Hearth-Bringers crossed the rest of the way to Rosen's office speedily. As soon as they entered the office space, Leo closed the door then turned towards his parents, put his hands up, and said, "I can explain everything."

"You better, young man. Do you even know what you have done? We have tried so hard to stay out of their traitorous dealings for so long, and now you just volunteered our services? How could you do that, Leo? You have no idea how much we have lost and how much we have suffered to achieve the small amounts of peace and freedoms that we have today. So, how can you throw all that away?" asked Calaren while finally expressing his shock and anger at what had transpired.

"Anyways, it won't work. They won't honor their end of the deal. We are going to lose another child, Cal. We can't let that happen. Do something to stop them. Please do something!" begged June while holding on to Calaren for dear life with shaky hands.

"Explain yourself, Leon Hearth-Bringer. Now!" said Calaren, his voice low but frightening.

"I did what I did because it was the right path to choose," Leo said earnestly.

"You are just ten years old. All you know is what we told you before, which was the bare minimum! So, you have no qualifications to choose any kind of path. All you did was just waste our years of sacrifices with your over-smartness," said Calaren in an utterly frustrated tone.

"No, Pa and Ma. I know this is the right choice, the right path, because in addition to my Hearth-Bringer healing powers being completely activated, my Pathfinder powers just fully activated as well," said Leo, taking off his t-shirt and turning his back towards his parents while also showing the back of his right hand to them. There on his back was the symbol of the Pathfinders; the nine-pointed star was glowing red, and on the back of his hand, the circle denoting the Hearth-Bringer mark was glowing white.

"All of the Veiled Ones, in general, are losing our powers at an alarming rate. It is not only limited to the Gainsworths and the Cursebinders. What once happened to the Pathfinders is happening to all Veiled Ones now. However, I know that I can help them. But don't worry; we won't need to team up with Edwin Gainsworth and Emanuel Cursebinder to do so. Something will happen during this event that will give us the chance to get away to a safe place. So, we won't even need to go back and negotiate the rest of the deal with them," said Leo enthusiastically while putting his t-shirt back on.

June and Calaren looked at their son's completely healed face and thought of the activated Pathfinder and Hearth-Bringer marks in awestruck quietness until finally an astonished June spoke up. "Please start making some sense, boy! I don't know what your newly activated powers are telling you, but I can tell you this: no matter where we run off to, that Edwin Gainsworth will find us. He always finds his prey. There is no escaping him," said June as she rocked herself in an attempt to calm her fears.

"No, he won't. None of them will be able to reach us where we will be going. I can guarantee that," said Leo confidently.

"How are you so sure, and where exactly is this place that is safe from the Anons? You just activated your powers. As it is, there isn't much information about Pathfinders and how their powers work in the first place. So, how are we supposed to trust you in this?" asked an irritably confused Calaren as he started pacing throughout the space.

"Pa, it's this feeling in the gut. The same subconscious prompting you get when you use your Hearth-Bringer powers. Trust me. All we have to do is wait for that right moment during the ceremony to slip away," said Leo.

"Slip away to where?" Calaren asked again. "Do you even have an inkling about this safe heaven we are running away to, or does this mythical place only exist in your imagination?"

"What are our other choices? You tried running all this time, and look where it landed us. We cannot just keep running away. Think about it logically. The Elementals were born on Ragonia, the Anons on Harbor, and the Veiled Ones on Yonder. Solem, though, is a world that was supposed to belong to all. You once told me, Pa, that you came here because this place was relatively safer for Veiled Ones. However, even here we Veiled Ones suffer humiliations, violent beatings, and killings every single day. So, it's time we leave in search of a better place to recuperate and plan our strike back," Leo said with conviction.

Leo took his parents' silence as an invitation to continue. "The sanctuary we are escaping to won't be our permanent destination either, but it will be a resting place where we can prepare our counterattack safely. We just need to listen to my instinct and follow where it leads us. Also, even in the worst-case scenario where we don't make it out, we'll still have the option to join the high ranks of the Anon forces where we can dismantle them from the inside."

"What are you saying, child? Are you out of your mind? Stop with this nonsense of fighting back. The Elementals, strongest of all the primordial races, lost to the Anons. We Veiled Ones are barely surviving even after accepting all of their demands, and now you think you can somehow defeat them. Ridiculous!" said a terrified June.

"I'm not the only one who thinks this way, Mother. Goddess Anorea must believe this to be possible too; otherwise, she wouldn't have helped me activate my powers and know all these things. So, no matter how ludicrous this seems, just trust me. Everything will be fine as long as we take the opportunity presented to us in today's event to run away from here," Leo said earnestly.

"Fine. Let's say for a moment we believe you. However, you are so sketchy on the details that we are sure to miss this precious opportunity you speak of. I mean, how will we even know when it is the right time?" asked Calaren, finally giving into his son's plan.

"I don't know of all the details either. However, I know that something big will happen during today's event that'll create havoc. We just need to use that chaos to get inside the Mother's Womb, and once we get inside, what to do next will become clear. So, just go on stage and perform like you were originally supposed to, Pa. Ma and I will watch you from the audience. Then when mayhem ensues you will head straight for the womb on your own, and Ma and I'll make our way to the womb separately from you as well," explained Leo.

"No, no, no! This is not going to work. There will be guards and traps everywhere. We won't be able to get away from here alive," said June while clasping Calaren's hand tightly.

"We will get outta here and no one, and I mean no one, will be able to stop us. Trust me, Ma, please," Leo pleaded confidently.

Calaren signaled Leo with his eyes toward the water jug resting on the table behind them alongside a couple of empty glasses. Leo nodded, grabbed an empty glass, filled it with water, then walked up to a June and held the glass to June's lips. Leo urged her to drink the water to calm herself, which she did. "We have to believe in what he says, love. There must be a reason why both of his powers are fully activated today. There must be a reason for us to remain unscathed even after Leo stood up to both Edwin and Emanuel. There must be a reason we are sitting in this damp, dark, cramped room and plotting our escape from the clutches of the Anons and their loyalists. Also, at this point, if what Leo said doesn't happen, we still have the backup plan," said Calaren while caressing June's cheek with his one free hand.

"The backup plan of betraying the Anons after joining their ranks? Don't be ridiculous. Leo is a child, Cal. He doesn't know what the Anons and their followers are capable of, but you and I do. Have you forgotten about the Amassings? If they ever get a hint of our true intentions, they'll make us fodder to that. Do you want us to end our lives that way?" asked June with tears in her eyes.

"Amassing? What is this Amassing?" asked a confused Leo.

"It is not easy to maintain a curse, especially a curse put on the primordial races. So, Amassing is the ritual that provides the necessary energy in maintaining the power draining curse put on us Veiled Ones. However, the sacrifices needed to perform this ritual are horrifying," said Calaren while growing pale.

"Why? What sacrifices are part of this Amassing ritual?" Leo asked suspiciously, his curiosity growing.

June and Calaren looked at each other with fear and extreme discomfort before glancing back at their son to answer his question. However, before they could say anything, someone knocked on the door.

"Cal, are you guys done yet? We are out of time. The performance arena is already open to the public. The King and his party have also arrived and are taking their seats as I speak. So, you have five to ten minutes at most before your performance begins. I need you backstage right now," said Rosen hurriedly from the other side of the door.

"We don't have any more time. I have to go. We'll answer all your questions about the Amassing another time. Meanwhile, just know that it is a horrible thing, and hope you never have to come across it," whispered Calaren before heading to the door and opening it. "Hey, Rosen, I'll go backstage right away. Umm, but can you make sure to grab some seats for my wife and kid please?" asked Calaren as soon as he opened the door.

"Well ok, but they need to hurry. I need to open the ceremony ASAP," said Rosen before briskly walking away.

Calaren turned to Leo. "Follow him quickly. We'll go by what you said. It's not much of a plan, but it's all we got. So, for all our sakes, I hope it works."

Leo nodded. He put away the half-full glass of water he was still holding and grabbed June's hand.

"Let's go, Ma," said Leo, pulling June's hand to make her get up. June looked at Calaren for one last look of assurance before getting up and following quickly behind Rosen with Leo as Calaren strode off towards the backstage.

CHAPTER FIVE

R osen led the mother-son pair to a couple of empty seats towards the front, but they were on the end of the row without proper views of the stage. These seats are very close to the Mother's Womb entrance. So, we'll only have to cover a short distance to the Mother's Womb when the time comes, thought Leo.

"This is the best I can do on such short notice. It's going to be a full house today. Cal told me before that Leo was coming. So, I saved a seat with a good view for him. However, since you are here now too, June, I needed to find a pair of seats and this is all that's left. Your father is very famous, and almost all the seats are going to be filled because everyone wants to hear your father sing. You should be proud to have such a talented and popular father, Leo!" said Rosen enthusiastically.

"Oh, I am! We both are. Right, Ma?" asked Leo.

"Yes! Yes, we are very proud of Cal," answered June after being jolted out of her still shocked state by Leo's question.

"You still look a little pale, June. You sure you are going to be fine?" Rosen asked, concerned.

"Yes, she is not feeling very well, but we just didn't want to miss Pa's big performance. So, here we are, haha. Don't worry, though. She'll be fine once the event gets over and we get to our place," answered Leo on behalf of June.

"Well, I don't blame you for not wanting to miss this once-in-a-lifetime event. It truly is a miraculous day with the Mother's Womb giving birth and all. Anyways, I gotta go and put on my suit before getting up there and hosting today's event. Gotta look good, you know," said Rosen smiling while walking away from June and Leo.

"Alright! Also, thanks for seats," said Leo loudly while waving goodbye to Rosen. "Let's sit down, Ma, and don't worry. Everything will be fine. Just trust me and follow my lead," said Leo as he made June take her seat before sitting down himself. After sitting down, Leo started looking around. Rosen was telling the truth. The whole arena was almost filled to the brim. The one or two seats that were still empty were being held for people. To Leo's left sat a wealthy noble Anon family. The whole row except the two seats at the end was occupied by the members of that family. Many of them were eyeing Leo and June with looks of disgust and condescension.

These rich, privileged, bigoted assholes... I'm sure right now they pity themselves for having to sit next to us. Just because you have more money and are part of the ruling class that systematically thrives off of oppressing others doesn't make you better than us. It just makes you weak, thought an outraged Leo.

The arena lights started to dim. It's about to start! Good! Now neither they have to see us lowly people of color nor do we have to tolerate their racist gazes.

After the arena grew dark, a spotlight was directed at the middle of the stage. In that light stepped in a very well-dressed Rosen, ready to entertain the crowds. "Ladies and gentlemen, boys and girls, and of course our most venerable king and queen along with their esteemed guests, welcome! Today's grand festivities are to celebrate the greatest event in the history of creation—the birth taking place in just a while, here at the Mother's Womb. We have a great show planned for you all, but before that, let me give you a brief rundown of how everything will progress!" exclaimed Rosen.

"We have a lineup of incredible acts being performed by the most amazing artists—which just will not stop. Then we all bear witness to the second-largest Amassing in memory, broadcasted live on the magic mirrors above. After that, our most beloved king and queen will give a celebratory speech while distributing the amassed power, before heading into the Mother's Womb with the chosen to welcome the newborn," said Rosen theatrically while pointing towards a strange device in the middle of the arena.

As soon as the Amassing was mentioned, a nervous murmuring spread to all corners of the arena. June grasped Leo's hands, and even in the dark Leo could feel his mother asking him to keep quiet and not to ask any questions about the Amassing.

"Now then, it is time we begin our performances, and to start we will have the magnificent, the dazzling and the most fabulous singer born in this century Calaren Hearth-Bringer entertain you all. So, please put your hands together for everyone's favorite Calaren Hearth-Bringer!" announced Rosen enthusiastically before handing off the center stage to Cal.

Art in any of its numerous forms has always held the attention and curiosity of the masses, especially if the artist is powerful enough to completely command that attention and curiosity. Calaren Hearth-Bringer was one such worthy artist. As soon as he got on stage the whole arena grew silent in anticipation of hearing his melodious voice.

"Hello, everyone. Hope you all are doing well, and thank you for joining us in celebrating this extraordinary occasion. Ever since the first Primordial races took birth, this will be the first time another powerful being will come into existence directly by Anorea's will. Through this, the powers and opportunities of new creations, that were thought lost, have come back, and we are all fortunate to be spectators of this. We pray that Anorea's latest creation will be a savior and shepherd of Areliam just like the Anons have been," said Calaren somewhat forcibly. "So, to honor this new beginning, I'll start by presenting a special arrangement prepared only for today. It is a simple tune, easy to hum along after just hearing it once. So, after you have heard me sing it once, please feel free to join in with me. Alright?" Calaren asked the audience invitingly.

"Yes!" answered the crowds watching both in the arena and the ones who were watching the broadcast in their homes.

"Excellent," said Calaren while cueing the musicians to start playing as he launched into his song.

Glorious days of the past
Cometh back again today
What was once thought as lost
Takes rebirth right here and now (X2)
The mother who gave birth to us
Sends her gift to one and all
So, come one and come all
To see this miracle

The Mother's Womb will give birth today
To a future bright and tall
Lights of hope ablaze anew
For everyone near and far
For everyone near and far
Glorious days of the past
Cometh back again today
What was once thought as lost
Takes rebirth right here and now (X2)
Today's the day we rise again
To march to our marvelous future
There's nothing to fear anymore
With joy and faith as our strength
So, let's rejoice night and day
In honor of our savior today
The moment of birth draws near
So, let's all voice our cheer
Glorious days of the past
Cometh back again today
What was once thought as lost
Takes rebirth right here and now (x3)

By the end of the last verse, the audience was singing along with Calaren. In those moments it didn't matter that Calaren was a Veiled One and most of the audience members were Anons. Both the Anons and the Veiled Ones joined in singing together in harmony and happiness. Leo looked on in awe as the same Anons that were snubbing him but a few moments ago were cheering on his father's performance. *I guess music and art, in general, are universal.* When I grow up I'll be just like my father, an awesome praiseworthy artist that can unify this hate-filled world, thought Leo.

Alas, these positive thoughts and pleasant atmosphere didn't last for long. All of sudden, the magic mirrors on top of the arena lit up and in them showed the reflection of an unknown planet being ripped apart. The strange thing was as the planet shown in the mirror was dying, the device in the middle of the arena was coming alive. It seemed like somehow the machine in the arena was draining the life source of the planet and storing it as raw power within it.

Something is wrong, Leo thought. "What is happening? Why is that planet being destroyed? Is there a way to stop this destruction?" asked Leo, his concern growing.

"The...the Amassing, why is it happening so soon?" asked an anonymous person from the crowd nervously.

Did he just say the Amassing? This is the same Amassing Ma and Pa warned me about. Also, didn't Rosen say something about the amassed power being distributed later? So, that means the Amassing destroys already living things just to use their life force as raw power. The Anons then use this power to do whatever they want, like the curse, thought Leo. No, this is wrong! You can't kill beings just to use their deaths as food for your monstrous actions. Help me, Anorea—please stop this Amassing. The lives of every being living on that planet are at stake here. You have to save them, prayed Leo.

As Leo was silently praying to Anorea, small tremors started rocking the arena. Soon, the tremors grew into a full-grown earthquake. Then, complete mayhem engulfed the whole arena.

The same magic mirrors that, but only a few moments ago, showed the destruction of a planet far away now started to crack and fall on the crowd below. The Anons of Earth present in the arena were trying desperately to create shelters as the Anons of air were trying to hold up the broken pieces of the mirror to keep them from hitting the people. But no one's power was working. People started screaming and running into each other as they frenziedly searched for cover. But there was nowhere to hide. The panic only increased as the floor of the arena started to crack and people began falling in. The giant door to the arena caved in, killing many who were trying to get it open to escape outside. At the same time, a fire broke out backstage, only compounding the terror of the situation.

Among all the blood, casualty, misery, and horror, there was only one good thing that happened. The entrance to the Mother's Womb was left unguarded, and Leo noticed it immediately. Everyone, including the guards formerly stationed at the entrance, were trying to run outside, leaving the entrance wide open. Also, just like no one's powers were working anymore, all of the cave admittance blocking traps stopped working as well. So, this is our chance to escape, thought Leo.

He looked up at the stage to find his father. He saw Calaren lying flat by the edge of the stage hanging on for dear life while searching the crowd for a glimpse of his family. Calaren and Leo's gazes met for just a second, which was enough for Leo to point towards the entrance of the Mother's Womb to his father. Calaren nodded in response and started running towards the Mother's Womb. Leo did the same with June following right after him.

It was easy to enter the Mother's Womb after all the traps lost the power to operate, and all the guards ran away to save their lives. Once inside, the family finally had a chance to catch their breath. Strangely enough, inside the Mother's Womb there was no trace of the earthquake that was ravaging the grounds outside. What was even more strange was that the entrance closed as soon as the Hearth-Bringers entered. As if today out of all the people present, the Mother's Womb thought the Hearth-Bringers to be the only worthy ones to be saved.

CHAPTER SIX

T he actual entrance to the Mother's Womb was small and slim, but it got bigger and branched out deeper inside. "So, this is what the Mother's Womb looks like from the inside. Honestly, it didn't look like much from the outside, but guess the inside is a different story. You can fit a whole castle inside this place," said Leo, looking around curiously.

"Don't be fooled by what you see. This place connects all of creation. Every corner hides a secret passageway that could lead to anywhere in Areliam," said Calaren with respect in his voice.

"Leo, if you are done sightseeing, and Cal, if you are done playing tour guide, then can we please figure out our next move. I don't wanna be stuck here when everything calms down and they realize we bailed on them. Knowing them, they'll probably blame the whole thing on us and put a kill on sight order on us," said June with worry in her voice.

"Don't worry, a lot of lives are being lost outside as we speak. With all the cave-in wounds and glass cuts, most of the dead will be unrecognizable. With any luck, they'll think us dead," Leo said calmly.

"That still leaves us to figure out where to go in this maze of a place," June said frustratingly.

Before answering his mother, Leo closed his eyes for a few moments, lost in deep thought. Then he raised his right hand and uttered, "When surrounded by darkness, look to the stars for guidance," all the while still keeping his eyes closed. As he said those words, nine-pointed star symbols, etched in the cave wall on the right lit up. Leo opened his eyes. "We have to follow where those symbols lead us." Then, he ran inside the womb following after the path shown by the stars with Cal and June right at his heels. The Hearth-Bringers kept running deeper and deeper inside the womb, until finally they reached a large rock with a huge phoenix symbol in the middle of an infinity symbol on it blocking the way forward.

"That phoenix is the being representing the Pathfinders, and the infinity symbol represents Anorea and the Paradigms," said Cal while catching his breath.

"So, the nine-pointed star is not the only symbol of the Pathfinders? Then do all Veiled Ones' families have multiple symbols, and who are the Paradigms again, Pa?" asked an intrigued Leo.

"No, son. Some like the Gainsworths use their animal representation of cats also as their symbol. As for this Pathfinder symbol, if you think about it, it makes perfect sense, as we Veiled Ones respect our lineage. That is why we are the only ones who have last names to honor our clans, while the Anon and Elementals do not. It is said that the pathfinders were the first to discover phoenixes and tame them. Since then, the Pathfinders started using the phoenix symbol in addition to the nine-pointed star as their symbol. As for the Paradigms they were one of the Veiled One clan of old." answered Calaren.

"Boys, this is not the time for a history lesson on Veiled Ones. Since the path led us to this dead-end, we need to find another way to get out of here first," said June. Ever since they entered Mother's Womb June had looked back uncountable times in fear of someone coming after them. All she wanted to do was reach the safe place Leo alluded to before. Any delay in that, including Calaren and Leo's chatter about Veiled One symbols, irritated her immensely.

"Have no fear when Leo is here, mother. If I'm not mistaken, phoenixes represent fire, right? Well, stars represent fire too. So, let's light one, shall we?" said Leo while reaching into his father's pockets to take out his lighter. Once he had the lighter, Leo lit it and went over to the phoenix symbol to check it more closely. As soon as he drew near, the symbol caught fire from the lit lighter. After catching fire, the whole symbol blazed brightly for a brief moment before the symbol parted midway, creating a doorway to enter the chamber inside.

As the whole family went inside they heard the door shut behind them and saw the chamber they stood in being filled with mirrors with the nine-pointed star symbol etched in them. "So, all the mirrors here were created by the Pathfinders." stated Leo.

"All the magic mirrors in existence were created by the Pathfinders for various reasons, chiefly among them was to travel to different places in Areliam. These mirrors are reflective of Pathfinder teleportation abilities. See, the fastest thing in the universe is thoughts. It used to be that, once you think of a place to go in your mind, the magic mirrors reflect it and you can enter the mirror on your side and come out of any reflective surface on the other side. However, after the Pathfinders lost their powers, travel between places is only possible through magic mirrors. Each of these mirrors must represent places all over Areliam. Now, all we have to do is just figure out which one to use to get to safety," explained Calaren.

"Boys, it's still not the time for lectures of any kind. Let's talk about how we know which mirror pathway leads to safety instead?" said June sternly to keep Leo and Cal on point.

"That one in the leftmost corner of the room," said Leo.

"Oh, and how do you know that?" asked June.

"It's a hunch, and since all my hunches have been right so far, this one will be right too," said Leo confidently while walking towards the mirror. However, he stopped midway to look at the mirror in the middle of the room. It was showing a bizarre scene. The king of Anons was standing over a baby girl with a knife in hand.

"Oh, Anorea! What is he doing? Why is he trying to kill a baby?" asked a horrified June, unable to look away from the scenario. However, as soon as the king was about to strike the blow, the earthquake, that up until now only affected the grounds outside, came inside the Mother's Womb. All the mirrors started to rattle, a couple of them began to crack.

"We don't have the luxury to worry about others. We have to get out of here fast before everything collapses," said Leo before taking both his mother and father's hands and somehow making it to the leftmost mirror. He pushed June inside the mirror first; Calaren went next instead of Leo, accidentally losing his footing and falling into the mirror due to the earthquake. Leo followed him but not before he took one last look at the mirror in the middle showing the baby girl whose life was endangered by the Anon king. "Live, you little troublemaker, live," said Leo as he plunged into the mirror.

CHAPTER SEVEN

T he floor was cold. Leo breathed in the stale air and opened his eyes. He pushed himself off of the hard, white marble floor and took in the view. They were in some sort of underground temple. A pure white structure dedicated to the worship of Anorea surrounded by cave walls. The whole space was well lit with light crystals, so Leo could see the towering black statue of Anorea on the altar in front of them. The temple was eerily silent. Not a person in sight. Someone must take good care of this place, because it's too tidy to be left alone. But why isn't anyone here now? Oh no! Forget about others, where are Ma and Pa? Did they not make it? Leo frantically searched until he found his dad in a corner passed out and bleeding in his mothers' lap.

"He hit his head hard when he stumbled out of that mirror," said June, pointing to the mirror behind them.

Leo glanced back and saw a mirror, cracked and broken all over, leaning against one of the huge white temple columns. Well, at least no one will be able to follow after us through that anymore. It is a miracle that we were able to travel through it. Where are we, though? Is this another part of the Mother's Womb?

"Who disturbs my peace?" asked a little girl's voice coming from the altar.

"Who's asking?" Leo retorted back.

"It's I Anorea, of course."

Leo rolled his eyes and said, "Drop the act. The all-knowing Goddess would've already known who we are. Also, I can see part of your blue dress sticking out from behind the statue."

There was a long silence before a little girl, white as snow with straight silver hair, peeked out from behind the statue.

Her blue eyes filled with guilt at being caught. She hid away again after she saw both June and Leo staring at her.

"It's ok, sweetheart. We are not mad. We know you were just playing. So, will you please come out and introduce yourself? It'll help us out a lot because we are new here and don't know anyone else," said June in a gentle and loving voice.

"New here! You can't be new here. You sure you weren't just hiding?" the little girl asked in surprise as she finally came out from behind the statue.

"Yes, we are very sure that we are new here. Now, will you please get over here and explain everything?" said an irritated Leo.

"Manners, Leo! Be nice to the sweet girl!" said June as she beckoned the girl with open arms and a smile on her face. The little girl hesitated and kept twirling with her hair in nervousness. Eventually, she stepped towards them. As she came out of the shadow of Anorea's statue, June noticed how thin and malnourished she was. However, at that moment, June had to take care of her own family before she could think about anyone else. "My husband is injured and we need to find medical help for him right away. So, can you please help us?"

"Ok! Let me go get the healers."

"Wait! At least tell us your name first!" said Leo.

"I'm Desdemona of the Destruction Elementals. But my friends call me Des," said the little girl.

"The Elementals! Aren't all of you dead?" asked Leo.

"The ones up top, yes, but not the ones down here," replied Des.

"Up top, down here. You don't make any sense. Where exactly is down here? Where are we right now?" asked Leo.

"We're in the Sanctuary. The underground metropolis of Ragonia, to be exact," said Des.

"The underground metropolis of Ragonia! That means the Elementals survived!" said a dazed Calaren as he tried to stand up on his own.

"Watch out, honey! Your head is still bleeding from the fall!" June said while helping Calaren stand up.

"Fall, yes fall! You guys must've fallen from the mirror I put together. They told me it wouldn't work, but I knew it would. Well, not anymore I guess, 'cause this time it's too broken even for me to put back together," said Desdemona with tears in her eyes.

"Sweetheart, thank you so much for making that mirror whole; without it, we would've never been able to get away," said June.

"I see you are still a coward that runs away from problems, Calaren," said a male voice with a deep base in his tone from the entrance of the temple.

Leo noticed that the tall white man, with the same blue eyes as Desdemona, was abnormally thin as well. He looked weathered, with his blonde hair tied back in a ponytail. A deep scar ran down from the bottom of his left eye to the tip of his lip. The dirty black clothes he was wearing were worn-down and torn in parts. His stance, though, had a sense of power. It was like he was ready to jump into battle at a moment's notice like a well-seasoned soldier.

"Papa! They came from the mirror I put back together," said Des as she ran towards the man.

"I told you not to put it back, Des. We have to deal with these cowards now because of it," said the man curtly.

"Atlas! You can insult me as much as you want, but leave my family out of it. Also, for your kind information, it takes more courage to conclude things peacefully rather than fighting to the bitter end," said Calaren.

"Man! Things you say to yourself to sleep better at night. It is only because of you that your father, mother, grandmother, and brothers have died a horrible death at the Battle of the Behemoths," said Atlas with vitriol in his voice.

"You know that's not fair! I had left the family long before that!"

"Yes, but you could've come back and helped us. With someone of your caliber, we could've turned the tide. Instead, you kept yourself hidden in Solem, out of harm's way. And now you and your cowardly family wiggled yourselves into our Sanctuary."

"Stop it, Atlas!" Calaren spat.

June had to step in. "Honey, calm down. You are not in a good shape. Atlas, was it? Can we please have this conversation after Calaren receives treatment for his wound?" asked June earnestly.

"No, we don't have enough resources for ourselves, let alone for someone like him. Ragonia's environment has been destroyed. The only reason we survived is by working very hard to keep the air in this sealed city clean. It's been ten years since then. Now our inventory is depleted, and we all have been starving for the past few days. So, we can't spare any resources or energy on you."

"But Papa, can't the healers take a look at him? Please, he is hurt."

Atlas glanced at Des. "No. Stay out of this, Des. You have made enough trouble as it is." Then he eyed all the Hearth-Bringers scornfully. "You need to go back."

However, the heavily damaged mirror that transported them to Sanctuary chose that moment to break apart completely. Diminishing any hope of being used ever again.

CHAPTER EIGHT

G rumble, grumble.

On and on went the noises in Leo's empty stomach. It had been a day since they arrived in the Sanctuary. However, in this short while, the start of another Primordial war seemed imminent each time Calaren and Atlas locked horns. After the mirror had completely broken apart, all ways of exiting the underground metropolis of Ragonia were blocked. The Hearth-Bringers were trapped. And no one was unhappier about this than Atlas. Things had come to blows several times. Violent bloodshed was avoided only because June and Desdemona stepped in.

Desdemona, or Des as she insisted on being called, was a completely different creature than her father. Even though resources were scarce she still brought them pillows, blankets, and water. The situation was dire. Food had run out and the water supply was dangerously low. People were eating insects for survival and were in no mood to entertain three extra mouths to feed. Des had suggested the Hearth-Bringers stay hidden in the temple to avoid other hostile occupants of Sanctuary.

Meanwhile, Calaren's head injury made him weak and feverish. June dressed the wound and tried to make him as comfortable as she could, but it didn't help much. As hours passed his fever got worse, and there was nothing they could do. Now, he didn't even have enough energy to argue with Atlas. They put all the blankets together to create thick bedding for him so the freezing floor wouldn't bother him. He lay flat, with closed eyes and staggered breathing. Calaren's pain was reflecting in June's eyes. She kept looking up at Anorea's statue but said nothing. Still, Leo felt like Anorea was listening to June's silent prayers. The sheer fact that they were still here even after the unfriendly Elementals had every reason to get rid of them was proof of that. *Mothers are so amazing. They don't even need words to convey their emotions*, thought Leo as he rocked himself to sleep on the cold, hard floor at the foot of Anorea's altar.

Darkness encased Leo. He moved his hands around to try to feel his surroundings. Nothing but air touched his fingertips. However, a few steps ahead was an illuminated spot in the dark, from where a chicken was watching him. Leo started walking towards the light until he was close enough to touch the bird. He went up to the chicken and grabbed it. Then, he bit it.

"What? What are you doing? You stupid kid!" screamed the strange chicken.

"Mr. chicken, I'm sorry that I'm trying to eat you while you are still alive. But I'm starving, and this is a dream after all. So, please at least let me eat you like food in here. Now, can you just die and come back as a roasted chicken on a platter? It'll make you easier to eat," said a hungry Leo.

"Chicken! Did you just call me a chicken! Listen, moron, I'm a phoenix. I said, I'm a phoenix. You hear me? Also, I happen to be your ancestor as well. What kind of descendant tries to eat his ancestors? I didn't know the Hearth-Bringers were cannibals!" said the ticked off phoenix.

"We are not," said another voice from within the darkness.

Leo looked in the direction of the voice and saw a pair of glowing green eyes. Slowly the owner of the voice emerged from the shadows. A beautiful blue wolf entered the spotlight and approached Leo.

"Let him go, Leon. You cannot eat your ancestors no matter how hungry you are," said the wolf calmly.

Leo ran his tongue over his lips and kept holding on to the phoenix chicken tightly. The look in Leo's eyes made the phoenix chicken shudder. He peered at the wolf and said, "Kendall, call off your grandson this instance!"

"Leon Hearth-Bringer! Dorian over there is the reason for the activation of your Pathfinder powers. He is the one who guided you subconsciously on the path to getting out of Solem. Even now he is here to grant you more powers. You should thank him instead of trying to eat him. So, put him down!" ordered the wolf called Kendall.

"This is such a weird dream. Why are animals trying to act like my ancestors?" said Leo out loud.

The wolf sighed and went up to Leo, raised his claws, and scratched his leg. "Ow!" said Leo in pain as red droplets of blood appeared on his leg, and he finally let the phoenix go. The phoenix took advantage of this and flew away to the farthest corner of the well-lit area. "So, this is real?" asked an astonished Leo.

"Yes," answered Kendall.

"So, you guys are the reason I have these awesome powers! Thank you! Thank you so much!" said Leo gratefully.

"That is only part true. While it's true that Dorian has blessed and passed on part of his Pathfinder powers to you, I am not the one who activated your Hearth-Bringer powers. You awakened a part of your Heath-Bringer power on your own. Even if we left you unattended you would eventually become one of the most powerful Hearth-Bringers in history. Your healing powers are so strong that it overcame the curse and the power loss of the Pathfinders. It also allowed us to contact you. We only hastened the process to your full awakening by sharing more powers with you." Said Kendall.

"So, you are saying my powers have not fully awakened yet?" Asked Leo.

"No, they haven't. Your Pathfinder powers specifically haven't awakened at all and it is only because of Dorian that you can use any Pathfinder abilities." Said Kendall while pointing at the chicken phoenix known as Dorian with his snout.

"However, you are sharing your powers with me in an attempt to awaken them fully?" Asked Leo.

"Yes." Answered Kendall.

"Does that mean I will be able to use all your powers if needed?" Leo asked.

"With enough time and practice you will be able to do that However, for now you can only handle limited amounts." Said Kendall.

"That's great! Thank you so much for sharing your powers with me!" Said Leo.

"I am not sharing my powers with you. I don't even have healing powers to pass on. I just came here to stop you from trying to eat Dorian," clarified Kendall as he watched Leo's wound heal.

"Really? Then who is sharing the healing powers?" asked Leo excitedly.

"Prime ancestor Areon Hearth-Bringer. He'll come to meet you when you are ready." As Kendall spoke, a pair of purple eyes glowed brightly far away in the darkness.

"So, you are here to pass on more powers to me now because you know I'll use them to free our people, right?"

Kendall twisted his wolf snout to something resembling a smile. "Dorian was here to do that, but maybe he changed his mind now."

"Nooooooo! I'm so sorry, ancestor! I didn't mean to hurt you," said Leo while running towards Dorian.

A panicked Dorian flew away from Leo and landed on Kendall's back before saying, "Stop! I've had enough of your antics. You're lucky there are no better candidates to inherit my powers. Otherwise, I would've never shared my powers with someone as dumb as you."

"I said I was sorry," Leo said in embarrassment.

Kendall interjected, "What is done is done. We cannot change it. Just keep in mind to never do it again. Also, before Dorian passes his powers on, we need to discuss some things."

"Ok, tell me. I'm listening."

"The Anons are destroying all of creation with their Amassings. Nothing in nature operates alone. By destroying the Elementals and taking away the powers of Veiled Ones, they have made sure no new life can take birth. Today they are reduced to recycling the already created energy in the universe. Alas! They are doing a poor job at that too. The Amassings must be stopped if life is to survive in the universe. Before freeing our people, you need to put Areliam back into balance first."

"No problem. Just tell me what I need to do, and it'll be done."

"This won't be easy. You are far too young and weak to make a difference right now. Even if we give you more powers, you cannot use them properly," said the chicken turned phoenix, Dorian.

"You need to find Ivan Renegader. The most powerful Veiled One alive, and your great grandfather," said Kendall.

"My great grandfather? Why is he a Renegader and not a Hearth-Bringer? Also, he must be like a hundred and fifty.

So, how will someone that ancient be of any help?" asked a confused Leo.

"So, in addition to being a cannibal, you are an ageist too! That's it, you need to be taught a lesson," said Dorian as he flew over to Leo and started to peck at him hard.

"You sure you are not a chicken? 'Cause you sure have its pecking skills." Upon hearing this from Leo, Dorian accelerated his pecking with more force than before. "Stop! It hurts," said Leo while trying to fend off Dorian.

"Alright, both of you behave! Leon, I don't have time to explain our family linage or inter-clan relationships of the Veiled Ones. Just ask Calaren later. He'll be happy to explain everything to you. As for Ivan Renegader, even at a hundred and twenty-three, no living Veiled One can match his powers. You need him. But to get to him you need to teleport to the planet Kracten. So, without wasting time, Dorian, pass on your teleportation powers to Leon already," Kendall said, irritated.

"I don't want to anymore," said the grumpy Phoenix.

"You don't have a choice. Let me remind you, we Hearth-Bringers have many descendants to pass our powers on to. However, June and Leon are the only viable options for you. June's connection to the ancestors is too weak to bring out her powers. So, either pass on your powers to Leon or watch the Pathfinder line completely die off," warned Kendall.

"Fine," said Dorian.

"Teleportation! Yayyyy! What an awesome power to have!"

"Shut up, before I change my mind."

"Yes, ancestor."

"Listen very carefully."

"Ok."

"Dang it, kid. Keep quiet until I'm done explaining. Just nod your head up and down if you understand." Dorian continued after he saw Leo nod. "Good. Now in a few moments, I'll be transferring my teleportation powers to you. It has been a long-standing tradition amongst Veiled Ones to transfer powers to each other. However, I cannot give you too much because you can't handle it. Using my powers constantly will help you awaken your own, until eventually you won't need to use my powers at all. Any questions so far?"

"Yes! How powerful is this teleportation power? How does it work? Is it at least cool looking? Can I go to places I've never been before? Can I take Ma and Pa with me too? Also, what are the side-effects?"

"Oh, Goddess Anorea, please save me! You are definitely Calaren's son. You'll grow up to be more annoying than him for sure. For future reference, anytime anyone asks if you have any questions, they are secretly hoping you have none."

"Dorian..." Kendall Interjected.

"Argh...alright then. The teleportation ability is extremely powerful because it can take you anywhere. Even to places you have never seen before. All you have to do is think about a destination, and a *cool looking* smoky portal will open to take you there. I suggest in the beginning you take no more than one other person with you. Taking more than that would be very taxing on your body. You can transport more people and things when you get familiar with this power and awaken your own. Lastly, your eye color will change to blue whenever you use Pathfinder powers. Now, let's get this over with." Dorian blew a stream of black fire on Leo.

The flames consumed him. He felt excruciating pain as the black fire penetrated his skin and spread to his insides. Leo opened his eyes screaming, only to find himself and Desdemona falling through the skies.

CHAPTER NINE

"**H**ey, Leo! You should have your eyes blue all the time. It looks so cool!" yelled Desdemona as she and Leo were falling through the skies of Solem.

"Thanks! I'll add that to the bucket list if I survive!" said Leo right before they hit the waters of a manmade lake. Leo had been dipping in this lake since he was four. So, he would recognize these waters even in his sleep.

Solem is an oceanic world with only one triangular island on it. The three sides of this landmass were occupied by three unique sites, each belonging to one of the Primordial races. In the north resided the Prophetic Caves of the Veiled Ones, near the Anon temple. The west coast had the Anon crystal mines. The rich Anon nobility lived in that area in their wealthy countryside estates. The south side had beautiful uninterrupted beaches and a port, where ships stayed anchored until they were set free to roam the waters. The port also served as a refueling station for Ascendance. The east side, however, was filled with mountains. The dormant Volcano of Creation, representing the Elementals, sat amongst those mountains.

Even though the Volcano of Creation was dormant, it still created a lot of heat. Due to this, the east side of the island was dry and mostly lifeless. So, naturally, the Anons decided to house the Veiled Ones there. The makeshift Veiled Ones' encampment existed halfway between the Volcano of Creation and Shalom. The campsite was close enough for the Veiled Ones to see jubilant views of Shalom while being way out of reach for them to ever hope to live there.

Leo had lived all of his life in the Veiled Ones' camp. Many nights he used to stay awake and stare at the brightly lit

Shalom, wondering how awesome it would be to live there. He thought Shalom was the city that welcomes everyone. Leo believed Shalom to be a place where people lived out their lives happily. However, after everything that happened during the Mother's Womb birthing event, he no longer wanted to live in Shalom. It was a rotten place. All the opportunities, acceptance, happiness, and benefits were reserved only for the Anons. Veiled Ones like Leo were not welcome there. Soon the Anons were planning to turn the whole universe as unhospitable as Shalom for the Veiled Ones.

Desdemona and Leo finally immerged from the lake. Wet as dogs and coughing like old men, they laid on the banks of the lake. After a while, Leo sat up and took a look around. Supposedly, his father had made this lake. It had taken a year, but Calaren encouraged Veiled Ones to dig a large space for the lake. Once the digging was done, he sang the ancient Hearth-Bringer song to bring down rain until the lake was full. Since that time his father had brought down the rain whenever the water levels were low. Hearth-Bringers were always powerful. Even after the loss of their legendary healing abilities, the bountiful uses of their artistic powers kept them at the top.

Leo looked at his own body and saw the scratches made from hitting the underwater rocks after he had fallen to the lake healing. He smiled. Now I have Pathfinder teleportation ability in addition to my Hearth-Bringer healing powers. I just need to form a plan on how to use these to free all Veiled Ones from Anon rule while simultaneously saving Areliam.

"Ouch," said Desdemona as she finally got up.

She must've been close to me when I accidentally activated my teleportation powers during the dream meeting with the ancestors. "Are you alright?" asked Leo, coming out of his thoughts.

"Oh yeah! Don't worry about me. I have a sturdy body! I'm one of the Destruction Elementals after all," Desdemona replied proudly.

"Shh. Don't make too much noise. I'm sure Veiled Ones are close by and are heading this way after they saw us fall from the sky. We need to make our way out of here as soon as possible."

"Where is here? I mean, I have never been here, so I have no clue. Actually, I've never been anywhere. So, you have a lot of explaining to do."

"I will, but let's get away from here first."

"Ok, where are we going? Can we please go somewhere with food? I'm really hungry."

Leo smiled. "Of course! I know just the place."

The Snack Stop was a prominent attraction of Shalom. One could taste snacks from all corners of creation here. Be it the shrimp skewers of Solem, to chicken samosas of Yonder, everything was there. Vegetarian snacks like rice dumplings or banana crackers were also available. However, Leo's favorite part of the shop was where the candies were kept. He had visited the shop just once with his parents on his ninth birthday. Before the events at the Mother's Womb, it was the most memorable day of his life. Today was Friday. New shipments for the store were coming in from all around the world. Desdemona and Leo hid in one of the large shipping boxes to gain entry to the shop.

"Uh Jeriah, make sure to check the goods thoroughly. After the Mother's Womb incident, it is hard to get any goods delivered. All the merchants are afraid. They fear some other catastrophe will happen and they'll be stuck in it during the delivery. However, we are running low on everything. So, I had no choice but to buy these from Brennon. That shoddy motherfucker. Last time, half of the stuff he delivered was bad. Let's see what he gave us this time," said Victor, Jeriah's boss.

"Ah, yes, boss. Let me check everything and see how much of it can we actually use," said Jeriah.

"You do that while I go tend to our special customer," said Victor as he walked out of the storage area.

As soon as Victor left, Leo and Desdemona popped out of the big box they were hiding in. "Uncle Jeriah!" said Leo.

"Holly Mother Anorea. Please save me!" yelled Jeriah.

"Keep quiet, it's just me, Uncle!" exclaimed Leo.

"What happened, Jeriah?" asked a concerned Victor as he hurriedly made his way back.

Leo and Desdemona quickly went back inside the box but not before Leo signaled Jeriah not to oust them. "Nothing, boss. It's just that the state of the delivered goods are so bad that it almost gave me a heart attack."

"What? No wonder that bastard made me sign a no-return vow. No matter. I'll get him punished at the merchants' guild for this. You just try to salvage what you can and keep it down, will you? We shouldn't disturb our precious guest."

"Yes, boss," said Jeriah, doing his best to maintain a calm demeanor until Victor left.

Once Jeriah made sure Victor was not in earshot, he said, "You can come out now. He's gone."

This time both Desdemona and Leo exited the box slowly and walked up to Jeriah. "Sorry, Uncle. Didn't mean to scare you. But please don't tell anyone that we are alive," said Leo.

"Boy, I'm just happy that you are alive! Where are your parents, though?" Jeriah asked joyfully as he gave a tight hug to Leo.

"Well..." Desdemona wandered out to the inside of the store while Leo was busy explaining everything to Jeriah.

The inside of the store was huge and magnificently designed. The walls were painted in vibrant colors. Each corner of the store was staged with either unique snacks and colorful lights or funny candy dispensing statues. The glass floor was so shinny Des could see herself reflected in it. The delicious aroma of food permeated throughout the store. So much so that Des couldn't help but drool. Des inhaled the delightful fragrances of different dishes as she passed by them. The smells alone gave away the tastes of those food items. Des could taste the spice in the chicken teriyaki and the sweetness of the cream rolls as she whiffed past them.

If only I had money. I would've bought this entire place! But why is it so silent and empty? Maybe because of the events of the past couple of days that Mama June was talking about. Desdemona reached the middle of the store as she pondered the reason behind the deserted store. There was a carousel in the smack-dead middle of the store, and a young Veiled One boy was riding on the teacup inside it.

Before she could reach out to the only other current inhabitant of the store, the front door burst open. "Where is he? I want to see him right now!" said Anon Guard Boyle as he stood firmly with his arms crossed like he owned the place.

"Sir, I told you that you cannot keep barging in here like this," said the shop guard.

"You are an Anon! So, act like one. How dare you take the side of a Veiled One. Hand over that Jeriah Gourmetdine to me right now," said Boyle while stomping his foot.

"But he hasn't done anything wrong," said the guard.

"I was humiliated because of him, and that is reason enough. Hey, you. Veiled One kid, you must know where that Jeriah is since all of you stick together like a nest of cockroaches," said Boyle.

The boy remained quiet, but Desdemona spoke up on his behalf. "Don't talk to him like that!"

"Stay out of it, little girl. Didn't your parents teach you not to talk over adults, or are they too poor to know any manners to pass on?" asked Boyle, after sneering at Desdemona's ragged clothes.

Des moved like a strong gust of wind. As soon as she reached Boyle, she kicked him in his nether regions. When he doubled over in pain Des punched him several times in quick succession. Lastly, she finished him off with a strong headbutt. Boyle fainted on the spot. Desdemona of the Destruction Elementals was taught how to fight from a young age by her warrior father. So even though she was only twelve, she could take down men twice her size easily.

All this commotion brought out Victor. "What is going on here?" asked the shocked store owner.

"He was harassing the poor little boy over there," replied Des as she pointed at the boy.

"What? I'm so sorry, sir! I promise he won't bother you again. I'll throw him out right now," said an incredibly frightened Victor as he and the guard dragged Boyle's unconscious body out of the shop.

The boy remained unmoved even after all the commotion. Desdemona walked up to the boy and saw him holding uneaten beef jerky while riding the carousel. He looked like a soulless husk; dead eyes stared into the void while he sat lifelessly. Desdemona entered the carousel and sat inside the same teacup the boy was sitting in.

"You look like you have lost something or someone very important. You are a Veiled One, so you probably don't know that Elementals and Anons don't have last names. My father told me it's because we are more independent. But I think it's because we believe in practicing detachment, as one day we'll all die alone. However, you Veiled Ones are lucky, in that you are never separated from your own. You have a whole ancestral realm from where your ancestors watch over you. Just think of how much pain your loved one is in seeing you like this. So, you need to take good care of yourself on his behalf," said Desdemona while feeding parts of the jerky to the boy.

The boy still didn't say anything, but his eyes slowly became alive as he stared at Des while eating the jerky.

"Oh, look at the time. I must go now, but remember that you are never alone. You are loved and cherished now and always," said Desdemona after she finished feeding the jerky to the boy. However, before she left to join Leo, Des turned around, smiled, and planted a kiss on the boy's forehead. Then she left swiftly.

The boy raised his hand to hold onto her, but she left before he could. So, after Des left, the boy finally broke his silence. "Leander, put that guard who was making trouble earlier into mine protection duty for the rest of his life and find out everything about this girl."

A shadowy figure hidden behind one of the statues replied, "As you command, Prince Ethan."

CHAPTER TEN

"**S**o, let me get this straight. You had the golden opportunity to go out and bring back food for all of us—yet, all you brought back is junk food," said an exhausted Atlas.

"Father, look at these here. They have a lot of fiber. See?" Des held up a nutty bar where almonds, cashews, and peanuts were glued together with melted jaggery.

"Desdemona, I have no need for your commentary at the moment. So, please keep quiet," said Atlas.

"Leo is just a child after all. He could only think so far," June spoke up to defend her son.

"Not true! I know I'm young, but I'm extremely smart for my age. The reason I couldn't get more food is because I had no money. I had to pull in a favor with Uncle Jeriah to get what little we have now," Leo said defiantly.

"Fine. I understand. We have enough gold coins to buy a small nation. So, let's go back and get more food for everyone," said Atlas as he got up and signaled a few men to accompany him.

"No. I'm too tired to access my teleportation powers right now. I think I'm coming down with a fever after wearing my wet clothes for so long too. Also, I don't think it is safe for you Elementals to roam freely in Solem. Lastly, I can only take one other person with me. Even transporting back these extra boxes was hard. So, I don't think I can handle another teleportation for today," said a tired Leo.

"Leo is right. His Pathfinder powers just activated, and it's too soon to have him transporting large amounts of things and people. By the way, how can you ask for our help when you were so hostile to us before?" asked Calaren.

"Let me remind you, Calaren, that the only reason you are still alive is because I defended you in front of the others. They wanted to have you killed the moment you stepped in here, to preserve the secrecy and resources of this location. So, it's time to pay back this kindness by helping us get food and other resources from the outside."

"I think we have done more than enough by providing these food items for you," retorted Calaren.

"I'm not surprised by your answer, knowing your history of selfishness and cowardice," replied Atlas.

"Atlas!"

"Calaren!"

"Stop! We don't have time to fight amongst ourselves. Anons are slowly killing Areliam, and I was chosen to stop this. However, I can't do this alone. I need all of you to help me out," said Leo.

"What!?" asked everyone in unison.

Inside the imperial palace of the Anons, secret rooms were reserved for training the Anon royalty. Power dampeners were employed throughout the space to make it a secure spot to practice dangerous powers safely. Today both Anon princes, Ethan and Zine, were training with Karenitz, the daughter of warlord Kaint Swordsbane. They were sparing inside a sandy enclosure.

It was Zine's turn to spar with Karenitz. The warlord, Ethan, and his bodyguard Leander watched over them from the protective zone. The blond-haired, blue-eyed Karenitz inherited the wind Anon powers from her father and was easily defeating Zine. The newest prince of the Anons, brown-haired and hazel-eyed Prince Zine, was supposedly born out of the Mother's Womb. The same way the baby Princess Lore was—on the same day Ethan's father died.

The official story was that the leftover Elemental forces had staged a desperate attempt to sabotage the birth at Mother's Womb. However, Anorea supported the Anons and sent Lore and her guardian Zine to save the day. Many deaths occurred in the process, though, including that of Edwin Gainsworth.

Ethan could see several holes in this story. Such as if Zine and Lore were both born out of the Mother's Womb, then how come Lore was far stronger than Zine? Also, how did the ragtag group of rogue Elementals gain the resources to sabotage an event that had utmost Anon security? Not to mention, if Anorea was truly on their side, then why did so many of their people die? Why did my father have to die? Why?

"Ahh!" Zine yelled loud enough to draw Ethan out of his thoughts.

Ethan saw Zine thrown face down on the sandy floor of the training area. He immediately got out of the protective zone and ran to him. Ethan helped Zine get up and handed him over to Leander, who had followed him out of the protective zone as well. On Ethan's orders, Leander left them to assist Zine get back safely to his chambers. Then he turned to face Karenitz, who was standing proudly after her victory over Zine.

"These are just practice sessions. Please refrain from using your full power."

"Look at this! One loser is trying to protect another! It's hilarious."

"We should end this session here today," said Ethan as he tried to make his way out of the training zone. Before he could take a step, though, sharp bursts of winds stronger than any blades made deep cuts in the sand before him.

"What's wrong? Afraid you'll lose to me too?"

Ethan didn't answer and started walking out. Karenitz got angry and directed big gusts of wind towards Ethan to knock him off course. But he used his earth Anon powers to create a barrier of sand to protect himself.

"Coward! Face me directly, or are you like your father? Always hitting people from the shadows."

Ethan stopped in his track. He dropped the sand wall and looked Karenitz in the eye. "Fine. One round and no retakes."

"Oh, there won't be need for more than one sparring round. I'll have you bent over on the ground in no time."

"Enough talk; start sparing or I'm leaving."

"Oh no, you are not," said Karenitz as she launched at Ethan. She used her wind-controlling powers to make herself speed up exponentially.

Ethan barely had enough time to erect a wall of sand again. However, this time the wall was no match for Karenitz's forceful impact. Ethan was knocked back several paces before he could use his power to ground himself. Ethan covered himself in the sand and changed its density to make it rock solid. Once inside his stone tomb, he felt the tremors in the earth to determine Karenitz's exact location. When he found where she was, he increased the gravity of that spot to an extreme level. Karenitz's body couldn't handle the increased gravity, and she pummeled down to the ground. She could no longer move and even the air around her was too heavy to be used freely.

"Fuck you, Ethan! Father, he must've cheated! There is no way he could bring me down otherwise," Karenitz spat, enraged.

"Don't be a sore loser, daughter. He is just in a different league than you. Only challenge him again after you have become good enough to avoid his gravity trap. Ethan, release her now," said warlord Swordsbane.

"Yes, sir," replied Ethan as he released Karenitz.

As soon as Karenitz was released she sent most of the air in the room hurling at top speed towards the stone tomb Ethan was in. However, the stone tomb remained unscathed. Finally, exhausted and humiliated, Karenitz ran out of the training ground crying.

Ethan changed the density of the stone tomb into that of sand again and let it fall away. His ordeal wasn't over yet though. As soon as Ethan dropped his defenses, a bolt of lightning struck him. His unprepared body couldn't handle the jolt of electricity and he flew to another side of the room. Kaint Swordsbane, the one with the lightning Elemental powers, had struck him. All power dampeners can be overwritten with enough force. The force of the warlord's attack was so great that Ethan was slowly losing consciousness while his body succumbed to the side effects of the lightning strike.

Anons and Elementals usually don't have last names, except in special cases. One of these special cases was Kaint Swordsbane. The reason he was called Swordsbane is that his Elemental Lighting Sword can destroy all other swords. The only one who can match up to him is Ethan's uncle, the Anon of fire Orias. Orias the Great, as most called him, is also known as the Commander of Flames. If only he was here, was Ethan's last thought as he lost his grip on consciousness. However, the last voice he heard was not of Kaint Swordsbane's; it was Emanuel Cursebinder's, who uttered a curse to make the warlord immobile.

"Gugu Gah Gagaga," said the nine-month-old Princess Lore of the Anons as she sat by Ethan's shoulder.

Ethan opened his eyes slowly. He was back in his room. Like him, his room was simple. It was minimalistic with peaceful white walls. It had a modest but sturdy bed with white beddings and a big plain desk in one corner of the room. The only fancy thing in the room was an ancient mirror left to him by his father Edwin Gainsworth.

Everything had gone wrong after his father's death. It had been over nine months since the incident at the Mother's Womb. Afterward, Emanuel Cursebinder had taken over the Gainsworth clan supported by Uncle Ran and Uncle Ori. In the meanwhile, Uncle Ran had said that they all would have died if it weren't for Lore and Zine, who were both born out of the Womb that day. So, Lore and Zine became the new princess and prince of Anons as a result of their 'good deed'.

"What happened?" Ethan asked Leander, who was standing by his bedside.

"The warlord suddenly attacked you. His excuse was that of teaching you to always be prepared. However, we all know he just wanted revenge for Karenitz. Mr. Cursebinder anticipated what would happen when he saw Karenitz run out crying. So, he came in the nick of time to save you. I'm sorry, sire. I should've never left you alone," said Leander with a pained and shameful expression on his face.

"It's not your fault. Like father, like daughter. Both vindictive. They'll go to any lengths to harm anyone that bested them. I'm surprised, though. Cursebinder cared enough to come to my aid?"

"He has to keep up the appearance that he cares a lot for you, as the new head of the Gainsworths."

"You are correct. Anyways, we will discuss politics later. Please inform everyone that I'm alright now. Also, return the princess to her room."

"I don't think that will be possible, sire. She hasn't left your side since yesterday when the Queen Adayna brought her to see you."

Ethan looked at Lore with soft eyes and smiled. "Fine, leave her with me and go inform the others."

Ethan did some stretching after Leander left. Then he picked up Lore and walked to the balcony. The drapes fluttered gracefully in the gently blowing wind. Lore reached out and grabbed hold of one of the drapes and started twisting it between her fingers. The one good thing that happened between all the chaos was the unconditional love Ethan received from Lore. As a prince of the Anons, Ethan knew of the Anon political games very well. There was more to his father's death than what was told. Ethan had vowed to find the whole truth. But amongst all the secrets and manipulations, Lore was the only one who genuinely loved and cared for him.

Well, she isn't the only one. There was one more. I never did find out more about the girl I met at the Snack Stop. I wonder who she was. Where is she now? As Ethan had these thoughts, the ancient mirror left by his father showed a peculiar scenery. The girl Ethan had been looking for all this time was walking towards the edge of the Volcano of Creation.

Chapter Eleven

It was midday in Solem. The guards stationed at the foot of the Volcano of Creation were all knocked unconscious with Desdemona's power. The ancestors were right. The Volcano of Creation is attracting Desdemona, and soon she will be able to extract the Creation Flames from it.

It has been over nine months since the Mother's Womb incident. All this time Leo was forced to help out the people of Sanctuary. Even after explaining that Areliam was in danger, no one, including his parents, agreed to help him. Instead, the idea of Leo trying to save Areliam scared his parents so much that they willingly cooperated with Atlas.

After a decade of living in isolation, the people of Sanctuary no longer wanted to be connected to the outside world. So, they came to a compromise. The Hearth-Bringers would help them gather resources to stay alive, and in return, they'd be allowed to stay in Sanctuary. Over the last several months Calaren used his sources to acquire various resources. Then they worked Leo to the bone to transport everything back to Sanctuary, all the while keeping a tight eye on Leo to make sure that he didn't run off to Kracten. If the Hearth-Bringers negated on their end of the bargain, they would pay with their lives.

So, Leo had to figure out a plan to counter the Anons in secret. It wasn't easy. However, by combining his smartness with the knowledge of his ancestors, Leo knew what to do. To bring Areliam back to balance, all the three Primordial races needed to be in top shape again. The Primordials gain strength from their home worlds. Ragonia was destroyed, and Yonder was under the Anon's oppression. Out of the public eyes, the Anons kept polluting Yonder, killing it little by little.

Currently, however, there was no way to free Yonder, as it was hidden away in a secret location. So, Leo had to start the counterattack by rejuvenating Ragonia first.

It is a great thing that the curse doesn't affect the Elementals. So, once Ragonia is healed, the remaining Elementals will be able to use their powers fully again. Then they will be indebted to Leo and will have to help him in saving Areliam and freeing his people.

The first step to achieving this is rekindling the Creation Fires at the Meadow of Origins. Only an Elemental can do that by acquiring sparks of the Creation Flame from the Volcano of Creation. Nature itself wants that to happen. That is why as soon as Desdemona neared the Volcano of Creation she was entranced to approach it.

The ancestors told Leo this would happen. So, for months he had been trying to travel to Solem with just Des. This task was extremely difficult given that he was always accompanied by a suspicious adult. Today Des convinced Atlas and Leo's parents to let them go for a quick trip to Solem so she can visit the Snack Stop again. Only this time. Leo tricked Des into coming near the Volcano of Creation. He told her they would be collecting local fruits to make snacks themselves.

Leo looked at Desdemona walking in a trance in front of him. She had used her powers subconsciously to destroy the energy of any guards she met on the way here. Most people took Desdemona's carefree and kind nature as a sign of her weakness, but Leo knew the truth. Des was far more powerful than the average Elemental, yet for some reason, she hid this truth from others. Not anymore though. Once she obtained the Creation Flames, everyone would know her might.

Leo silently followed Des, who by now had reached the mouth of the volcano. He watched as she walked down the jagged pathway to get to the boiling lava. Step by step she grew closer to the fiery magma until finally she stood a pace away from it. The heat increased, jets of fire rose, and Des put her hand in one of them. The fire didn't burn her though. The moment Des put her hand into a jet of fire, it disappeared. The fire slowly assimilated into Desdemona, her body glowing orange like the fire it absorbed.

This process went on for a few more minutes. Jets of fire would connect with Desdemona only for them to become one with her. After a while, Des couldn't consume any more of the fires, and she fell to the ground as her knees gave in. By now, the Anon authorities must have been making their way to the volcano. Or they would have if Leo hadn't broken all the mirrors that could have provided them an easy entrance. He had left only one of the mirrors intact, and that mirror was showing movement now.

Finally! He is coming! Good thing the ancestors stimulated the mirror in Ethan's chamber so he saw what was going on here and responded. Thought Leo. Ethan jumped out of the mirror with Lore holding on to his back. He looked around to find Des and saw her unconscious body by the lava. He ran at full speed to reach Des. Once near her, he bent down and scooped Desdemona in his arms. *No guards around him only the toddler princess ancestors mentioned before. Well, this makes my job easy*, thought Leo.

"Hey wake up! What's wrong with you? Wake up. Wake up, please." That was the last thing Ethan said before Leo pushed him along with Lore and Des into the portal he opened right in front of them.

Ethan hit the floor of Anorea's underground temple in Sanctuary. He found himself surrounded by Elementals who were extremely surprised to see him there. He could feel Lore holding onto his neck tightly. She had latched on to him when he bolted to reach the girl in his embrace and hadn't let go.

"Take them into custody. He is a prince of the Anons, Ethan Gainsworth, and that baby is Princess Lore of the Anons. They followed us back!" said Leo.

"What? No! You were the one that..." Ethan started saying but was interrupted.

"Look what he did to Des," said a man from the gathered crowd.

"How dare you hurt my daughter?" asked Atlas.

"GET HIM!" yelled a woman.

"GUGUGAHGAHGAGAGA!" said Lore loudly before she used her powers. All the stored water in Sanctuary came alive to aid her. The temple was flooded with water and people were having a hard time staying afloat. The only dry place was near Ethan.

"Damn this monster child. She wasn't part of the plan," Leo blurted out.

"Plan? What plan?" asked June.

"Leo...what did you do this time?" asked an enraged Calaren.

"Forget about me and do something about that demon baby. It took almost nine months for me to haul all this water in here and increase the reserves. Please, you can't let her waste it all!" Leo pleaded.

"Fine, but you better have some good answers to our questions later, or else..." threatened Calaren.

"Save me from this deranged kid first," said Leo as he and the others were being sucked into a whirlpool.

Calaren started to hymn loudly. Calaren Hearth-Bringer was the man with a magical voice. The power of his voice made the impossible possible. Words and sounds coming out of his mouth could bring down storms or hypnotize the enemy. Cal used his powers to lull Lore and Ethan to sleep. Once Lore was asleep, the turbulent waters dispersed throughout the tunnels. The people who were drowning but a moment ago now had the chance to collect themselves.

Calaren got on his feet and walked to Leo, who was coughing his heart out. He grabbed Leo by the neck like a cat and pulled him to his eye level. "Start explaining," Calaren demanded angrily.

CHAPTER TWELVE

T hings were finally calm inside the temple of Anorea. After Ethan and Lore were put to sleep, they were constrained with power dampeners first then put in the dungeon. Little golden bracelets that self-adjusted to the wearer were used. These power-limiting bracelets were the work of the Veiled One clan of Craftmasters, the group of people that once imbued mundane objects with magic. The architects of all the palaces, temples, cities, and other marvels of architecture in existence. The same people who have now been reduced to slavery by the hands of the Anons.

Calaren looked at Leo trying to clean up with the others. "Do you believe what Leo told us?" Calaren asked June.

"Are you crazy? You know better than to trust Leo and his elaborate plans. Remember that time when he lit a nobleman's house on fire? Or that time when he convinced the Anons that the Veiled One lake was haunted?"

"I remember all his plans worked. The cruel nobleman mistreated the Veiled Ones working under him. However, once his house was burnt he had to pay them triple to get it rebuilt in a hurry. Also, the Anons would've taken the lake away from us if Leo didn't spread the rumor of it being haunted."

"Still, other people's children will grow up to be healers and saints while our son will be a conman."

"Oh, that he already is! Leo can give the best black-market swindlers a run for their money. However, more good than bad always comes out of his actions. We would still be stuck at Solem if it weren't for him."

"Yes, but this time it's far too dangerous to let him follow his ideas."

"June, Leo has a hundred percent success rate. None of his ideas have ever failed. Not to mention, he'll do it even if we say no. So, let's not be typical parents, restricting our child's potential in fear of harm."

"But..."

"No buts, dear. You left a life of crime and I left a life of luxury to be free to love each other. Now our son is trying to bring freedom to all of Areliam. We have to help him."

June looked at Calaren for the longest time before finally saying, "You know I can never say no to you."

Darkness. Cold, wet, silent, sleek blackness that no light could penetrate. That was the place Ethan opened his eyes in. It took a while before he got accustomed to his new surroundings. Ethan felt shackles on his hands and legs. He reached out to the ragged cave wall behind him and used it as support for standing up. He felt nauseated. The putrid smell inside the space didn't help either.

"Veiled One. Are you up yet?" asked Des.

"Who? Who is it?" asked Ethan while scouring the darkness with his hands.

"It's me, the girl you met in Solem. I'm really sorry you are going through so much trouble because of me," Des said apologetically.

"If you are sorry, then show yourself and apologize face to face," demanded Ethan.

A small candle was lit close to Ethan as Desdemona came forward to meet him. She looked ethereal in the candlelight. Her eyes were sympathetic and remorseful as she observed Ethan's state. "I'm really, really sorry. Please forgive me. I had no intention of dragging you in here and making you suffer," said Des.

Ethan was mesmerized by Des and couldn't speak for a while. "What is your name?" he asked once he got back to his senses.

"I'm Desdemona of the Destruction Elementals," said Des.

"I am Ethan Gainsworth. So, where am I? Where is my sister? Why were we brought here? I remember being in some kind of underground temple after being transported from the Volcano of Creation. I found you unconscious inside of it."

"Yeah...that's about it. I have no clue what happened. I have no memories of what happened for most of the day. I just remember being with Leo and..."

"Wait, Leo as in Leon Hearth-Bringer? No wonder everything is messed-up. The last thing I remember is hearing his voice accusing me earlier. It's his fault. He caused all of this. Where is he? Bring him here right now!"

"Oh, come on. My son isn't that bad," said Calaren Hearth-Bringer from a dark corner of the room.

"You! You too are involved in this? What is all this? Some sort of stupid revenge plan? Father was right; Hearth-Bringers really don't know when to give up. Unfortunately for you, none of your pathetic schemes to bring the Anons down will work."

"Ah, I see we have a lot to talk about. Des, sweetheart, will you please keep an eye out for the other Elementals heading this way."

"Of course, Uncle Cal."

Cal waited silently as he watched Ethan achingly looking at Desdemona leaving the room. Cal knew the feeling behind Ethan's expression. He too had felt that pain of separation from the woman he liked a long time ago. "Don't worry, you'll get plenty of time to spend with her soon. Once you get out of here, of course."

"Have some shame. Even we didn't harm or threaten children of your clan."

"That's right! You didn't need to, because once all the adults were dead, controlling the children was damn easy. However, I'm not here to talk about the past. We need to discuss the future."

"Oh yeah? What atrocities will you make me and my toddler sister go through? Will it be a quick death or a long, drawn-out painful process?"

"Believe it or not, I'm here to save you from the brutalities. The Elementals wanted to skin both of you alive and send your bodies to the Anons, but I convinced them otherwise. So, they've agreed to release you and your sister topside instead."

"Release us to the poison-filled atmosphere above? Are you kidding me? How is that any better?"

"You can use your Gainsworth powers to protect yourself and your sister."

"No, I can't. I...I have almost completely lost my Gainsworth powers. Also, even if I could use them, these dampeners won't let me. I have used my Anon powers while being restricted by dampeners before. But these are different. They are too powerful for me to overcome. Also, I doubt the Elementals would take these off before throwing me out there."

"Don't worry. I'll help you activate your powers despite the dampener's effects. I just need some information from you first."

"So, that is what all of this is about, huh! You just want to get information out of me. Well, I'd rather die than tell you anything."

"Son, don't go on my face. I'm a lot older than you, and as such know much more than you can ever imagine. If I wanted to know the inner secrets of the Anons, no one—including your father—would've been able to stop me. What I need to know is information about how you specifically use your Veiled One powers."

"I just told you I don't use my Veiled One powers because I can't access them."

"Fine. Let's start from the core of things. The Gainsworth clan is divided into three branches. The main family, the Spellcasters and the Cursebinders. All members of the main family can use both spellcasting and curse-binding. So, originally you must have been able to use both of them too. Now all that's left to figure out is which of the six senses is your power trigger."

Ethan stared at Calaren for a while in silence before saying, "My power triggers are sight and sound."

"Two power triggers, that too at such a young age! Very impressive! Now, sight I cannot help you with, but I can help you with sound." Calaren walked up to Ethan, took out his ring, and put it in Ethan's front pocket. "Put this ring on as soon as you are by yourself. I'm sure you know of protective spells and curse words already. Utter them while wearing this ring, and your powers will activate."

Ethan was dragged through the muddy tunnels of the caves that formed the underground metropolis of Ragonia. The air felt stuffy. Maybe it was because of all the negative energy everyone was directing at him. Ethan looked over his shoulder and saw a peacefully sleeping Lore tied to his back, from the corner of his eyes. No one would say this was the same baby that panicked everyone just a few hours ago. The mucky floor of the tunnels was a result of the dispersed water from Lore's earlier show of power. If Calaren Hearth-Bringer hadn't stopped her, then a lot of people could have drowned today.

It was their good luck that they survived. Just as it was Ethan and Lore's bad luck for being stuck here. Yet for some reason, Ethan's eyes still looked around the crowd for the cause of his bad luck. Alas, he couldn't spot Desdemona, who was secretly eyeing him while hiding herself. Ethan and Lore were escorted by guards that protected them from the murderous horde following them. A few elaborately dressed men ahead of the guards led them to a huge cave. They're going to take advantage of our captivity to brag about their might. How typical.

Sure enough, as soon as they reached the middle of the cave, they stopped. One of the richly dressed men came forward and said, "My friends, today is the day we get revenge! The cruel and wicked Anons have destroyed our planet, our homes, and our people. However, Mother Anorea is just. She is fair. So, today she allowed us to destroy the coming generation of the Anons. We have here the prince and princess of the Anons, who we will send topside. There they will die of the same poison that our planet has died from. This will leave the Anon royal family out of heirs. And that will be our biggest victory!"

The crowd cheered. Everyone seemed to forget that they were sending children, who had nothing to do with the war, to their deaths. However, that wasn't enough. The people wanted to kill them with their own hands.

A few among the crowd yelled, "Stop!"

A man said, "Their kin killed ours, so let us avenge them by offing them ourselves."

"That's right. Let me at them!" said another.

"Let us kill them ourselves!" yelled many.

"They deserve it," said many more.

This is not going to work. The plan was to get topside and make our escape from there. But we'll never make it! This is the end! thought Ethan as he looked on in horror at the crowd rushing in to kill Lore and him.

CHAPTER THIRTEEN

M urderous cries echoed through the walls of the cave. Ethan hurriedly took a few steps back. He eyed the now mindless people, thirsty for his blood, breaking through the guards and accelerating to them. A paralyzing fear gripped him. He had never seen so much anger and hatred for himself in others. All this commotion had woken Lore. She was confused, not knowing what to do. Ethan didn't know what to do either. He needed to save himself and his sister, but his body was frozen. Try as he might, he couldn't even move as death came running towards him.

"STOP!" yelled an Elemental girl who used her powers to bring the crowd to their knees with a clap of her hands.

Ethan saw Desdemona's face as she turned around and pulled him up. "We must leave before they regain their energy. There are too many of them for me to render motionless." And so, they ran for their lives. Ethan followed Desdemona blindly through the jagged earthy hallways of Sanctuary, bumping into corners and tripping and falling several times. Only to get up right away in terror of the homicidal mob behind catching up to them.

Finally, they left the narrow underground hallways and approached a long and wide staircase. It was the stairway that led to Sanctuary's exit. Guards were stationed at the foot of the stairway who looked alarmed from all the commotion. They tried to stop the trio, but again Desdemona brought them down with a snap of her fingers.

They ascended quickly through the stairs until they reached the towering iron door blocking their way. Desdemona spotted the turning wheel controlling the door. "You both need to get out the door as soon as I lift it. Then quickly go as far away from the gate as possible. Also, don't forget to activate your protective powers as soon as you get out," she said while running towards the turning wheel.

"But what about you?" asked Ethan.

"Don't worry about me. Leo and I will join you very soon. Trust me. Now go," said Des as she turned the wheel and opened the door.

Ethan ran to crossover to the other side immediately but stopped abruptly, turned around, and said, "thank you, Desdemona."

Desdemona smiled at him and said, "Des, all my friends call me Des. So, call me Des the next time we meet. Okay, Ethan?"

Ethan smiled back at her and nodded before plunging into the unknown world outside. Des closed the door behind him and came down the stairs to face the wrath of the masses. She didn't need to wait long, as the furious crowd had been gathered at the foot of the stairs for a while now.

"Traitor! Why did you help the enemy?" asked a random person.

"Enemy! What enemy? They were children like me. One of them is just a baby who is not even a year old!" replied Des.

"Nonsense! That is no baby. It's a demon who tried to drown us all," said a woman.

"She only did that because we were trying to hurt her," said Desdemona.

"It doesn't matter if she is baby or not. She is an Anon, and that in itself is a crime worthy of death," said a man from the crowd.

"Well, you got your wish. They will probably die very soon now that they are outside Sanctuary's protective environment."

"But we wanted to kill them ourselves!" said yet another man from the crowd.

"How can you be so cruel? Is it not enough that they'll die a slow and painful death outside?" asked Desdemona.

"Be quiet, child! You have no idea what we have been through because of the Anons."

"I know we were at fault too! If the Elementals, correction, if the Creation Elementals didn't claim authority over creation, none of this would've ever happened!"

"How dare you say that," said an elderly man as he stepped up to slap Desdemona. However, Atlas intercepted his raised hand.

"Keep your hands and feet to yourself, old man Gino. Remember, you are standing on the land of Destruction Elementals. The same land where you Creation Elementals first exiled us, then came to seek refuge in. Wars and massacres don't happen on their own. The Creation Elementals made many, many mistakes of their own that led to our downfall. So, don't you dare fault my daughter for wanting no more bloodshed."

"What right do you have to object when your daughter is the one who brought them here?" asked a lady.

"That's right! I say we make her pay instead!" said another angry woman, riling up the whole crowd against Desdemona.

"Calm down, everyone! Ragonia can come back to life because of what Des did," Leo said as he stepped between the angry gathering and Desdemona.

"What new rubbish is this?" asked Gino.

"Think about it. Destroying a primal planet is no easy feat. It is known that Ragonia represents the Eternal Mother's body, while Yonder is her conscious mind, Harbor her heart, and Solem her soul. Even now, Ragonia is constantly trying to recover. It just needs a bit of help."

"What does this have to do with sparing those kids?" asked someone from the crowd.

"They are the prince and princess of the Anons. They have the authority to release the seal around the First Fire Pit and set Ragonia free to heal. Once they do that, feel free to punish them whatever way you see fit."

"Even if that happens, all the Creation Fires were drowsed by the Anons. So, neither Ragonia nor we would ever be able to recover our power," said Gino.

"False, the Creation Fires still burn in the Volcano of Creation," said Leo.

"Yes, but that's in Solem. Who'll go face the Anons there and bring the fires here?" asked a woman.

"It's already here! Look," said Leo while holding up Desdemona's hands. There in the middle of each of her palms, two little orange crystals had materialized. The crystals were outward manifestations of the Creation Flames Des had absorbed inside the Volcano of Creation.

"No, it can't be! The creation flames chose a Destruction Elemental!" old man Gino mumbled aloud.

"Yes, now all that is left to do is for us to go out and convince the prince and princess of the Anons to release the seal. So, we can rekindle the Creation Flames at the Meadow of Origins.

"Absolutely not! My daughter is not going out in that toxic environment!" said an anxious Atlas.

"Even if she goes now, those Anon children should already be dying from the toxic air outside," said Gino.

"She will be protected by the Creation Fires within her. Also, she is not going to be alone. I'll go with her. My Hearth-Bringer healing abilities will protect me from the poisonous atmosphere outside. Also, the Anons and Gainsworths have some inbuilt resistance to the toxicity. They originally made it so that they won't be affected by it. However, as time went on, it became too much for even them to handle. All this is to say they will remain alive long enough to get the job done," replied Leo.

"No, it's still too dangerous. There are other obstacles out there," said Atlas.

"Yes, but that is a risk worth taking for saving Ragonia. What say you all?" Leo asked the crowd.

"Yes! Save Ragonia! Save Ragonia!" chanted all.

It was pitch black and cold, save for the faint blue light of the protective shield around Ethan and Lore. Ethan had put on Calaren Hearth-Bringer's ring as soon as he got out of Sanctuary. The ring had a lot of power. It rendered the dampeners on him useless and awakened his Gainsworth powers as well. It even lessened the effects of Lore's dampeners. Speaking of Lore, she had been more than accommodating throughout the ordeal. She kept quiet throughout the chase inside Sanctuary earlier, then fell asleep again when she felt things had calmed down.

It had been several hours already, and Ethan had put quite a distance between Sanctuary and them. Should I stop here and wait for Des to catch up? But she did say to go as far away from Sanctuary as possible. Let's just walk a little farther for now. Ethan kept looking back hoping to see Des.

An eternity seemed to have passed walking in the darkness before finally a portal opened in front of Ethan. Leo and Des walked out of it holding light crystals.

"Told you we'd meet again soon," said Desdemona as she ran over and hugged Ethan. Ethan's body relaxed and he wholeheartedly hugged Des back. He closed his eyes and smiled fully. Anger came back, though, once he opened his eyes and saw Leo standing in front of him. Ethan gently released Des and furiously marched to Leo.

Ethan grabbed Leo by the collar and asked, "Why did you kidnap my sister and me? What are you after? Tell me honestly, or else..."

"Ok, ok, ok! No need for threats! We are all friends here!" said Leo casually.

"Friend!? I'm no friend of yours, and I will never want to be friends with someone like you!" Ethan replied.

"Don't be too certain. You will change your mind once you hear what I have to say. So, if you are ready to hear the truth, let me go," said Leo as he looked unabashedly into Ethan's eyes.

CHAPTER FOURTEEN

T hings calmed down a lot inside Sanctuary after Leo
convinced everyone to follow his plan. Afterward, the
Elementals equipped him and Desdemona with all the
necessary tools to reach the Meadow of Origins safely. Like
always, Leo made people believe everything would work out.
Now, the same people who were willing to kill children a short
while ago were acting normal. They were peacefully cleaning
the muddy tunnel floors caused by Lore's power outburst. The
temple of Anorea was cleaned first out of respect, and it
was easier. Cleaning the tunnel floors, though, was more of a
challenge. The floor was mopped then big rocks were placed
in the middle to create a pathway.

Calaren straightened his back after putting down a rock.
"Alright, that was the last one for me. All people have to do is
wait for the mud to harden and travel using this rocky walkway
in the meanwhile. What about you, honey? You done yet?"
Calaren asked June.

"Oh, I was done way before you. Am waiting on you, honey,"
said June, poking Calaren with her elbow and smiling.

"Yeah, yeah, I get it. Calaren Hearth-Bringer doesn't know
how to work fast and efficiently due to his elite upbringing.
That is what you want to say, right?"

"How well you know me, sweetheart."

"Let's head back to the temple. You can taunt me all you
want there."

"Do we have to? It'll be lonely there at this time of the day.
Also, I think after what Leo pulled off, the Elementals will
happily let us stay with their main group."

"Yes, but I don't want to face Atlas. We are used to Leo's
antics, but Atlas isn't. He looked extremely angry at how

everyone sent Desdemona out. I'm sure he blames me for all of this. If he wasn't called for emergency water rationing, he would be at my throat already. I want to have a few moments of tranquility at the temple before he comes for me."

"So, you are going to run away without taking responsibility like always. Well, not this time. You are going nowhere until you answer my questions," said Atlas from behind them.

Calaren heaved a huge sigh and massaged his temple before turning around to face Atlas. "Run away, that too from you? Never! I wouldn't even dream of it. Ask away. I won't move a muscle until all your questions are done," said Cal.

"All of this was planned by you, wasn't it?"

"No."

"Lies. If not you, then who?"

"It was Leo."

"Using your child as a shield for your nefarious plans is low even for you. Just admit that it was your plan, but how dare you use my daughter in your schemes."

Calaren took a deep breath and replied, "Atlas, my son is wise and capable beyond his years. He makes the impossible possible. From the moment we stepped in here to the moment Leo and Des left to heal Ragonia, it was all him."

Atlas swiftly crossed the short distance between him and Calaren and punched him in the face. "You despicable excuse for a living being! How do you call yourself a father? First, you put your child in harm's way, then you claim it was your son's fault!"

"Enough!" said June as she moved between Atlas and Calaren. "Ever since we came here, you have been constantly berating my husband. You know nothing about him and what he has been through. Did you know he saved countless lives during the Primordial War? He is the reason this place remained safe from the Anons' advances."

"Honey, please! He doesn't need to know all this," said Calaren as he put his fingers to June's lips.

However, June moved his hand away with force and continued speaking. "You think it is coincident that Calaren knows people who can supply a whole Elemental city with resources in secret? During the war when all of you were killing each other it was Calaren that helped the ones left behind. He is the wartime hero Wandering Soul."

"What?" asked a surprised Atlas.

"Don't believe me?" asked June as she revealed Calaren's unique Hearth-Bringer symbol with a nine-pointed star inside it. "Cal helped everyone while hiding his face, but people knew him from this symbol. Also, it was Cal that led the surviving Elementals to Sanctuary's gates. He would've joined the Battle of Behemoth too, but his father Kendall Hearth-Bringer forcibly sent him back."

"I...I can't believe this!" said Atlas.

"Hmmph," scoffed June. "Wait till you hear what we got in return for all his good deeds. They bound him with a promise on the Mother to stop him from going against the Anons. Not only that, they killed our first child in my womb and made me drink potions that were supposed to make me barren. It was only after years of tears, pain, and prayers that Anorea blessed us with Leo. Yet Cal still let our only son risk his life to revive your dead planet. So, after today I never want to hear you demean my exemplary husband ever again. Because I promise to rip your head off if you insult him one more time," said June as she punched the nearest cave wall. A huge gapping hole appeared where June punched the wall. Upon seeing it, Atlas became extremely thankful for the wall being there to take June's punch instead of him.

The metropolis of Sanctuary was hidden deep underneath the surface of Ragonia. A long stretch of land existed between it and the entrances to the Ragonian underground. Once upon a time, light crystals illuminated the underground passageway. However, with time all of them lost power. Currently, only a blanket of darkness engulfed the whole passage. Nowhere was this eclipse more profound than in the area surrounding Leo and Ethan. It seemed Ethan's anguish and frustration directed at Leo served to deepen the shadow around them, and the two light crystals held by Des and Leo didn't help lift the dark either.

Des wanted to prompt Ethan to let Leo go right away, but Leo signaled her not to interfere. Instead, he stared back into Ethan's venom-filled eyes for what seemed like an eternity. Finally, Ethan let Leo go. "That's more like it! Now before we have our chat, let's brighten up this place, shall we?" asked Leo as he took out a box from the back sack he was carrying. Several mechanical fireflies came out as soon as he opened it. "A marvel of the Craftmasters. Little stars that create light in the darkness." The fireflies flew to far-away corners and relit dead light crystals on the walls.

A special ability of the mechanical fireflies was to supply and siphon powers to and from other objects. As the space they were standing in came to light, a horrible scenario greeted the children. Traps were littered everywhere. From walls aligned with hidden spikes, barb wires sticking out from the floor to guillotines hanging in the air, and parts of the floor giving away to deep spear-filled holes, death was beckoning from all corners.

"How did you manage to avoid all of these in the darkness?" asked an astonished Desdemona.

"A safe pathway exists between the traps. My protective shield changes to red each time danger is near. So, I just moved in the direction where the shield's color remained blue. However, how are you surviving out here without a shield? Isn't the air outside Sanctuary toxic?" Ethan asked Des.

"Yes! It is! Both Leo and I are immune though. I acquired the Creation Flames back at Solem which nullify the effects of most destructive things. As for Leo, he is using his healing Hearth-Bringer powers to remain unaffected from the toxins in the air," replied Des.

"I see," said Ethan before turning to Leo. "Mr. Hearth-Bringer made me a promise to hear you out in exchange for his help in escaping. So, start talking about this great truth that has been kept hidden from me," said Ethan while crossing his arms.

"The Gainsworths' loss of power is directly linked to the Cursebinders putting the power-draining curse on all Veiled Ones. It is Anorea's punishment to the Gainsworths for their role in the Primordial Wars. The Anon king and Emanuel Cursebinder knew of this but let it happen anyway. The only way you can stop this is by helping me restore balance to Areliam," said Leo solemnly.

"You are full of shit. If what you say is true, then our whole clan would've lost complete power already. It has been over a decade since the war ended, yet a lot of us still have our powers. Uncle Emanuel remains especially powerful. He is the strongest, not only within the clan but also among all other Veiled Ones," countered Ethan.

"Emanuel Cursebinder is draining the Gainsworth ancestors to remain in power. Have you not wondered why your connection to your ancestors has been broken? Why you haven't been able to contact your father's spirit through the death-link rituals?" asked Leo.

The death-link rituals were a common practice between Veiled Ones, at least it had been before the Anons outlawed them. It granted the living Veiled Ones brief periods of contact with their deceased ancestors. However, special privileges were given to the Gainsworths to keep practicing it. But, it wasn't working. All communication with Gainsworth ancestors had stopped. Ethan was visibly shaken by Leo's knowledge of this.

"You must be wondering how I know all this. My ancestors told me. See, this has happened once before. Anorea took away powers from the Pathfinders when they abused them. Back then, the Pathfinders didn't have a chance to get it back. But you do. The question is whether you'll take it or not."

Chapter Fifteen

The walls of the royal Anon castle at Ascendance never looked so calm and peaceful. Yet, the environment inside was no less than a funeral. The whole castle was put under high alert. Guards were posted outside every chamber. Plain-clothed security guards patrolled the nearby areas of the castle. Even the number of housekeepers was limited. Behind closed doors, very secret meetings discussing the disappearance of Ethan and Lore were happening constantly. One such meeting was going on currently in a small hidden room of the castle among five men.

"What do you mean you still don't know where the portal led?" Orias asked while punching the table so hard that a part of it broke off.

"We are still figuring out how the portal opened up in the first place. As you know, all traces of portal transportation magic disappeared with the Pathfinders. So..." Leander fell silent, having nothing more to add.

"None of this would've happened if you didn't bully Ethan, Kaint! Then he wouldn't be left alone to deal with the intruders at the Volcano of Creation. Neither would Lore and he be missing right now. How lowly of you to roughen up a child. My nephew!" Orias accused warlord Kaint Swordsbane venomously.

"That boy is not worthy of your bloodline. He couldn't even withstand one attack!" answered Swordsbane.

"You attacked him without warning to take revenge for your daughter's defeat. I know because I was there!" said Emanuel Cursebinder.

"Well, a true royal should've been prepared for anything," retorted the warlord.

Orias created a fire spear from the fire burning in the fireplace and hurled it across the table at Swordsbane. The warlord used his wind Anon powers to split the spear, only to have parts of it clasp him tightly.

"What happened, Swordsbane? Couldn't dodge that one? Maybe it's you who is no longer worthy to serve as the warlord of the Anon empire," taunted Orias.

Kaint used his wind Anon powers again to suppress the fire and took out his lightning sword. Before he could strike, though, the room grew cold. Ice engulfed the bodies of both Orias and Kaint, freezing their movements. King Ran, the Anon of water, used his powers to rein in Kaint and Orias.

"Although both of your fighting might is impressive, now is not the time to show it," said King Ran of the Anons.

"But..." protested Emanuel.

"Enough! Kaint, Ethan's caliber is high enough for him to head into danger without backup. Also, he is the second most powerful young blood in the Anon empire. I'm sure you know that. Otherwise, you wouldn't need to bring him down in your daughter's stead. Am I correct?"

"Yes, sire," replied Kaint Swordsbane with his head held low.

"Good, now I need you to go and protect Zine. We must keep him safe at all costs, as he is the last of the young royals left in our care. Am I making myself clear?"

"Yes, sire," said Kaint without raising his head.

"Alright, then you may leave." Ran waited for the warlord to leave before turning to Emanuel. "Is there truly no way to figure out where Ethan and Lore were taken?"

"There is one, but it is tricky." Emanuel stopped speaking and glanced over to Leander. King Ran understood the signal and sent Leander out.

"Now speak freely," ordered King Ran.

"The regular wards placed on them have vanished. Either someone forcibly removed them, or the situation they are in is dangerous enough to exhaust all the wards. I can use the ancestral magic to pinpoint his location, but they are being uncooperative. So, I have to use force to make them help, which will anger them further," said Emanuel.

"Whoever kidnapped Ethan and Lore is powerful enough to avoid detection. It must be the same people who attacked us at the Mother's Womb," Orias spoke up.

"If that was the case, then Lore's powers would've surely kicked in by now to protect both of them." Said King Ran.

"Not necessarily. Lore had the home ground advantage that day, of being born inside the Mother's Womb. So, she could overpower the assailants. However, her powers will be significantly weaker when placed in hostile environments outside of Solem. She may have the powers of a first-generation Anon, but she is still just a toddler," replied Emanuel.

"Fine, no more delays then. I want you to do everything you can to figure out where they are and how to get them out. In the meantime, please try to remotely place protective wards on both of them again," said King Ran.

"I will do so. However, one good thing is that Ethan's life force is still strong. So, he is still alive. I'll use the ancestors' magic to make sure he remains that way until we find him. Also, I'll research all known facts about how the Pathfinder portals work, to find out where they were taken," said Emanuel.

"Great! If Ethan is alive, then Lore must be too. Ethan wouldn't let anything happen to her," said Ran with relief in his voice.

"Why do I feel like you are more worried about Lore than Ethan? Remember, Ethan is the only one related to us by blood. I can understand your love for Adayna makes you care for Zine. But what is your concern over Lore's safety? Isn't she just one of your pawns?" Orias asked Ran.

The atmosphere inside the room changed dramatically with ice spikes growing out of the walls. "Now, now! This is not the time to discuss such things," Emanuel desperately tried to interject to calm things down, but to no avail.

"Lore is my daughter. She is an integral part of my life despite how she originally came into it. Now, my life is incomplete without her. She is just as precious to me as Ethan and Zine," replied King Ran while staring down Orias.

"That's funny. Didn't you want to kill her off at birth in fear of her becoming too powerful later?" Orias asked amusingly.

"Yes! And it was you who repeatedly stopped me at that time. Reminding me how wrong it would be for me to kill an innocent baby girl. Especially a powerful Anon born out of the Mother's Womb," said Ran.

"I still stand by my words. However, I'll always choose my flesh and blood over others. That is why I'm more concerned about Ethan. Have you forgotten the curse of Calico Paradigm on our line? We cannot father children. Even if we do, none of them survive. It is a miracle Ethan has lasted so long, but..." Orias stopped before finishing his sentence, in fear of it becoming true.

"No! Nothing will happen to Ethan! Calico Paradigm might have been the all-powerful head of the Paradigms, but she is still just one being. As long as I'm alive I'll pour all the Gainsworth resources into protecting him. I'll make sure he survives no matter what," proclaimed Emanuel, who had unknowingly gotten quite attached to Ethan after Edwin's death.

King Ran chuckled and said, "You don't always have to be related by blood to call a child yours, Orias. Emanuel of all people has understood that fact. It's time you do the same."

The children's journey from Sanctuary to the surface exit of Ragonia was a hard one. The menacing and deadly underground passageway tried their patience at every turn. A lot of traps remained active closer to Sanctuary. Maneuvering around them took time. They mostly followed Ethan, who found the designated safe path for them.

However, years of no maintenance made some of the traps lose control. For example, a lava canal blocked their way at one point. The levers controlling the lava flow had long been broken. So, the lava had proceeded to flood over the safe pathway too. In another instance, a glitch in the controls made electricity run through a whole portion of the passageway permanently, when originally it was only meant to send out electric shocks every few minutes.

Leo used the fireflies to cut powers to such machines permanently so they could pass through them. He then redistributed the power to light crystals along the way, so they wouldn't travel through absolute darkness.

Ethan remained mostly silent throughout this ordeal. Leo's revelation of the Gainsworth ancestors being taken hostage to supply the living Gainsworths' power shook him. He knew Emanuel Cursebinder was bad news, but Ethan didn't think he would go so far as to abuse the dead to get what he wanted.

Ethan only opened his mouth to tell an extremely concerned Lore, who stuck to him like glue, that he is ok. Or he spoke up to say thank you to Desdemona when she provided him with food and water brought from Sanctuary. Des and Leo mostly left Ethan on his own. They wanted to give him space to be alone with his thoughts.

Finally, Leo and the gang reached the last obstacle before the gate leading to the surface. A giant mechanical pyramid stood before them, dead bodies spread all around it. Some of the bodies belonged to Anon soldiers who tried to gain entry to the underground. However, most belonged to Elementals who wanted to take refuge inside Sanctuary. Now it made sense why the children didn't encounter any bodies on the way. None of the people trying to reach Sanctuary had ever made it past this machine.

CHAPTER SIXTEEN

A silver-colored mechanical mound in the shape of a pyramid stood before the children. At the foot of it laid countless dead bodies or what was left of them. A decade is long enough for the flesh to decay. However, the bones, clothes, and accessories remained. Before the children was a mountain of carcasses. Behind it was the exit to the surface of Ragonia. Leo, Ethan, and Desdemona quietly stared at the structure and its surroundings for a long time. Even Lore, who had no clue about what was going on, looked on with a gaping mouth.

They remained this way until Desdemona broke the silence. "I think I'm going to be sick," she said before running over to the side to puke.

Leo, who had seen death and destruction at the Mother's Womb event, was more composed. However, he too was shaking with fear. Sensing all the fear and dread in the air, Lore gripped Ethan tightly while burying her face on his chest. Only Ethan, who had received royal training about how to handle such situations, remained calm.

Ethan walked up to Leo and grabbed him by the arm. Then they walked over to Des. Ethan sat Lore by his feet and focused on Des. "You better now?" Ethan asked Des, who had just finished throwing up.

"No," replied Des.

"What about you?" Ethan asked Leo, who had finally stopped shaking.

"Never better," said Leo with a weak smile.

Ethan smiled back at Leo's bravado and said, "Great! So, how do we get over to the other side of that?" Ethan pointed at the machine stopping their way. "Surely we didn't come all this way to go back now.

"So, you are fully on our side now?" asked a hopeful Leo.

"Not completely, but your words have some truth in them. I'll continue to help until I figure out the whole truth for myself," replied Ethan.

"That's complicated speech for you being one of us, right?" asked Des.

"Temporarily, yes," replied Ethan.

"Good enough for me! By the way, Leo, you sure you can't just portal us to the Meadow of Origins?" asked Des.

"Listen, if I could, I would have done it already. I mean, I'd love to, but it hasn't even been a year since I discovered my powers. So, I don't have enough practice to use both of my powers simultaneously. Even if I could, the power dampeners placed all over this planet severely hinder the use of my powers. You must feel your powers being suppressed as well. It was different inside Sanctuary where wards are placed to offset the dampeners. Currently, I can barely survive in this poisonous atmosphere. Thank goodness for my healing powers; otherwise, I wouldn't be able to handle this toxic environment," Leo explained.

"Shouldn't it be thanks to the ancestors in your case?" joked Des.

"Haha," Leo mocked Des.

"Ok, back to the topic. The ring your father gave me is losing its power. I can feel the protection weakening. At most, it'll last for two more days. After that, it'll no longer help me in activating my protective shield. Both Lore and I will die at that point," said Ethan to bring the team back on track.

"Alright! Let me tell you what the Elementals told me about that machine. It is an ancient creation. It has nine levels. The first layer disperses electricity, the second throws knives, third dispenses rotating round blades, fourth shoots laser beams, the fifth layer has hidden mechanical arms that come out to grab people." Leo stopped to take a breath and continued, "Fireballs come out of the sixth, arrows are thrown out of the seventh, a force field is generated from the eighth layer." Leo took another brief pause and said, "The last layer activates teleportation to teleport people who escaped back to itself."

Ethan and Des remained tongue-tied as they heard Leo's description of the death trap in front of them. Des kept blinking her eyes in disbelief while her jaw dropped, leaving her mouth wide open in shock. Even Ethan's eyes grew bigger while listening to Leo.

"Holy Mother Anorea! How are we supposed to get through all of that?" asked Des.

"Can you use the fireflies to siphon power from it?" asked Ethan.

"Power siphoning won't work on that machine," answered Leo.

"Why not?" asked Des.

"Because it has a continuously replenishing internal power source," said Leo.

"What?" asked Ethan and Des in unison.

"Inside the machine, several powerful amassing stones should still be supplying it with power. It also has a siphoning stone that draws powers from the machine's victims. So, as soon as we step inside its operating area, it'll start sucking our powers. However, the good news is none of this will be a problem as long as we get out of its operating area in time," said Leo enthusiastically.

"Alright, then what is its operating area?" asked Ethan.

"Uh, it should be one mile every which way," replied Leo.

"And what is the time limit we have to cross it?" Ethan asked.

"Umm...anywhere from nine seconds to one minute and a half," Leo said timidly.

"Are you out of your mind? How are we gonna get out of here in such little time? How?" yelled Desdemona as she started to shake Leo violently.

"Hey, stop! Don't hurt the messenger. I'm not the one who created this thing!" said Leo as he got Des to stop shaking him.

"What else did the Elementals tell you about it? They must have told you how to deal with it," said Ethan.

"Ah, yeah. They told me I should destroy the eighth layer from a distance first. Then use the same tactic to keep destroying layers from afar. However, we have to be careful that the arms don't grab us first, as their reach is far more than the one-mile operating area. Here, they gave me these crossbows to destroy the machine with," said Leo as he took out three crossbows from his back sack.

Ethan picked up one of the crossbows to examine it. In the world of Areliam, energy was used to power weapons.

The crossbows were light and well-oiled. Amassing crystals were integrated inside the bolts to be used with the crossbow. The crystals should supply enough strength to the bolts to have them go long distances. However, these weapons were old. Who knew whether the crystals still had power? Not to mention finding and aiming the bolts at the right target would be difficult.

"These will not work. We have to go back and get more weapons," said Ethan.

"I don't think that'll work. They already gave us all they could," said Leo.

"Then they knowingly set us up for failure," replied Ethan.

Leo went silent for a while and looked at the heap of skeletons between them and the machine. All those people were alive once and they tried their best to stay that way. However, no matter how much they struggled, that machine killed them. Then it used its mechanical hands to pile up the dead bodies around it as a warning. If we try to cross now, we'll end up dead too.

"You are right. Let's go back and bring better weapons to destroy this machine," said Leo while slumping his shoulders.

"Yeah, but we don't have any more weapons. Most of the weapons and machines were broken down to create new devices that purify the toxic air. Others were used to weaken the effect of the power-dampeners," explained Des.

"Well, then I just have to teleport out of Sanctuary and get more. It's gonna take a lot more time, but what other option do we have?" said Leo.

"However, you have to teleport Ethan and Lore out of here before we go back. Otherwise, there'll be lots of trouble." Said Des.

"I know. I will use my teleportation power closer to Sanctuary. We need Ethan to get us through the traps on the way back." Said Leo.

"Fine. Let's go back," said Ethan as he bent down to pick up Lore. "Wait! Where is Lore?" Ethan panicked.

Lore had disappeared. One moment she was sitting by Ethan's feet, and the next she was gone. Frightened by her disappearance, the trio frantically looked for her everywhere, yet she was not seen anywhere. Until they heard a distant, "Gugu Gah Gagaga."

While the older children were talking, Lore had been attracted by a shiny object closer to the machine. So, she had quietly walked on all fours to get to it. Currently, she was joyfully biting into it.

"How did she get so far?" asked Des.

"Bloody troublemaker!" said Leo.

"I have to go get her." Ethan said.

"No! Right now, she is very close to the machine's operating area. Look how close the pile of the dead is to her. We might accidentally trigger the machine if we get too close. So, we have to bring her back here without risking ourselves," said Leo.

"How do you suggest we do that?" asked an impatient Ethan.

"Well... let's try to call her over. Pspspspsps. Come here, baby. Come on. Who's a good baby? You are. Yes! You are. 'Cause you are gonna roll over here, aren't you?" cooed Leo while clapping his hands and making all kinds of weird noises. So much so that even Lore had a look of bewilderment at what Leo was doing.

"My sister is a toddler, not a dog. By the way, even dogs won't answer if you call like that. Now step aside, idiot," said Ethan as he knelt and extended his arms towards Lore imploring her to come to him.

"But I'm very smart," mumbled Leo.

Lore understood Ethan wanted her back desperately. So, she threw up her hands in excitement. However, she accidentally hit the giant bone hill behind her while doing so. As soon as the pile of bones was hit, it started to crumble down towards Lore. A terrified Ethan promptly got on his feet and ran to save his sister.

"Lore!" yelled Ethan as he rushed over to her.

"No! Stop!" said Leo as he ran after him.

"Be careful!" Yelled Des as she also ran after Ethan.

Ethan dived in to protect Lore as all of the bones fell over them. The sound of a mountain of bones crumbling down was not the only sound present, though. There was another sound, the soft humming sound of an old machine coming back to life. By the time Ethan and Lore emerged from within their bony burial, the machine was activated. Ethan looked at the machine and then back at Des and Leo, who were frozen in fear.

Ethan knew if he didn't do something quickly they would all die. So, he pointed the finger with Calaren Hearth-Bringer's ring first at Leo and Des, then at Lore and himself. "Connect!" Ethan ordered the ring, and a ray of blue light sprang forth and branched out to attach to all of them. Then he pointed upwards and said, "Fly." This made them levitate. Ethan set the destination of their flight towards the exit and they flew towards it at top speed.

The children were able to get off ground just in time before a wave of electric current hit where they were previously standing. The electric wave generated so much heat that it blew apart the hills of bones piled everywhere. So, now besides avoiding the various attacks from the machine, the children also had to avoid being hit by exploding bones. The ring generated shield protected Ethan and Lore, but Leo and Desdemona suffered some damage. One of the sharp pieces of bones cut Desdemona's hair and the back of her shirt. Also, Leo's pants caught fire from the heat and friction of a small piece of bone that hit his pants.

"Fire! Fire!" Leo kept yelling as he was doing cartwheels while flying to drowse the fire in his pants.

"Shut up and let me focus," yelled Ethan as he concentrated on getting all of them out of there as quickly and as safely as possible. It was an arduous task as the number of projectiles trying to harm them increased by the seconds.

Ethan navigated their flight to avoid the knives, arrows, fireballs, and other projectiles, to the best of his abilities. However, completely avoiding the arms proved to be impossible. They had several near misses. Until finally they avoided being grasped by one of the arms, only to be smacked by another one that sent them on a high-speed collision with the machine. Shortly before they collided with the machine, Ethan commanded the ring again. "Energy blast." A ball of energy shot out of the ring that blew a hole in the top part of the pyramid. The kids entered the pyramid through that hole right before the machine's protective shield covered it completely.

Chapter Seventeen

Orias stomped through the grimly silent corridors of the royal palace, completely ignoring Emanuel calling him from behind. Orias marched to his chambers and slammed the doors hard behind him. Emanuel Cursebinder came running after him within a few minutes.

"My love, please calm down," Emanuel managed to say while catching his breath.

"Calm down! My nephew, the only one to carry our blood into the next generation, is kidnapped and no one is doing anything. Yet you still want me to calm down?' asked an enraged Orias.

"That is not true. The King and I are doing everything in our power."

"Ran is only trying to save his beloved daughter, and you need to protect the heir of the Gainsworths. I'm the only one trying to save him earnestly."

Emanuel peered at his lover with hurt eyes. "You know I've always been fond of that child. Ever since Regal passed away I've been taking special note of him. My love and care for him has only grown after Edwin's passing. I see my childhood in that boy. I would never let anything bad happen to him," said Emanuel as he slowly approached Orias.

"Then what are you doing to get him back?"

"Everything in my power. The Gainsworths are scouring all of Areliam looking for Ethan. I've also locked his energy to mine. I'll know the moment Ethan will be in mortal danger. I'm also persuading the ancestors to help locate him. I will bring him back safely. I'll bring both him and Lore back safely. Trust me, my love," said Emanuel, caressing Orias.

"I worry for him, Emi. I worry for our whole family. So much of the family is already lost as payments of our sins. I don't want to lose the remaining few. With Ran favoring his adoptive children more than our blood, I have to protect him. You understand?"

"I do, my love! Also, don't worry. I consider Ethan as my adoptive son. And you know I can do anything and everything for the ones I love. The crown, the power, and all of Areliam will be our Ethan's. Just wait and watch. He will be back by our side very soon."

"You promise?"

"I do."

Orias smiled and pulled Emanuel closer. "Only Anorea can help your enemies. No one can best you. I'm so lucky that you love me."

"That you are, my love," said Emanuel as he shared a passionate kiss with Orias. However, the kiss ended abruptly as Emanuel jerked away.

"What happened?"

"It's Ethan. His life is in danger. I can feel it!"

The children hurled down the darkened interior of the machine. Their small bodies smacked into several mechanisms operating it. After what seemed an endless amount of time falling, they finally hit the bottom. Leo felt the bitter taste of blood inside his mouth. A few of his teeth were knocked out and blood flooded his mouth. The rest of his body felt shattered as well. Near him, Leo heard the sounds of Des moaning in pain and the desperate cries of Lore. Yet Ethan remained silent.

Leo reached for his backpack with shaky hands and took out the fireflies. The fireflies powered the internal light crystals. Once light illuminated the space, the damage was seen. Des was all bent out of shape, her body dangling from one of the lower ledges. Her legs were bloody and twisted, and her right hand was broken. Ethan's condition was far worse. He laid unconscious, face down on the ground in a pool of blood while holding on to Lore.

"No!" yelled Leo as he crawled over to Ethan. He waited for his Hearth-Bringer powers to fully heal him. Once that happened, he started helping the others. He turned Ethan over to see his belly pierced by multiple sharp parts of the machine. Leo quickly pulled out all the big parts and bandaged his wound with clean clothes. Then he took out healing potions from his backpack and pushed one down Ethan's throat. He looked up at the still weeping Lore and said, "Shut up! It's all your fault."

Next, he ran to Des with another potion in hand.

As Leo was tending to Des, he felt weak all of a sudden. Dang it! With our entry, we already took out the teleportation device placed at the top, but the siphoning stone is activating now. We will be drained of all our energy and left to die unless that stone is either destroyed or disconnected from the machine.

"Ancestors, please protect me," Leo called out and immediately felt his body revitalized again. He took out the crossbows and started equipping them while trying to find the siphoning stone. It didn't take him long. In the middle of the triangular-shaped floor laid a giant clear crystal. It was protected by an electric fence and surrounded by numerous amassing crystals powering it. By its side was another fenced-off mechanism that operated the shield around the machine. That device was also powered by the numerous amassing stones around it.

These crossbows won't do much damage. Did the Elementals know it wouldn't work but still sent us to our doom? Was Ethan right about them wanting us to fail? No, that can't be it. Atlas won't risk Des's life. They gave us everything they could to take down this machine, but it just wasn't enough. Plus, the exact make of this machine is not common knowledge. If it was, there wouldn't have been tons of dead Elementals who didn't know how to stop it. Des and Ethan are both down, and that troublemaker Lore won't be of any help either. Then...I guess I need some help from above.

Leo moved Des, Ethan, and Lore to a tucked-in corner then walked out to the middle of the floor and looked up while smiling. He pointed the crossbows upward and shot. He specifically targeted joints of the nuts and bolts holding bigger mechanisms in place. This commenced a downpour of debris and heavy parts falling.

Leo ran for his life as parts of the giant arms used to kill many fell right beside him. He barely escaped from being cut in half under a falling rotating blade. He managed to jump just in time before another huge part of the machine crushed him. Once he reached safety, Leo looked back to see if the siphoning stone was destroyed. It was, along with all the other stones besides it. The mechanism powering the protective shield was also damaged. All that stopped the children from leaving the machine was its thin walls. So, Leo used the rest of the crossbow bolts to create another hole on the lower wall that led outside.

Leo used that hole to drag his injured friends out. He laid Des and Ethan right by the exit to the surface. Then he fed them the rest of the healing potions. After that, Leo proceeded to get some food for himself. He fed Lore some as well. Next, he tied Lore to himself. "Don't want to take any chances with you, troublemaker. Too bad your brother didn't get to see my heroics back there. But you saw everything, right? You know I'm very smart. I can get us out of any trouble, but I would rather rest now. So, will you please keep out of trouble for a while?" asked Leo.

"Gugugagagagagah," said Lore as she curled up beside Leo to sleep. Leo laid down and took one last look at the exit as he closed his eyes. Soon, very soon, was his last thought as he fell asleep.

CHAPTER EIGHTEEN

Ethan opened his eyes in complete darkness. As soon as he tried to move, pain shot up through his stomach area. He touched Calaren Hearth-Bringer's ring on his finger and felt the energy left in it. Damn it! Not even ten percent remaining! The ring must be working only to protect Lore and I from the toxic air now. No wonder it didn't protect me against collisions with sharp objects inside the machine. Neither will it help me heal my physical wounds.

"Urgh, it hurts so much, and this damn darkness doesn't help either," said Ethan as he tried to sit up.

"Darkness is the great equalizer. It's light that discriminates. At least that's what Father says," said, Desdemona.

"He didn't have any dealings with the Anon royals before, did he?" Ethan asked jokingly.

"Well, there was this one time at the Battle of Behemoths where he barely escaped death at your uncle's hand," replied Des.

"It must have been Uncle Ori who let him escape. He would be long dead if it were Uncle Ran," said Ethan grimly. "By the way, I've been wondering, why have you always been so kind to me? Given the history of our races, you should've been hostile, yet...you have been nothing but helpful."

"I guess it's just my nature, and maybe because I know the truth."

"What truth?"

"Ok, story time!" Des said excitedly. "Yes, it's because of the Anons that we are trapped inside Sanctuary. However, we have always lived under the shadows of the Creation Elementals. Father says long ago, the Creation Elementals treated us as equals. In time, though, they started to fear us. So, they exiled us underground while they reigned above. They only accepted us after the Anon victory seemed imminent."

"So, you are nice to me because you think the Anon attacks helped Destruction Elementals regain their status in Elemental society," stated Ethan.

"Oh, hell no. Anons killed my mother. So, a part of me will always hate Anons. But my mother, who was a Creation Elemental, would've never met my father if it weren't for the Primordial Wars. Also, you are not your father. Why would I hate you based on your father's actions?"

A stunned Ethan looked in the direction of Desdemona's voice. He had never imagined someone persecuted by his family would allow him such understanding. Unknowingly, he stretched his hands in search of Des.

However, Desdemona reached out and touched his hand first. She took his hand in hers and said, "I don't want to hate you out of fear. I always wished that people would give each other an opportunity to work things out. If Creation Elementals accepted us Destruction Elementals from the beginning then my parents could've met earlier, and I could've spent more time with my mother. Alas, that didn't happen. So, I guess I'm trying to do the right thing now by giving you a chance. I mean, to be honest, you seem just as much a victim as us. You know, with all your Veiled One powers being gone because of your uncles and all. Are my ramblings making any sense, or should I shut up?"

Ethan smiled and squeezed Desdemona's hand. "You are the only one that makes sense. Thank you for being genuinely nice to me. Also, you are right. I'm tired of all the secrets, lies, and politics. The reason I hate darkness is because I feel like I have been trapped in it my whole life. I believed the wrong people for the wrong reasons. The light helps unmask these people. So, I wish I had more illumination in my life."

"Yeah, but darkness has its advantages. You need it for rest and rejuvenation and to protect yourself. Sometimes you need to hide to survive, and that's when darkness really comes in handy. For example, if the Anons knew about Sanctuary, they would kill us all. So, we need to hide in the darkness of the underworld for survival."

"You have a point there."

"You are not going to tell them about us when you get back, right?" asked Desdemona while tightly squeezing Ethan's hand.

"Don't worry, your secret is safe with me."

"Really! Thanks a lot. I knew I could trust you. Tell you what, let's make a deal. You who love light and I who love darkness will work to build a world where both are equal. Then there would be no fear of darkness or misuse of light."

"Done."

"Great, now that your conversation is over, will one of you please clean Lore's diaper! It stinks!" said Leo, who had been patiently holding his nose while waiting for Ethan and Des to finish talking.

The royal palace of the Anons had many elaborately designed rooms. However, the room Emanuel was currently using was empty. It was a clean room with dark drapes on windows to not let any daylight in. In the middle of the room, a fire was burning under a portrait of Ethan held up in the air by magic. A few hours had passed since Emanuel felt Ethan's life force dwindling. Since then, he holed himself up in this room, casting protective spells over Ethan's essence. Finally, after hours of effort, Emanuel could feel Ethan's life force coming back to normal.

"Ancestors! For how long are you going to ignore me! I know I have bound you against your will, but it was all to protect you! If the other Veiled One ancestors got a hold of you, they could've seriously damaged your spirits! However, it's no longer just about me. Ethan is in grave danger. Edwin, at least you should help me find him. Please!" pleaded Emanuel.

Suddenly, the raging fire under Ethan's portrait burned low. Frost appeared all around Emanuel and the room grew exponentially darker. Then Edwin's ghostly voice rang out. "What have you done, Emanuel?"

"Me! What have you all done? Why have you been so unreachable?"

"So, it is not enough for you to drain us dry! Now we have to be on your beck and call, too!"

"Edwin, it's not like that. If I didn't bind you all to our portion of the ancestral plain, the other dead Veiled Ones would've harmed you!"

"Rubbish! The Pathfinders before us made the same mistakes and were made powerless as punishment. However, even they were not tampered with after death. The rest of the dead Veiled Ones let them rest in death. But you didn't even give us that peace. You are continuously draining us and using our powers as your own. You don't even share it with the rest of the clan."

"Why should I? You all treated me horribly! Always made me feel like an outcast. So, why should I share my powers with others?"

"Forget about others. You didn't even tell me you were doing this. We had to approach the Hearth-Bringers for help in regaining our powers when you could've shared the ancestral powers under your control. You forget it is not your power, Emanuel. It's the power of the ancestors. It should be wielded now more than ever by all living Gainsworths with dwindling powers."

"No! It is mine because I came up with the spell to channel the ancestors' energy. Just like in time I'll find out a spell to return the powers of all Gainsworths. Having the Hearth-Bringers, especially that kid Leo, on our side would've made things easier and faster. No matter, though; I'll still figure something out by myself. For I am that talented and powerful. Anyways, I didn't call you here to discuss the morality of how to use MY power. You must know by now that Ethan was kidnapped. I need you to find him ASAP."

Edwin remained silent for a long time before answering, "We can't."

"What nonsense is this! Are you going to keep your son in danger to get back at me?"

"Emanuel, we really can't."

"Don't make me force you!"

"You are not understanding, Emanuel. It is not like we haven't been trying. Ever since Ethan and Lore were kidnapped we have tried to locate them. However, a power much superior to ours is blocking the attempts to find them."

"A power more superior... Do you mean other Veiled One ancestors are interfering in this?"

"No, it is not them. The one I speak of is far more powerful than all of the Veiled Ones combined, living or dead."

Back at Ragonia, Leo was being forced to help Ethan change Lore's diaper. Meanwhile, Desdemona was cooking dinner. By now Leo had used the fireflies to relight all the dead light crystals in the area. So, the triumph of the children over the machine was in full display. The huge machine that killed hundreds of people now lay destroyed behind them.

Leo smugly looked upon the machine before turning back to see Lore's dirty diapers. "Why do I have to do this? Just ask Des for help like usual."

"I don't need anyone's help."

"Awesome! I'm off then!"

"No. You are not. We need to talk."

"Can't we talk later?"

"No!"

"Fine. You win. What do you want to talk about?" asked Leo, making a disgusted face.

"So, you said the Gainsworths are losing powers because of helping the Anons destroy Areliam. I can help reverse it by helping you save Areliam. Correct?"

"Yes! Absolutely!"

"You also said Emanuel Cursebinder is draining the Gainsworth ancestors to stay in power and Uncle Ran knew about this. Did my father also know about this?"

"I don't think he did, but I'm not sure."

"I knew my father far better than you. So, believe me when I say he would've never gone against Uncle Ran. He would've remained quiet even after knowing everything because he could never win against King Ran. Yet, you think we children will be able to win against the king of Anons! I mean, we barely survived that machine back there. Also, even if we do win, what guarantee is there that the Gainsworths will regain their power? If it was so easy, then why didn't the Pathfinders ever recover their power?"

"Wow! I've never seen you talk so much about anything. So, that means you are serious about joining me in making everything right again," said a hopeful Leo.

"Just answer my questions," replied Ethan while crossing his arms.

Undeterred by Ethan's suspicions, Leo spoke confidently. "Look, no one said it was going to be easy. However, we can do it. What other choice do we have? Just wait till the Anons bleed all of Areliam dry? Someone has to do something sooner or later, and that someone is us! Both the Pathfinders and the Gainsworths will gain back their powers after we set Areliam back in balance."

"How are you so sure?"

"I'm the first Pathfinder in generations to gain teleportation powers and the Gainsworths still hold a lot of power. You were gravely injured. Some of the wounds didn't heal even after using up all the potions. However, your ancestors must have cast more protective spells on you to have you up and running so soon. It means they want you to help us too, right?"

"Do you even have a plan?"

"Yes! We are going to go to Kracten after reviving Ragonia. There is someone who will help us there."

Upon hearing this, Ethan let out a long sigh. "Leon Hearth-Bringer, I never liked you, nor do I trust you. I've followed you this far because I promised your father I would and because I have no other choice. Still, I want to believe you. I have suspected things have gone wrong for a long time. If I can help fix it, I will. However, all this will fall apart without a solid plan. So, I'll help you heal Ragonia and accompany you to Kracten. You have until then to come up with a solid plan. If you do not, then I'll return to my family and keep helping them instead."

"Ok, but what will you do if I do come up with a plan to make everything work by then?"

"Then I'll help you till the end, come what may."

"Either way, you won't disclose Sanctuary's location or divulge our secrets to the Anons, right?"

"Correct. However, there are other things we need to discuss."

"Whatever it is, it has to wait until after dinner, 'cause I'm starving. Now, let's eat something. We'll figure out the rest later."

"Ok."

"Alright. Des, is dinner ready yet?" asked Leo while looking around for Desdemona, who seemed to have disappeared into thin air.

Chapter Nineteen

Ragonia, like all the four original planets, is a water world. It has two enormous landmasses connected by the meadow of origins. The Creation and Destruction Elementals each took one of these landforms as their home. The region occupied by the Creation Elementals was known as Optimum. It was full of stunning cities, marvelous buildings, and magnificent temples of Anorea. Nature, however, ruled the land occupied by the Destruction Elementals, called Primal. Once they too hoped to build great metropolises, but the Creation Elementals rejected these ideas. Instead, lush forests flourished in the Destruction Elementals' territory, supported by the tropical climate of Ragonia.

In an attempt to keep them in check, the Creation Elementals forced the Destruction Elementals to live underground. They were only allowed to have a few above-ground outposts.

Alas, during the Anons' attack, all the cities and monuments of Creation Elementals were destroyed. The creation fires that supplied all Elementals and Ragonia itself with power were put out. Huge cylinder-shaped machines that both dampened powers and made Ragonia's air toxic were planted everywhere.

Elementals were hunted all over creation. The few survivors were thought to have died off on their own. The Destruction Elementals suffered heavy losses as well. All of their on-ground bases were destroyed. Sanctum, the sister city of Sanctuary in the Optimum underground, was demolished.

Sanctum was the place where important Destruction Elementals lived. It was located beneath the Ragonian capital

Magnum. So, the Anons utterly ruined it while burning and pillaging Magnum. However, they were unaware of the underground city of Sanctuary. Once a place of exile for Destruction Elementals, now the last refuge of all Elementals.

Sanctuary was placed in the middle of the Primal subterranean area with many concealed routes leading in and out. One of these hidden roads led to Sanctum, which was sealed to protect the retreating survivors. The Primal underground also had several exits opening up near the above-ground Destruction Elemental settlements. Currently, the children were at the exit by the Dollin outpost closest to the meadow of origins.

Desdemona kept peeking outside through the ajar exit doors while cooking dinner. Something out there was calling her name—constantly. It was easier to ignore it earlier when she was resting to heal her body. However, now that she was completely healed, it was bothering her.

Des felt the strength in her body return to normal. It seemed like the Creation Fires she ingested at the Volcano of Creation could work miracles. It not only saved her from the toxic air but also healed her broken body. The healing potions Leo fed her also helped speed up the process. If only the Creation Fires allowed me to use my Elemental powers as well, thought Des as she kept looking at the exit.

It was night outside. Blontzar, the current star Ragonia was rotating around, had already set. Des remembered something about Leo saying not to go out at night no matter what, but she just couldn't help it. The voice calling out to her grew desperate with each passing minute. Well, maybe if I just get close to the door, I can see what all this is about, Des thought as she got up and walked towards the door.

Desdemona opened the heavy doors as far as she could and peered outside. It was a dismal view. A sea of skeletons surrounded the exit. A lot of them were of Elementals, evident by the climate-appropriate light, flowy clothing on them. However, most were dead Anon soldiers. Yet, there was one particular skeleton that attracted Desdemona the most.

It seemed like the body of a female hoisted up in the air by numerous stakes running through its body. No doubt the work of the twenty or so Anon warriors whose skeletons lay at her feet. Not a lot was visible in the night. However, as light spilled from inside the exit, Des could see it being garbed in the light brown armor of the Creation Elemental warriors.

Desdemona felt a strange pull to that skeleton. So much so that she unknowingly grabbed the adjacent light crystal and started walking towards it. By this time Leo, Ethan and Lore were actively looking for her inside, calling her name loudly and repeatedly. But she couldn't hear them. All her focus was directed at that special skeleton.

Des walked over several dead bodies. Some of the carcasses broke beneath her weight, but she didn't stop. Foul energy was surrounding the whole area, disturbing the dead and invoking a feeling of foreboding. But she didn't stop. As she grew closer to the skeleton, she saw its mouth moving. Is it saying something? Is it calling my name? Leo, Ethan, and Lore finally spotted Des and were frantically yelling at her to come back inside, but she didn't stop until she reached where the skeleton was.

Desdemona put the light crystal down by her foot. Then, she used all her might to pull the stakes out of the skeleton. As she diligently worked on pulling out the stakes, the corpses surrounding her were slowly coming back to life.

Click clack, Click clack. That was the sound the skeletons were making as they got up—one by one.

However, Desdemona was oblivious to what was going on around her. Feverishly, she worked until she freed the skeleton. Then she drew near it to hear what it was saying. A bone-chilling cold made Des shiver alone in the middle of the dead once she finally heard what it was saying.

Desdemona must survive! The skeleton kept repeating endlessly. An awestruck Desdemona reached out for one of the skeleton's hands. On it, she noticed a bracelet. As she was going to check out the bracelet further, an Anon soldier's skeleton came up behind her. It raised a sword to cut her down. Before it could swing it down, Ethan rushed in and scattered the skeleton with one punch.

"Gugugahgahgagaga!" yelled Lore from her strapped position on Ethan's back to draw Desdemona's attention.

"Des, Des, snap out of it! We have to get back inside. NOW!" said Leo, who had also come with Ethan and Lore to get Des back. Nevertheless, it was too late. The way back was blocked.

All the skeletons in the area, except the ones inside the underground, had woken up. They were closing in on the children from all sides now. "Damn it," said Leo.

"We can't fight all of them to get back inside, especially with Des like this," said Ethan while pointing toward Desdemona, who was still in a trance.

"I know. You try to talk some sense into her while I try to handle this," said Leo as he called forth his ancestors. A ghostly blue aura encompassed the area as several wolves and phoenixes materialized to protect the children.

"You were told not to venture out at night. Negative energies are in full power in the darkness of night," said Leo in an unnatural tone with glowing green eyes, an indication of him being possessed.

"Who are you?" asked Ethan.

"Kendall Hearth-Bringer," replied Kendall currently controlling Leo's body.

"Well...we didn't do it on purpose," said Ethan.

"On purpose or not, you have put yourselves in grave danger," said Dorian, in the shape of a phoenix that landed on Leo's shoulder.

"Ok, but what can we do now?" asked Ethan.

"Well, there are too many of them for us to handle, and more are on their way. The best we can do is mask your energies," said Dorian.

"What are you talking about? Aren't you the great Hearth-Bringers and Pathfinders? Can't you deal with this?" asked Ethan.

"We are limited to act with the amount of energy Leo can handle, which isn't much at this point. So, the best thing we can do now is stay quiet and wait until daybreak. You can make a clean run for the underground in the morning. Until then, stay still," answered Kendall.

Dorian looked at Kendal speaking through Leo, and had a thought. *I wish Leo had more power. If only he had the powers of a first generation Veiled One.*

In the world of Areliam, everything is dependent on the use of energy. Each Primordial is born with a fixed capacity for controlling these energies. Their bodies act as conduits to manifest and manipulate energies in desired ways. Each Elemental has an innate capability to create a certain Element. Anons can bend elements to their will, while Veiled

Ones use their specific powers, depending on their clan power specifications. For example, the Gainsworths manifest energy as spells and curses while the Hearth-Bringers manifest energies as healing and artistic powers.

Under certain conditions, the limiters can be extended or surpassed. The power dampeners are one example of how powers are subdued. On the other hand, one of three ways to increase one's power is by lifelong practice. The other is to use artifacts with stored power that extends a user's power. The third is to forcibly remove the mental and physical limiters on one's body. However, doing so almost always results in the death of the user, as the body cannot handle the burst of energy. So, this technique is only used as a last measure.

The first-generation Primordials, though, were different. They had an almost infinite amount of power. Their power came from being born directly out of the Mother's Womb, which imbued a lot of the eternal Mother Anorea's power in them. Leo could never have that level of power; so, it was futile for Dorian to want that to happen. Still, he couldn't stop himself from wanting his descendant to be more powerful. *Having a first generation Primordial on our side would've been really beneficial, thought Dorian as his gaze fell on Lore.* Before he could think of anything else, though, Desdemona thrashed around and made weird noises in her uncomfortable stupor.

"Hey, bring that girl back to reality and fill her in on what's going on. Can't have her acting on her own again to mess everything up," added Dorian.

"I'm trying, but it's not working," said Ethan as he looked at Des, still in a daze.

Desdemona was stuck in a nightmare, as everything around them worsened. She was reliving the last moments of her mother's life. The moments before she heroically died defending the retreat of her father and herself along with other Elementals into Sanctuary.

"Diandra, honey, it's impossible to shake all these Anon dogs off. Here, take Desdemona and make a run for Sanctuary. I'll hold them off for as long as I can. Here is the remote for the machine. Activate it when you are halfway to Sanctuary. That should give the rest of the Elementals enough time to clear the machine's operating zone," said Atlas, as he tried to hand

off Desdemona to Diandra, a beautiful Creation Elemental warrior with the same features as Desdemona.

"No, honey. Your family has been ruling Sanctuary for decades. She has the best chance to survive there if you take her. Otherwise, they will discriminate her for the Creation Elemental blood she received from me."

"But you are the strongest. With you by her side, no one will dare lay a hand on her!"

"Atlas, my dear, when will you learn? We live in a world where lesser men thrive off the miseries of the strong. The Elementals were the strongest in the universe until the weak Anons decided to win by underhanded techniques. Just like how you Destruction Elementals were stronger than us Creation Elementals—yet we pulled you down. Made you second-class citizens in your own homes. So, now that we'll be dependent on the Destruction Elementals, they will make us pay for our sins."

"Honey, please, you did nothing wrong! Nothing bad will happen to you in Sanctuary. Just take Des and go. Please."

"You are wrong. I deserve this for being a cog in the machine that propelled injustice. However, I don't want my daughter to pay the price for my wrongdoings. Keep her safe. Make sure she and all other Creation Elementals receive just treatments. That is all I ask for, my love.

"Desdemona, look at me, sweetheart," Diandra continued as she cupped a terrified Desdemona's face with her hands. "Listen to me very carefully. I love you very, very much, so I need you to promise me that you will survive no matter what. Promise me. Promise me, Desdemona, promise me," said Diandra frantically.

A petrified Desdemona didn't understand what was going on or what her mother was asking of her. Still, she couldn't refuse her mother. So, Desdemona nodded her head in yes.

"Good. Take her away now," said Diandra with tears in her eyes.

"But..." Atlas tried to protest.

"No more arguments. There is no time left. I'm the stronger fighter. I can hold them off longer. So, leave already. Go. Now!" commanded Diandra as she charged forward.

Atlas saw Diandra leaving and then glanced at the horrified Desdemona in his arms. He knew what he had to do and why, but he didn't want to leave the woman he *loved. Yet, he had no choice. Atlas turned around and started running towards Sanctuary while saying, "I'll always love you, Diandra of the Creation Elementals."*

It is said that sometimes the universe communicates true intentions of beings to each other without contact. Maybe this was one of those times. As Diandra ran towards her death, she smiled and said, "I'll always love you too, Atlas of the Destruction Elementals."

CHAPTER TWENTY

As the night progressed, more and more of the dead came crawling. The Hearth-Bringers and Pathfinders created a safe zone for the children to hide in. The temperature dropped below freezing. However, inside the protected area the children remained relatively safe. Their living aura was masked by Leo's ancestors. So, the other dead did not take notice of them yet. Ethan continuously tried to make Desdemona conscious again. However, she was still deeply engrossed in the last memories of her mother.

Diandra ran to the front at full speed. There she regrouped with the last of her team still fighting to keep the pursuing Anons at bay. She stopped for a moment to talk to the Veiled Ones helping the Elementals. "Edward, how is the spell coming along?"

"I still need at least twenty more minutes," said Edward Gainsworth, father of Edwin Gainsworth and grandfather of Ethan Gainsworth.

"Well, obviously we don't have that much time. Your allies will overrun us far before then."

"Former allies. Remember, I'm going against my clan to help you keep Sanctuary safe."

"Will it work though? Your son..."

"My son is the best the Gainsworths have to offer. However, even he doesn't know all the spells and curses. Don't worry; we are sealing this whole area. No harmful energies, dead or alive, will be able to get through once we are done. Even partially done, this spell will protect Sanctuary for at least a couple of decades."

"You seem awfully calm while facing death."

"Death is just a long pause in our journey to become one with the Mother again. All I want is to make her proud. That is why I chose to do the right thing till the end. Plus, we Veiled Ones have a long afterlife. Unlike Elementals who turn back into the elements you used in life."

For a moment, Diandra silently watched the last of her men fall at the hands of the pursuing Anons. She then took in her surroundings. It was a nice day. Blontzar was shining bright, and a cool breeze blew through the beautiful plain of Primal. Everything was fine, except for the screaming, fearful crowds of Elementals fleeing underground, hunted by the Anons. The smell of blood, sweat, and tears permeated the air, a sense of dread was permanently settling in the hearts of all Elementals.

"It's over. They just dowsed the last of the Creation Fires. I can feel it."

"Don't worry. We have cast a spell that'll keep the coals of the First Fire Pit warm for decades to come. All you have to do to relight it is to bring a spark from the Volcano of Creation in Solem," said Edward while giving a nod to the five others on his team that risked their lives to help the Elementals.

"Do you think we'll ever surface again? Will the surviving Elementals ever take back Ragonia? Even if we do, can Ragonia heal from this utter destruction?"

"Have faith, Diandra. Both on the Goddess and on your home planet. Out of all the Primordial planets, Ragonia is physically the strongest. It is said Ragonia represents the eternal mother Anorea's body, unbreakable and everlasting. I'm sure one day it'll regain its full glory again. You never know, maybe it'll be your daughter that brings it back to life. Now go, protect her and all of your brethren." These were the last words of Edward Gainsworth, the third most powerful Gainsworth in history and an all-around remarkable being.

At that point, except Diandra, all other Elemental warriors protecting the mass retreat to Sanctuary were dead. The Anons were rushing to the underground entrance like starving hounds finally unbound. Diandra was the last defender against them. She closed her eyes for one brief moment to remember happier times with Atlas and Desdemona. Then, she leaped into action.

Diandra was special. Unlike regular Elementals, she controlled the rare element of energy. She sent out a burst of energy into the air in front of her in the shape of a wide *scythe. Her energy scythe cut through the front line of the Anon soldiers. She then gathered energy in her fist and struck the ground, causing a minor earthquake. This threw her enemies off guard.*

Next Diandra sent waves of energies towards her opponents. A lot of the Anon bodies couldn't handle the influx of high energy. It resulted in their bodies being torn apart from the explosion of energy within. Then she turned around and shot balls of pure energy at all the Anon soldiers that got past her, blasting holes in the Anons and killing them on impact.

After making sure no enemies remained behind her, Diandra once again turned to face the foes in front. Exhausted from a full day of fighting, she didn't have a lot of strength left. So, she used the last of her powers to materialize two energy scythes.

Diandra drove headfirst into the horde of enemies wielding her energy scythes like a madwoman. She cut down countless, yet many more took their place. Soon her energy scythes dissipated, leaving her to rely only on her sword.

Without the long-range attacks of the scythes, many more Anons got past her than before. Diandra glanced behind her briefly. Five of the Gainsworths were now casting offensive spells against the attacking Anons, leaving only Edward to work on the protective seal. This was bad news. While it granted more time for the fleeing people to make their escape, it prolonged the time needed to finish the protective shield. Damn it. I need to hold off more of them here, thought Diandra.

Abandoning all hopes of her safety, Diandra kept slashing and stabbing furiously. Earlier, she had been far more calculated in her attacks, making sure to kill as many of them as possible. However, now her objective was to wound them instead. This would give her a chance to engage more of them. Keeping the majority of the Anons occupied with her would, in turn, give more time to the Gainsworths to finish their spell, and grant more time for the escaping Elementals.

Nonetheless, doing so left her far more vulnerable. Her body suffered more and more wounds. But she kept fighting. Rivers of blood flowed out of her. But she kept fighting. A mace crushed her left shoulder. But she kept fighting.

Before long, her sword broke. So, she resorted to hand-to-hand combat. She broke the skull of a soldier with a headbutt. She punched and broke the nose of another soldier. She blocked a sword being swung at her with her right hand while kicking the life out of the assailant.

As one on one combat failed, multiple Anons attacked her together. They pinned her to the ground. Yet, Diandra didn't give up. She used her legs to squeeze one of her attackers until his spine broke in half. She lurched up and bit off the Adam's apple of another while kneeing an additional man so hard that he couldn't get up anymore. Following that, she clawed the eyes out of yet another. Then with an atrocious cry of rage, she got on her feet again. Ready to fight on, come what may.

Her fearless and suicidal fighting skills left the Anons scared and incapable of acting for a time. Alas, the period of inaction was short. New Anon reinforcements reawakened their fighting spirits while the vengeful wounded soldiers got up to slash and stab her repeatedly.

Without realizing it, Diandra had been pushed closer and closer to the entrance. By now all the Gainsworths except Edward were dead. Unfortunately, he too didn't survive for much longer. Soon she heard the dying scream of Edward behind her. Diandra didn't even have time to react before she was next. The soldiers staked her from top to bottom, making her unable to move before going underground to pursue the rest of the Elementals. In a last desperate attempt to fight back, Diandra released her power limiters. A tremendous amount of energy burst out of her, killing everyone in sight.

Yet, more Elementals and the Anons chasing them kept pouring in from all over Ragonia, but Diandra couldn't help them anymore. Incapable of continuing the fight and moments away from her death, Diandra activated the machine. She also crushed its control; no one could stop it.

Her dying thoughts were, <u>I have done all I can. The rest is up to you, Atlas. Keep our daughter safe.</u> **Desdemona must survive.**

CHAPTER TWENTY-ONE

I n an ocean of death, a small island of the living existed. Outside the Dollin underground exit in Ragonia, the shadows of the dead made the night even darker. The bluish hues emanating from the protected area of the Hearth-Bringers and Pathfinders were the only source of light. Kendall was still possessing Leo's body, and Desdemona was still out of it. Not for long though.

Very soon Desdemona awoke from her nightmare with a loud shriek. "No! Mother! You can't die. Momma, no!" yelled Desdemona while hugging the skeleton of her mother that was still muttering *"Desdemona must survive."*

"What are you doing? Stop her from attracting attention to us!" said a panicked Dorian.

Ethan clasped Desdemona's mouth tightly, muffling her screams. However, it was too late. All the undead eyes were on them now, a monstrous hunger emanating from them. Their desperate unfulfilled desire to live propelled them to obtain the lives of the children as their own.

The Hearth-Bringers and Pathfinders immediately used their power to create an energy dome to protect the children. And not a moment too soon. All the dead rushed simultaneously towards them, each toppling another in an attempt to get to the children faster. Their bony skeletons broke apart against the energy shield, cracking it upon impact.

"Damn it! We can't hold out much longer. Wish these Elementals would disperse into the elements already," said an irritated Dorian.

"They can't. The sudden and violent nature of their deaths keeps them tied to their current form. If the Creation Fires still burned, their energy would've been purified by now. Without it, they will remain like this forever. So, we need to get that girl over to the First Fire Pit as soon as possible," answered Kendall.

"I know, but we don't have enough energy to fend these numbskulls off while the children go there. So, what do you say we do now?" asked Dorian.

However, it wasn't Kendall that answered. It was Diandra's skeleton that acted. The skeleton got up on its feet, lugged Desdemona over her right shoulder and jumped. Diandra broke through the protective dome, scattering the bones of the dead trying to get in. She landed far away from the group of undead and started running towards the Meadow of Origins.

"Quick! Follow her!" commanded Kendall. So, Dorian and the rest of the phoenixes grabbed each of the children and flew out of the hole Diandra created. The rest of the dead followed them. The Hearth-Bringer ancestors tried to hold them off. They tore through the bones of the dead in their wolf form. They smashed into many of them, turning their bones to dust. However, there were just too many of them.

Soon all Hearth-Bringer ancestors except Kendall lost their energy and returned to the ancestral plane, leaving the hordes of the dead to chase after the children uninterrupted. Even though the children had a head start, they didn't get too far. By the time they got to Dollin, only Dorian remained from the Pathfinder ancestors. Everyone kept running at full speed to reach the First Fire Pit in the Meadow of Origins. Diandra with Desdemona in the front, Leo and gang in the middle, and a massive army of the dead behind them.

"How in the world do they still have the energy to chase after us?" asked Dorian.

"Remember, this is their world. They have more power here," answered Kendall.

"This is not going to work. We have to try something else. Hey, Gainsworth kid. Your sister is a first-generation Anon, is she not?" asked Dorian.

"Yes, but she is just a toddler. So, she can't use her full power yet," said Ethan.

"Oh, you don't worry about that," said Dorian as he took possession of Lore's body.

"What are you doing?" yelled Ethan.

"Gugugahgahgagaga," replied Dorian with Lore's voice.

As they kept running they passed the empty buildings of the Dollin outpost. It was a haunted ghost town filled with many dead who became alive after sensing the presence of the living. The ghosts inside the buildings came out and joined the army of the dead already chasing the children. Kendall released Leo and ran behind the children in his otherworldly blue wolf form to guard the rear.

"Dorian! Whatever you are going to do, do it now," said Kendall.

"Gugugagagahgahgah," said Lore possessed by Dorian while wiggling her index finger, signaling it's not time yet.

"Urgh, what's happening? Where are we?" asked Leo as he held his throbbing head while suffering from momentary amnesia. A side effect of possession.

"No, Leo! Don't stop running!" yelled Kendall.

"Wait, what? But why?" asked Leo, who had stopped running once Kendall exited his body.

"Look behind you, idiot—and also, make your ancestor stop possessing my sister!" Ethan yelled at him.

Leo took one look behind him and saw what was happening. Then, he let out a high-pitched scream before running like there was no tomorrow. Initially, the others got ahead of him when he stopped running to figure things out. Well, not anymore. He overtook Kendall, Dorian, Ethan, Lore and almost caught up to Diandra and Des in no time.

"Man! That boy can run!" said Kendall.

"Gugugagagahgahgah," said Dorian in agreement.

"Will you please stop using my sister's body!" exclaimed Ethan angrily.

"Gugugagagahgahgah," Dorian replied, shaking Lore's head.

"Damn it, Leon. Say something to him!" yelled Ethan.

"Can't. Too busy running for my life!" Leo yelled back.

"Like ancestor, like descendant. Both utterly useless!" Ethan mumbled under his breath.

"Gugugagagahgahgah," said Dorian via Lore while hoisting her little fists in protest.

The yelling and banter went on between the group as they reached the other side of Dollin. The Dollin outpost was nearest to the Meadow of Origins. So, as soon as they exited its main gates, they could see their destination.

Meadow of origins was a long, thin piece of land that acted as a bridge between the two continents of Ragonia. It was surrounded by the ocean on the north and south sides. Meanwhile, both of its other sides were occupied by Optimal and Primal. It also housed the Creation Fires. The First Fire Pit, one of the main sources of powers for Ragonia and Elementals, lay in the middle of it.

It was then that Dorian acted. Lore was a first-generation Anon. Even in her nascent stage, she commanded a lot of power. So, Dorian took advantage of this and used Lore's power over water to aid them.

The ocean rose and collided with the army of the dead, breaking them to pieces. Yet, more dead arose to take their place. So, Dorian employed another tactic. He utilized Lore's power to create a small piece of ice floating in the ocean then urged everyone to get on top of it as they neared the ocean.

"Gugugagagahgahgah! Gugugagagahgahgah!" kept yelling Dorian with Lore's voice.

"He wants us to get on top of the ice so he can transport us swiftly to the First Fire Pit," Kendall translated Dorian's intention.

Leo didn't need to be told a second time and was the first to get on. The others followed. All except Diandra and Desdemona, who were still making their way towards the First Fire Pit on foot. Once they got on, Dorian used Lore's power to carry the floating piece of ice on the waves, speedily ice-surfing to their objective.

"Wait! Is that Des being held captive by that skeleton? Is that why she is crying?" asked Leo as he heard Desdemona's cries.

"That skeleton is her mother. She was an Elemental warrior who is still trying to protect Des and Ragonia even after death," said Ethan.

"Really?" asked Leo.

"Yeah, she was calling it mother while crying earlier," replied Ethan.

"In that case... Hey, dead aunty, you are taking too long. Jump over here so we can get there faster!" yelled Leo while waving his hands at Diandra.

Diandra glanced to where Leo was and with one mighty jump landed on the floating ice. She plopped Des on the ice, who was still crying uncontrollably while hugging her mother. Leo was going to say something to ease the situation, but Ethan stopped him.

"Not another word, you insensitive moron," said Ethan.

"I'm just trying to help," Leo said defensively.

"Well, you suck at it. So, stop," Ethan said curtly.

"Fine!" grumbled Leo.

Time passed quickly and soon they were almost at their destination, till suddenly a skeleton of a huge fish jumped out of the ocean to devour them. Dorian made Lore evade the attack, which resulted in them being thrown off course.

"Connect! Fly!" Ethan commanded his ring and used it to fly the team the rest of the way.

"Couldn't you do that before?" asked an enraged Leo.

"No, because it barely has any power left," answered Ethan.

"Well, it's all because of you Anons. You didn't even let the wildlife survive. What, you thought they'd evolve into Elementals and come after you for revenge or something?" taunted Leo.

Ethan didn't answer. They kept running in terrified silence. Kendall was leading the way with blue light emanating from him, lighting the path. The rest followed. Numerous skeletons of people who died by the countless smaller Creation Fires rose up. Their motive was the same as the other dead: claim the lives of the children as their own. However, the dead didn't understand that there was no way so many of them could possess so few living bodies. Things would never progress to possession, though. For in their gluttonous attempt to seize them, the dead will rip the children apart first.

Finally, the team reached its goal. The First Fire Pit. The problem was, it was sealed off by a dome of impassable white light. So, the group was stuck facing a wall of light in front and a multitude of the dead behind.

CHAPTER TWENTY-TWO

T he glowing white dome of the light barrier sealing the First Fire Pit illuminated the night. Its blazing radiance and overpowering aura even stopped the dead in their tracks. The empty hole of the First Fire Pit stood just beyond the wall of light, daring them to approach it.

Leo glanced at the rest of his party. Dorian had finally exited Lore's body and was much smaller in size now, an indication of his loss of power. Kendall's wolf form also seemed much thinner and less bright than before. Soon both of their symbolized forms would disappear altogether. Ethan was catching his breath while Lore slept. No doubt the toddler was drained by Dorian's possession. Desdemona was still crying while hugging her mother's hips. Meanwhile, Diandra's skeleton kept gently caressing the back of Desdemona's head. Leo then looked down and saw his own shaking hands.

Click. Clack.

The dead started moving again, their desire to possess the children's lives outweighing their fear of the sealing dome. However, Leo's team didn't have the energy to fight back or run away anymore.

It was Diandra that acted first. She removed Des's hand, despite her heavy protest, and walked towards the dead. Leo took this moment to reach Des and held her back while Diandra faced her former countrymen.

Diandra stopped a few steps away from the crowd of the dead, making herself a shield for the children. Still ready to fight for her daughter's safety—even after death—constantly muttering, **"Desdemona must survive."**

The dead, however, felt no bond of kinship towards the living. All they wanted was to claim their lives as their own. So, one by one, all of them surrounded Diandra, the last obstacle in the fulfillment of their desire. Then, they attacked.

Diandra let out a mighty scream then grabbed the skeleton closest to her and used it to beat down the others. She twirled around and smashed the bones of many incoming skeletons with the one she held in her right hand. Once the skeleton in her hand was spent, Diandra resorted to hand-to-hand combat. She targeted different joints of the skeletons, hitting hard enough to crumble their bones to dust. It wasn't enough, though. More and more of the dead came. They tried to overwhelm her with their numbers again and again. However, Diandra stood her ground with nothing but sheer willpower.

The children, Kendall and Dorian watched the battle unfold before their eyes. Stunned speechless from the display of a mother's undying love—yet still scared to death. Even in the warm climate of Ragonia, cold sweat ran down the faces of the children. Fear gripped their mind and bodies.

She can't hold them off for much longer, thought Leo as he watched more dead approaching them from all directions. Then he looked around at his teammates. All of them were exhausted. Without Diandra, they wouldn't survive more than a few minutes. *We have to act now!*

"Mommy, please, please stop. You have done enough," Leo heard Desdemona say through her tears.

"You're right, Des. She is doing all she can, and we need to do the same. Look here, Des—look here. Do you want your mother to fall here trying to protect you?" asked Leo while turning Des's head towards him.

"No," said Desdemona.

"Then we need to get on the other side of this shield and relight the First Fire Pit. Ancestors, help us get through," said Leo.

Dorian and Kendall exchanged glances at each other before Dorian said, "We can't."

"What do you mean, you can't? If not you, then who?" asked a panicked Leo.

Both Dorian and Kendall looked at Ethan. This in turn made Leo and Desdemona look at Ethan too. Ethan, on the other hand, had no clue what to do. He had never been good at using his Gainsworth powers. Things went from bad to worse after Emanuel had restricted the powers of the Gainsworth ancestors for personal use.

Desdemona, who was on her knees crying her eyes out, finally got up and approached Ethan. She held Ethan's hand and said, "Ethan, please help. It was your grandfather whose spell has kept the coals of the First Fire Pit warm for us to reignite. Now it has to be you who gets us there. Please!"

Ethan wiped away Desdemona's tears and said, "I'll try my best." He then turned to face the sealed dome. The cursed dome was specifically created by Emanuel Cursebinder. Only Anons and Gainsworths were allowed entry. So, he and Lore could enter, but the problem was taking Des and Leo along with them.

Originally, the Anons and Gainsworth were immune to the toxins in Ragonia's air. However, as time passed, the toxins mixed with other environmental elements became toxic to Anons and Gainsworths too. That is why the Anons no longer monitored Ragonia like they do with Yonder. However, this meant both Lore and he were targets of this toxicity. Ethan and Lore would succumb to the toxins if he used the last of the ring's power to open a path for Leo and Des.

Even after knowing all this, Ethan pulled out the ring from his hand and checked its power level. *Less than one percent! It will be of no use to me.* He slipped it inside Lore's clothes. *If I stop using it now, then at least it'll protect Lore for a while longer.* As soon as he did that, blood started flowing out of his nose and his throat started burning. His body that already suffered so much damage inside the machine and was exhausted from all the running, could not hold on any longer. However, Ethan ignored the blood and pain and closed his eyes.

Eternal Mother Anorea, please help me! I know my clan has sinned. We have destroyed so much and so many. Yet now that I'm trying to rectify our mistakes...I can't. I'm powerless. I cannot make the others enter this dome with me. But you can! Please give me the strength to make it happen! Please make my Gainsworth powers work. Please grant me enough power to allow the rest of my team to enter the dome. I do not ask for this strength to benefit myself; I ask so that I can aid others. Please, Goddess Anorea, creator of all, help me help others.

As soon as Ethan finished asking for help from the Goddess, an image of a gap within the dome appeared inside his mind. Ethan then opened his eyes and imagined the same gap appearing in front of him. It worked! A gap opened up in front of him!

"Quick, everyone, enter!" yelled Leo as he pulled Des inside the dome. Once everyone was inside, Leo told Ethan, "Now close it. Hurry!"

"No! My mom is still outside!" protested Des.

"It'll all be alright once we light the fire, but we'll never get to do that if the dead follow us inside. So, close it already!" said Leo.

"I can't," replied Ethan.

"What? Why?" asked Leo.

"I don't know, but I'm trying," said Ethan as he tried to make his vision of closing the gap into a reality. However, it didn't work.

By this time, the dead had seen the opening and were bypassing Diandra to get to it. Diandra tried to stop them the best she could. However, a lot of them got through.

"Ok. Don't worry. We can still turn this around. Des, make a run for the First Fire Pit. We'll hold them off here for as long as we can for you," said Leo.

"Yeah, but what do I do once I get there?" asked a confused Des.

"Imagine transferring the fire burning inside you to the pit," said Leo.

"Wait, there is a fire burning inside me?" asked Des while hugging herself.

"You'll be able to figure everything out once you get there. So, get going already!" said Leo as he finished making a pile of rocks to be used as projectiles. "Ethan, forget about closing the gap. It's not working. Instead, throw these rocks at their legs. Breaking their legs will slow them down. Ancestors, you get more rocks to throw while we do that. Also, attack the ones we miss or just can't bring down." Ethan gave a nod of approval and gave Des a supporting glance before doing what Leo said.

Des stole a look at her mother, who was being overwhelmed. Then another at her fatigued teammates. Ethan was bleeding from his nose and ears. Lore was out cold while Leo was shaking all over. Leo's ancestors, on the other hand, had gotten much smaller in size and were losing luminosity. They could disappear any time now. *None of them will survive if I don't do anything soon. Please help, Anorea,* thought Des as she started running towards the First Fire Pit.

Des ran with all her might. She was all out of breath and sweating profusely when she finally reached the pit. She imagined a fire burning within her that magically flew out to light the fire pit, but it didn't work. She looked back to see a group of the dead pilling over her mother to stop her from moving. Des also caught a glimpse of Ethan's unconscious body falling to the ground. A lot of blood was coming out of his mouth. Leo and his ancestors were moments away from falling prey to the claws of the dead too. Des then turned back to the deep, dark pit in front of her and did the only thing her instinct told her to do. She jumped.

Her fragile body hit the bottom of the pit with a loud thud. Blood flowed out of her and onto the coals kept magically warm for a decade. A sacrifice. That was the spark needed to ignite the fire. Suddenly, an explosion happened. The shockwaves of the blast blew away the sealing dome and everything else for miles around. Kendall and Dorian used the last of their energies to protect the children. Then all went silent.

CHAPTER TWENTY-THREE

L ore woke up in a dark and uneasy quietness. She was still strapped to Ethan's back. So, she tried reaching out and waking the unconscious Ethan. When that didn't work, she kept repeating her famous line, "Gugugahgahgagaga," in hopes of someone getting up and answering her. However, both Ethan and Leo were in no position to reply, and the others weren't present. Desdemona was dead, and Kendall and Dorian returned to the ancestral plane after exhausting their energies in saving them from the blast.

Even though Kendall and Dorian's intervention saved the children's lives, it still left the boys severely burned. Ethan's body took most of the damage and shielded Lore from being burnt. However, he and Leo were in very bad shape.

Lore tried to use her powers to ice their wounds, but she too was running on fumes. Dorian's use of her power to transport the children had taken a toll. Also, Calaren's ring had run out of juice. So, the rest of Lore's powers were primarily being used to protect her from the toxic air. She would've succumbed to this toxicity already if she weren't a first-generation Anon controlling the healing element of water.

Feeling all alone and unable to help anyone, Lore started crying loudly. Her voice traveled far and wide in the silent and lonely night. However, it is said that no one is truly alone, for Goddess Anorea watches over all. The Goddess always aids those who remain on the righteous path. So, it was She who appeared in this time of need for the children.

Slowly, the darkness around Lore started to morph. It took a shape of a beautiful black woman, with long and brilliant black, wavy hair, and a pair of mesmerizing green catlike eyes.

"Do not cry, little Lore. For I am here for you now and always," said the Goddess as she scooped Lore in her arms. Next, she healed the severely burnt and toxic air filled bodies of Leo and Ethan. She then walked up to the First Firepit, now burning brightly. She reached out and a burning ball of fire flew out from the pit and landed on her hand. She breathed life into that fire and gave it the form of Desdemona, bringing her back from death.

Suddenly, the Mother felt the presence of another entity. Not living yet, not quite dead. **"Desdemona must survive. Desdemona must survive,"** said the half-broken skeleton of Diandra.

Diandra had survived the explosion. Or at least a part of her had. The blast blew away the other dead, holding her down. Unfortunately, it also blew away the lower half of her body. Still, she crawled her way to her daughter.

"Fret not, warrior. As one mother to another, I promise to look after your daughter. You can rest now," said the Goddess as she laid the bodies of each of the children by the fire.

Diandra took one last longing look at Desdemona and another at Mother Anorea. Then, many cracks appeared near both of her eyes which then spread to the end of her chin. It was like tears of sorrow were flowing down her face. A few moments later, Diandra's skeleton crumbled to dust.

After shedding a tear for Diandra's motherly love, Eternal Mother Anorea set Lore down and addressed the children. "My dear children, I'm so proud of you. For eons, most Primordials have done nothing but harm each other. It was hard for me. Tired of seeing them exercising their free will this way, I left. Never to return. However, your efforts and dedication to set things right called me back," said the mother Goddess, while smiling down on them.

"As a reward, let me give you gifts that will support you in your journey. To Desdemona, I give an indestructible body and powers of a Creation Elemental. To Ethan, I return the ability to use his Gainsworth powers and give the power to master the infinity spells. To little Leo trying to right all wrongs, I give everlasting energy and stamina. So, you can fully channel the Veiled One ancestors.

"Lastly, to Lore, the mightiest of Anons, I give the ability to channel my powers directly. Your race has done much wrong.

You will need access to my powers to fix it all. So, call upon me in your darkest hour. I will come to your aid."

"Now, my children, it is time for a change of place," said the Goddess, for She knew the Anons and Cursebinders must have sensed what happened in Ragonia by now. So, she decided to send them far away from their reach. With a snap of her fingers, She activated the cosmos traveling ability of Ragonia.

All four of the primal planets had a special ability, the power to teleport around the cosmos. Ragonia's capability to teleport was hampered due to the drowsing of its Creation Fires. However, with Anorea's help and the relighting of the First Fire Pit, Ragonia was once again cruising through the cosmos. Voyaging towards an unknown destination selected by the Mother.

Inside the royal palace of the Anons existed a beautiful garden full of blooming flowers and water fountains. Small seating arrangements enjoying the best views were placed throughout. One of these spots was hidden away from the rest. It was Zine's favorite place to be. That is where he went when he wanted to be alone with his thoughts.

Something is wrong! I haven't seen Ethan or Lore at all for the past few days. The palace is on high alert, and everyone has become secretive. "What is going on!" Zine spoke out loud.

"Aww, poor orphan boy doesn't know what is going on? No one cared enough to fill you in is it?" taunted Karenitz.

"Where did you come from?" asked a surprised Zine.

"Oh please! I've been around here a lot longer than you. So, obviously, I know every nook and cranny in this place. You can't hide from me in here!"

"Wasn't trying to hide. Just wanted to be alone..."

"If you want to be alone, then go to your room. Don't walk around everywhere with your gloomy face."

"Sorry."

"If you are really sorry, then get out of here and let me rest in peace. This spot is well-hidden, so no one can bother me if I rest here."

"Ok," said Zine as he got up to leave. Before he left, though, he couldn't stop himself from asking, "Excuse me, but do you know what is going on? Everyone is on edge and not answering my requests of meeting Ethan or Lore."

"I guess what they say is true. Blood is thicker than water. They would've told you already—if you were truly a royal. Guess they don't think of you as their own," said Karenitz haughtily.

"Who we call our own is none of your business, Karenitz Swordsbane," said King Ran, who heard the children's conversation quietly up to this point from behind a bush. Finally, he emerged to put an end to Karenitz's bad behavior.

"Your Majesty, I, uh..." Karenitz fumbled her words.

"Speak when spoken to. Did your father not teach you any manners?" asked King Ran.

"Um..." Karenitz tried to put an answer together.

"No need to say anything. Things are evident from the way you act. Next time you talk to any of my children like this, be it Zine, Ethan, or Lore, you will be severely punished. Do you understand?"

Karenitz nodded her head in submission.

"Good. Also, you are banned from entering the royal gardens ever again. Now go, get out of my sight," said King Ran in a grim tone.

Karenitz bowed low before sprinting away. Zine couldn't help but smile at her condition. Then he turned to King Ran and said, "Please tell me what is happening?"

King Ran looked down at Zine and smiled gently. "That is why I'm here, son. Come, let's have a seat first." King Ran took Zine's hand in his and guided him back to the spot. "Ethan and Lore have been kidnapped."

"What?" asked an astonished Zine.

"Shortly after your sparing session ended Ethan responded to a situation, and we haven't heard from him since. Unfortunately, at that time, Lore was with him too. So, both of them are currently missing."

"Why didn't anyone tell me about this before?"

"We didn't want to worry you, son."

"But..."

"Hear me out, son. It was my decision. I wanted to keep you safe and worry-free about this. I love you. I want to make you king one day. I also wanted to make Lore your queen and Ethan your chief advisor. However, you are the only one left to me now. So, I need you to be in good health in both mind and body. That wouldn't happen if you kept thinking about all this."

Zine kept quiet for a while before asking, "Any news on them?"

"Not yet, but all of you are our children. Your security is the most important. Trust me, I'll find Ethan and Lore if it is the last thing I do. However, I need you to remain safe by my side until that happens. So, you need to remain in your chambers, guarded by our best soldiers and protected by magic seals. Think you can do that, son?"

"Yes, Father," answered Zine.

"Good," said King Ran.

At that time, Emanuel and Orias rushed in calling out for Ran. "Ran, Ran, where are you?" Orias loudly called out.

"What is it?" asked an alarmed Ran.

"Ragonia. Ethan, and Lore are in Ragonia, most probably kidnapped by what's left of the Elementals," said Emanuel.

"How do you know this?" asked King Ran.

"It has to be Ragonia, because that is one of the only places out of our reach. So, the kidnappers knew we cannot easily chase after them there. It has connections to the attack on us on Mother's Womb as well. So, they must have found a way to survive the toxic environment. Also, most importantly, Ragonia has started moving again," said Emanuel.

"What? That could only happen if the First Fire Pit was relit!" said King Ran.

"Relighting the First Firepit requires Creation Flames from the Volcano of Creation. We believe Ethan caught them doing so and was abducted because of it. Then, they forced him to override the seal and relit the First Fire Pit. Setting Ragonia free again," said Orias.

"Well, then let's catch up to Ragonia as soon as possible," said King Ran.

"We can't," replied Orias.

"Why not?" asked King Ran.

"All the wards placed in and around Ragonia have been dispelled. Also, we have no clue where it is traveling to," said Emanuel.

It was just another day at Sanctuary. Atlas was taking stock of supplies inside the cold and dreary storage room. For most people, life remained the same as before Desdemona and Leo's departure. The same rationing of food and water. The same maintenance of the amassing stone-powered purifiers that kept Sanctuary's air breathable. The same age-old politics raged on between the Creation and Destruction Elementals as well. The only thing that changed inside the old, dark all-encompassing walls of Sanctuary was the tension levels of its inhabitants.

One indeed sees the world through the lenses of his or her characteristics. The Creation Elementals had always shunned and outcasted the Destruction Elementals. So, they couldn't digest that now their lives depended on the mercy of the Destruction Elementals. As a result, they were extremely dissatisfied living in Sanctuary. Many times, they falsely accused the Destruction Elementals of hoarding resources and discriminating against them.

A rebellion almost arose when Sanctuary ran out of food and other resources. Things had only calmed down when Leo had brought enough supplies to keep everyone happy. However, people became afraid again ever since he left to revive Ragonia.

At first, everyone was convinced by Leo's inspirational speech about resurrecting Ragonia using the prince and princess of the Anons. Today, though, people were more worried about what would happen if Leo didn't make it back. Not to mention the Creation Elementals were unhappy about Desdemona, a Destruction Elemental, being the carrier of the Creation Flames. Meanwhile, the Destruction Elementals are miffed with having to share the glory of reviving Ragonia with a Veiled One. Most, however, thought this to be a fool's errand. And no one wanted to lose Leon Hearth-Bringer, their primary supplier of resources, to it.

All of this was running through Atlas's mind while he finished his inspection of the food to be rationed out. *This much will not even last three months*, thought Atlas, as he grappled with the possibility of stretching their provisions if Leo didn't return. *They have to return, though!* Other than Atlas, no one else currently living in Sanctuary had to deal with that evil machine blocking the path. Thus, they didn't know of its destructive powers. So, Atlas, was the only one who knew that the meager weapons given to the children was nowhere near enough to bring it down. However, under the pressure of the masses, he had to let the children go and face it alone. *Everything can still turn out alright in the end, though,* hoped Atlas. *No one can survive that machine and the children will find this out too. Once they reach the machine, they'll understand they can't get through and will come back then.*

"You need to eat something. You haven't eaten properly since the children left. I'm sure Desdemona would want you to be in good health upon her triumphant return," said Calaren.

Atlas immediately wanted to give a snappy reply, but stopped himself in fear of June's retaliation. "Thank you for your concern, but I'll be fine."

"I don't think so. You aged a couple of decades in these past few days and your unhealthy eating patterns are adding to it."

"Since when do you care, and why?"

"As a parent of one unruly kid to another, I know the feeling of having your child out of sight. Don't worry. All of them will come back alive and well."

"You know nothing! This is not Solem where your child roamed around safely. Ragonia is a ruined planet with nothing but death to offer. It's filled with deadly traps and a toxic environment capable of killing able-bodied men in hours. Most importantly, the machine..." Atlas fell silent, remembering his escape to Sanctuary with the last of his people as the machine had become active.

"They are protected from the toxic atmosphere. Also, I'm sure you guys gave them the best resources to deal with everything."

"Resources! We never had much of anything to give away! Even before the fall, scarcity was no stranger to Sanctuary. This is where most Destruction Elementals lived like prisoners. Very few ever made it out, and the ones that did were mostly forced inside the golden cage of Sanctum. Why do you think there was only one unkempt and broken traveling mirror here? It was because we were only allowed to own one of them, which was not even maintained properly. All our lives, the Creation Elementals treated us like disposable items. Limiting our growth and abusing us for their gain. Yet in the end, it is us that kept them safe."

Tears rolled down Atlas's cheek as he finally buckled under all the pressure. He fell to the ground and started crying uncontrollably. Atlas of the Destruction Elementals, the man who had endured the destruction of his world and people, finally broke. Calaren signaled the rest of the people inside the food storage room to leave them alone. Once everyone left, he kneeled beside Atlas and said, "Everything will be alright. They will come back victorious."

"Are you out of your mind? They are mere children trying to accomplish what seasoned warriors cannot!" yelled Atlas.

"They are miracle workers. Healing agents of the Mother."

"No. Only my daughter is the healing agent. Your son is the source of all evil. I should've never let Desdemona hang out with him."

"Leo only starts up trouble to address and fix bigger problems."

"Horseshite!"

"Look, Atlas. Leo is a gift from Mother Anorea, born against all odds. As is Desdemona, she thrived even under such harsh conditions. She is the first Destruction Elemental in generations to hold the Creation Flame. They are also being aided by a first-generation Anon and a Gainsworth. If anyone can revitalize Ragonia, it's them!"

"Say what you want, but it is not their burden to carry! It's our fault. We should be the ones to fix all of this!"

"I think we have done more harm than good. So, the best thing we can do is not get in their way. However, we should always be ready to support them in whatever way we can. For that to happen, we have to keep ourselves alive and well," said Calaren as he offered a piece of bread to Atlas.

Atlas begrudgingly took the piece of bread and ate it. Once he was finished, he turned to Calaren and said, "Just so we are clear, I can take care of myself. The only reason I ate it was because I wanted to be polite. That and I do not want your wife to blow my head off on account of refusing you."

"Of course!" said Calaren as he broke into a smile.

"By the way, is it true that you helped us during the invasion of Ragonia? Are you really the Wandering Soul?"

"Yes, and yes."

"How and why?"

"It was the last act of defiance I had against the Anons. I aided in the escape of Elementals from Magnum to Sanctuary through Sanctum. I also went back to take care of the pursuers. Lastly, it was I that collapsed the tunnel way so no one could follow. If it weren't for father sending me back to Solem, I would've joined and fought on your behalf, too. As for why, I just wanted to save people, that's all."

There was a long silence before Atlas spoke up. "Thank you. It is only because of you that a lot of the Elementals made it to Sanctuary. However, are you sure we deserved saving?"

"Absolutely!"

"That makes one of us."

"What do you mean?"

"For my whole life, I have served the Creation Elementals. My brethren and I fought for them, bled for them, and died for them. We ventured into the toxic environment outside to find more survivors while they stayed safe in Sanctuary. Unfortunately, none who went came back. Still, it was never enough! Even now, after years of keeping them alive, the Creation Elementals plot against us in our own home. Before, when I got angry at you for letting Leo go, I wasn't angry at you. I was angry at myself for allowing Des to risk her life for these ungrateful nuisances. I'm sorry."

"Don't be. I understand."

"So, tell me honestly. You think our children truly have a chance of success?"

"Of course!"

"But they will turn back if they can't, right? I want my daughter back alive, and we need Leo to transport goods for our survival."

"Don't worry. They will succeed and return to us safely." As soon as Calaren finished speaking, tremors rocked Sanctuary.

Atlas and Calaren got on their feet and ran outside to find out what was going on. People were running towards them. Old man Gino and June were foremost among them.

Before Atlas or Calaren could say anything, Gino said, "The Fire is burning again."

June said, "Ragonia is traveling through the cosmos again."

Atlas and Calaren looked at each other. Atlas was dumbfounded, while Calaren wore a proud expression on his face.

CHAPTER TWENTY-FOUR

The renewed fire in the First Fire Pit burned brightly. It purified the immediate area of the toxic air, and the children slept blissfully in its shadow. Mother Anorea had disappeared by now. However, her presence still lingered, ensuring the safety of the sleeping children, for none could ever dare to hurt the ones under the Eternal Mother's protection. Time passed and Ragonia zoomed through the cosmos while the children remained asleep.

Ethan was the first one to open his eyes. It took a minute for him to remember where he was and what happened. He sprang to his feet as soon as he recalled their life being in danger. However, he breathed easily once he saw Lore, Desdemona, and Leo slumbering peacefully. Leo was snoring loudly, Lore was sucking her thumb, and Desdemona lay flat on her back. The last sound Ethan remembered before losing consciousness was that of a large explosion, coming from her direction. So, he checked to see if she was breathing. She was alive and well! All of them were alive and well! Not even a scratch remained on any of them!

It was almost as if nothing bad had happened. However, the terrain around them told a different story. Signs of a fierce battle were all around them. Scattered bones, clothes, and pieces of armor belonging to the dead were everywhere. However, it wasn't this recent battle that Ethan was thinking of. He was thinking of the Battle of Behemoth, where the Anons destroyed Ragonia.

My family was responsible for all this pain and suffering—all this death and destruction! We just relit one firepit, but what of the others? What of the people who died huddled around them hoping the dying embers would save them? What of the uncountable dead lifeforms of Ragonia? We killed everything! What have we done? thought Ethan as he gazed upon the destroyed world around them. His legs gave in under the sins of his father. Ethan fell to his knees repeating, "What have we done?"

Ethan's ramblings woke Leo. He was just as dazed as Ethan when he first woke up. However, after a while, Leo surmised that they had accomplished their goal and all was well. So, he couldn't figure out why Ethan was so destitute.

"Hey, Ethan. We succeeded! See, the toxic environment has been dispelled around here after the fire was relit. Soon, the whole planet will be healed. So, what are you so down about?" asked Leo as he approached Ethan.

Leo put his hand on Ethan's shoulder, only to have Ethan drag him down. "We'll never recover from what we have done. We destroyed a whole world! What have we done?"

"Ethan, it wasn't you. It was your father. You helped us set it right, and I hope you continue to do that. You need to get a hold of yourself first though. We aren't fixing anything with you like this. Are you listening to me? Please, I need you to calm down."

Leo comforted Ethan until he came back to his senses. Then they sat silently side by side for a long time until Ethan asked, "You will still go to Kracten next?"

"Of course! It is the only way to save Areliam. What we see here is just one example of Anon atrocities. They are destroying the rest of Areliam with their Amassings as well. So we need to stop them."

"And going to Kracten will help us how?"

"Ah, there is the good old naysayer Ethan. Couldn't hide for long, now could you?" jested Leo.

"Shut up and answer the question."

"Those are two contrary things you want me to do at the same time."

"Keep talking, Hearth-Bringer, but remember: I'm out if you can't come up with a viable plan even after going to Kracten."

"Oh, you must be serious about this. You know, since you are using my last name and all." In response to Leo's quip, Ethan gave him the evil eye, which made Leo chuckle. "Look, the plan is to meet Ivan Renegader, my great-grandfather, who will help us get back at the Anons."

"What? You are counting on getting help from that geezer? He and his band of pacifists went into seclusion after your great grandmother dumped him!"

"The ancestors never told me this!"

"Of course, they didn't. It's because they have done nothing but add to all the problems."

"What do you mean?" asked Leo. However, Ethan didn't get to answer, as both of them were shocked when suddenly daylight brightened the night. One moment Ragonia was undergoing the darkest of nights, the next it was experiencing a bright and shiny day.

"What in the world!" exclaimed Desdemona, who had finally woken up.

"Des! Des, are you alright?" asked Ethan.

"How did you survive the explosion?" asked Leo.

"Wow! The green sky is so beautiful. I never thought I would see it. Wait, what explosion?" asked Desdemona, having no memory of what transpired after she jumped inside the pit.

"There was a huge explosion when you leaped into the pit earlier. I think that is how you relit it," said Leo.

"I heard it too while losing consciousness, but then how did you survive?" asked Ethan.

"Don't know. Maybe the Creation Flames inside me saved me from the explosion. By the way, that blue star is not Blontzar. Blontzar is a little red star, not a big blue one," remarked Des.

"That means Ragonia's cosmos traveling ability must have activated after the fire was relit. So, it brought us somewhere new," deduced Ethan.

"Ok, but where and why?" asked Des.

"We are near Kracten. I can feel it," said Leo, sensing his destination was near.

"Really?" asked Des.

"Yes, it's almost like all of Areliam is telling us to go to Kracten. The question is, do we listen to it or not?" asked Leo while eyeing Ethan.

Ethan didn't answer Leo's question right away. Instead, he walked to a small pile of ashes a little farther away. The pile of ashes was Diandra's, evident from the upper part of her armor and bracelet. Ethan looked around everywhere to find the lower part of the armor. Once he found it, he returned the whole armor and bracelet to Des. Then he picked up Lore, who was still sleeping, and said, "Now we are ready to go visit Kracten."

Kracten was a jungle world with a red sky. Half of its surface was covered in dense forests; the other half was occupied by a turbulent ocean. Due to its high humidity levels, frequent violent thunderstorms drenched the planet. The high humidity led to reoccurring hurricanes ravaging the coastline. Luckily, the children didn't land in the middle of a thunderstorm or hurricane upon their first visit to the planet. Unfortunately, though, they landed near one of Kracten's more inhospitable inhabitants—a giant scorpion the size of a big house.

"Hearth-Bringer! Portal us out of here already," yelled Ethan as he avoided the scorpion's stinger while running for his life.

"Yeah about that... I'm very new at using my powers, so I don't know how to teleport moving objects or people yet. I can only teleport us when we stand still," said Leo while running for his life too.

"You are absolutely useless!" replied Ethan.

"Come now, friend! No need to be unnecessarily harsh!" said a hurt Leo.

"I am not your friend!" said Ethan.

"Meanie," mumbled Leo.

"Guys, focus! We have to bring it down if we want to live!" said Desdemona as she ran alongside them. Lore was sleeping soundly on Ethan's back, still tired from the ordeals of the night before.

"Fine," said Ethan as he stopped running and turned around to face the scorpion.

Ethan used his earth Anon powers to cause a landslide to stop the scorpion from moving. At the same time, Desdemona used her Destruction Elemental powers to drain the scorpion of its energy. However, the scorpion was too fast to get caught up in the landslide. It quickly moved away from the area affected by the landslide. Although slowed down by

Desdemona, it still rebounded right away and came after the children swiftly.

Ethan raised columns of the earth as roadblocks while Desdemona concentrated on draining energy from its legs. The scorpion's legs wobbled as it struggled to stay up. So, it used its stinger instead. It swung its stinger around to raze the earth columns into dirt again then sprayed venom towards the children.

Ethan protected Lore and himself by creating a wall of earth in front of him. However, Desdemona and Leo were still left unprotected. The venom spewing out was acidic, burning everything it touched. No rock, tree, or bush was safe from it. Part of the venom hit Des. She screamed in pain and fell to the ground.

"Des!" shouted Ethan from behind his earth wall, which was deteriorating each moment by the scorpion's acid.

"I got her!" yelled Leo as he ran towards the stationary Des to teleport her away to safety. He got to her just before another bout of poison shower hit her. Leo shielded Des from the venom as much he could while teleporting away. However, he was burnt in the process, so he couldn't teleport them far. His Hearth-Bringer power kicked in to heal his burnt skin, causing him trouble in using Pathfinder teleportation power.

Wounded Leo and Des landed just outside of the venom ejection zone, but not too far for the scorpion to catch up to them by foot. "Ethan, hold it off until I can teleport again!" said Leo while concentrating on healing himself before teleporting again.

"How is Desdemona?" asked Ethan.

"Heavily burnt and passed out, but she'll live!" replied Leo.

Without Desdemona, the scorpion regained its power and charged straight towards the now immobile Leo and Des. Easier targets than Ethan and Lore, as its venom couldn't penetrate Ethan's continuously regenerating earth wall. "Ethan, help!" called out Leo in desperation, but it was too late. The scorpion had already reached them.

The scorpion moved its sting to strike Leo at lightning speed. It was intercepted at the last moment, though, by a tall, muscular black man in black clothing with long dreadlocks. He shattered the scorpion's stinger with one punch, then proceeded to lift it by one of its legs and fling it far away. Only to run after it and jump on its head with enough force to crush it, killing it on the spot.

CHAPTER TWENTY-FIVE

A thunderstorm raged outside. The children were safe from it, though, as the mysterious man helped them find shelter inside a cave. Leo's wounds healed automatically due to his Hearth-Bringer powers, and Ethan and Lore were both unharmed. Des, however, needed time to recover. She was lying asleep in a corner. The man applied some miraculous ointment on her that healed her wounds completely. Yet, her mind and body were still exhausted from the happenings of the past few days. So, she was sleeping to regain her strength. The man also provided milk for Lore to drink.

"Taste this to make sure it's not poisoned," Ethan commanded Leo.

"Do I look like a poison taster to you?" asked an irritated Leo.

"If only you were that useful. Anyways, it was your idea to come here. So, take responsibility and make sure this is safe for my baby sister."

"Yeah, but what if something happens to me? I mean, this was given by the man who is roasting snakes for dinner," said Leo while pointing at the man.

The cave they were in also housed an enclosed area full of snakes. This mysterious savior of theirs loved snakes. He loved them so much that he created a snake pit inside the cave full of different types of snakes. He even took out a snake and offered it to them as food. Obviously, they refused. However, they still needed medication to treat Desdemona and milk for Lore.

"Look, I don't trust him either. However, we haven't had any food since yesterday. We can still endure hunger, but Lore can't. So, if this milk is safe, I need to make her drink it right away. Fortunately, you happen to be the best person to test it out. Your Hearth-Bringer powers will protect you in case anything bad happens. So, stop whining and drink it already!" said Ethan, glancing at the man with a lot of contempt even though he saved their lives.

"I'm sure since the ointment was fine the milk would be too!" said Leo, hoping to avoid drinking the milk.

"Leon Hearth-Bringer..."

"Ok. Ok." Leo gave in as he begrudgingly took a sip. His fear was uncalled for, though, the milk was fresh and tasty. "This is delicious!" said a pleasantly surprised Leo as he started to drink more.

"That's enough, leave some for the baby. Also, go find some clean clothes to use as diapers," said Ethan as he took the milk away from Leo and fed it to Lore.

"What? You want me to be a nanny for your sister now?"

"Again, if only you were that useful. You wanted to come here. Well, congratulations. We are here. Stranded on an alien world without proper supplies. So, make amends for your poorly hatched plan."

Leo couldn't argue with that. So, he heaved a long sigh and started searching for something that could be used as diapers. The man saw him looking around and said, "Hold on for now. You can resupply at my camp before leaving."

"Leaving? We are not going anywhere until we find the person we are looking for," said Leo.

"He is not interested in meeting you, Hearth-Bringer."

"How can you say that when you don't even know who we are looking for? Also, how did you know I am a Hearth-Bringer?"

"You are part Pathfinder for sure. However, there is only one Veiled One clan who had an innate ability to heal themselves. The Hearth-Bringers," replied the man.

"Just like there was only one Veiled One clan who chose to live in this forsaken place. They loved this place so much that their clan leader broke all the travel mirrors here so no one could teleport in or out. Of course, that wasn't until Isaac Renegader took half the clan to join the war. Isn't that right, Mr. Ivan Renegader?" asked Ethan in a hateful tone. The anger and hatred he had for this man were reflected in his voice.

"Ivan Renegader! Are you really Ivan Renegader?" asked an astonished Leo.

Ivan smirked. "Leave it to a Gainsworth to recognize a Renegader. Tell me, child, does my name still haunt your clan?" asked Ivan, remembering the long history of enmity between the two clans.

"No. Your name no longer means anything. Your second in command, though, is still on our hit list."

"Wait, who are you talking about?" Leo asked confused.

"Isaac Renegader, his son and second in command joined the Elementals and went up against the Anons. He was also the one who attacked Harbor and killed my mother," replied Ethan.

"And you are just telling me all this now?"

"You are leaving out the reason my son rode to war. It was because Gainsworths killed my granddaughter."

"She was working for the Elementals! She almost turned all the Veiled Ones against us."

"Nonsense. The Veiled Ones always remained neutral. They would've continued to do so if you hadn't wiped out the Paradigms."

"We had no choice! They attacked us first during peace talks!"

"You always have a choice!" yelled Ivan Renegader.

"Stop. All this is extremely confusing. Just explain exactly what happened. Please," pleaded Leo.

Ivan fell silent and looked away. Ethan's face was red with anger. The usually cool and collected Ethan was having a hard time expressing all his emotions. Meanwhile, Leo and Lore were the confused ones quietly looking at the faces of both Ivan and Ethan.

"Remember when I told you that I have things to discuss back in Ragonia. Well, this is what I wanted to discuss," Ethan finally said.

"Well, then, do tell more."

"It is true that the Anons started all of this. It was King Oran who manipulated everything behind the scenes. When my mother and uncles found out about it, they confronted him. They even gave him the death penalty for all his crimes. Then they voluntarily surrendered and asked for nothing but peace. However, the Elementals and the Paradigms attacked them during the peace talks and killed most of our forces. They decided to hunt down the last of the Anons and Gainsworths. We fought back and wiped out almost all of the Paradigms.

His granddaughter, Calico Paradigm, survived and managed to turn the Veiled Ones against us. Once again threatening our existence. So, we developed the curse as a last-ditch effort for survival," said Ethan.

"Don't lie! No one can come up with such a curse in a few days. You had that slimy Emanuel working on it for a long time!"

"No! It was a last-minute thing!" proclaimed Ethan.

"Lies!" Ivan countered, refusing to believe anything coming out of Ethan's mouth.

"Leo, listen to me. Even now his son wants to destroy us. The only ones who escaped the War of Behemoths were Isaac Renegader and his followers. They are the only ones powerful enough to cause havoc during the Mother's Womb incident. They must have been the ones to attack us during that event. They killed my father! I'm sure of it!" said Ethan.

"Rubbish! I do not know what you speak about. However, I know that my son isn't one to cause senseless deaths," Ivan objected.

"You have no clue what your son is capable of then. At first, I thought the surviving Elementals had a hand in it. However, seeing their poor shape I know it wasn't them. So, that leaves only them, the Renegaders, under your son's command. They are responsible for the Mother's Womb event," stressed Ethan.

"Wait. So, you helped us not because you want to save Areliam. It was because you wanted to get to the Renegaders, who you think are responsible for your father's death?" asked a hurt Leo.

"I do want to make things right and save Areliam. However, I can no longer stay quiet. This man is no better than his son. Can't you see he refuses to help us? He doesn't care what will happen to Areliam. None of these Renegaders are worth our time. If you want my help, then you have to stand with me against him," said Ethan passionately.

"But the ancestors said..." Leo started to mumble

"Forget about the ancestors! It's their fault in the first place. If they hadn't taken such exclusionary steps, then things wouldn't have gone so bad. Now they want to use us, the new generation, to fix their mistakes. How is that fair?" Ethan asked earnestly.

"On that one thing, we both agree, Gainsworth. With that, we have nothing more to discuss. Portal yourselves off my planet now!" demanded Ivan.

"Is that any way to talk to friends of your great-grandson?" asked Desdemona, with a mouth full of food. She regained consciousness during all the bickering, but instead of adding to it, she decided to fill her stomach. By this point, she finished eating all the cooked snake meat by herself.

Ivan didn't answer her but raised an eyebrow in response.

Des recalled how everyone freaked out when Leo mentioned coming to Kracten to meet Ivan Renegader was necessary to save Areliam. Then she overheard Calaren addressing Ivan as his grandfather in a conversation with June. Curious to know more she did some information hunting on the matter.

Her father told her, originally there were eight Veiled One clans. The Hearth-Bringers, Gainsworths, Pathfinders, Renegaders, Transenders, Warhammers, Keepers, and Craftmasters. They all had a common ancestor, Lapis Lazuli Hearth-Bringer. It was she who had created the last Veiled One clan of Paradigms, also called Channelers by some.

The Paradigms was a clan that included beings from all corners of creation. It was not restricted to the Veiled Ones only. Everyone was welcome, be it an Anon, an Elemental, a Veiled One, or someone from the other races of Areliam. Anyone could join after they passed certain trials. However, Paradigms still counted as a Veiled One clan, for it was established by the progenitor of all Veiled Ones, Lapis Lazuli Hearth-Bringer.

Like the Paradigms, the rest of the Veiled Ones tried to be inclusive too. Since all Veiled Ones came from the same source, people from one clan were often born with powers of another. In such cases, upon reaching adulthood, people were transferred to the clan matching their powers. Khalifa Hearth-Bringer was born as a Renegader. After her Hearth-Bringer powers surfaced, she was forced to transfer to the Hearth-Bringer clan. However, Ivan and she were childhood sweethearts and carried their relationship into adulthood. Their love was so great that both of them remained unmarried for the rest of their lives. At the time of transfer, Khalifa was already carrying Ivan Renegader's sons in her womb.

Isaac was born as a Renegader, and Leo's grandfather Kendall was born as a Hearth-Bringer. In time Isaac transferred over to the Renegaders while Kendall stayed behind. After separation from Khalifa and Kendall, a heartbroken Ivan kept himself secluded from all matters of Veiled Ones. The last he heard, all the adult Hearth-Bringers were dead and the rest of the Veiled Ones were enslaved. At that time, he didn't have any great-grandchildren yet. So, he thought none of his grandchildren survived to give birth to a new generation.

Des didn't bring all of this up to Leo before as she thought it was a family matter. Only Calaren or June should be the ones to tell Leo all this. So, she kept quiet. However, she revealed that information now to calm Ivan down. "What? Leo, didn't you tell him that you are the son of Calaren Hearth-Bringer, his grandson, yet?" asked Des.

"Calaren, one of Kendall's four sons..." Ivan muttered aloud as he looked closely at Leo. Finally, he understood why he felt called to save Leo earlier. It was his blood calling for his help. An emotional Ivan kneeled and hugged Leo, a display of emotion uncharacteristic to him. However, he couldn't stop the tears of joy that flowed out. *At least one of my grandsons and his line survived.*

"Oh, how cute! You just went from a roaring tiger to a happy kitty! But this is just the beginning. Your grandson and his wife are at Ragonia. We can go meet them once you hear us out. What do you think?" asked a hopeful Des.

"No one is going anywhere. I won't lose my last surviving great-grandchild at any cost. You'll always be by my side, safe and secure," replied Ivan as he caressed Leo's cheeks. Then he continued, "You all will live here with me until the end of your days so I can keep you out of harm's way forever."

"Wait, what?" asked a surprised Des.

"How will we save Areliam then?" asked a stunned Leo.

"Over my dead body," said Ethan.

Even Lore objected by saying the usual, "Gugugahgahgahgahgah."

However, Ivan Renegader didn't listen. He took out some white powder from his pocket and sprinkled it on the children. The powder was imbued with the dark magic of the Renegaders and was spelled to invoke a deep slumber in people. Ivan activated its power with his voice. "Sleep," he said, and all the children fell asleep in an instant. Becoming prisoners of Ivan Renegader in the process.

CHAPTER TWENTY-SIX

L eo enjoyed some blissful sleep. The type he hadn't had
since he left Solem. The mattress was firm, and the white
sheets were soft and comfortable. A whole day had passed
and daylight was just starting to bloom. The chilly morning
mountain air was being warmed by the fire burning inside the
fireplace, making the room have just the right temperature.

Leo opened his eyes and found himself lovingly tucked
inside the bedsheets. He got up and stretched. They were
inside a cozy little bedroom with a few bunk beds, in what
seemed like a mountain cabin.

He felt refreshed and smelled good, indicating someone
had washed him. It seemed someone had changed his clothes
too. Now, only if there was some good food that is not snake
meat.

"We need to save Areliam, he said. For that, we need Ivan
Renegader, he said. So, let's go to Kracten, he said. Well, you
got your wish! We are here," said Ethan.

"Hello, friend. I see you are doing well," said Leo as he
turned around and saw Ethan angrily eyeing him from the top
bunk of one of the beds. Ethan was bathed too and wore a new
set of clothes. As was Lore, who was sitting next to him and
playing with a toy. Des was by the window. She too seemed
fresh and had a new set of clothes on.

"Friends don't kidnap friends and get them imprisoned for
life!"

"Yeah... It's all part of the plan."

"Oh really? Then why don't you enlighten us with the details
of this brilliant plan of yours?" asked Ethan, while crossing his
arms.

"See, we already accomplished the first part, which was to find Mr. Ivan Renegader. Now we just have to do the second part, which is to convince him to help us at any cost."

Ethan got down from the bed and walked up to Leo. He stood mere inches away from Leo's face and held up his right hand. There was a power-binding bracelet on it. Then he grabbed Leo's hand and showed him the power-binding bracelet on it as well. After that, Leo took a closer look at the girls and saw them wearing the bracelets too.

"Ok, so what if we can't use our powers? We can still convince him with our words. All we need are the right words to persuade him to help us."

Ethan started massaging his temple in frustration. "What can you say to a stubborn man over a hundred years old to make him aid us?"

"You tell me. You seem to have more information about this whole situation. Who or what has the power to convince him to come out of isolation and join our side?" asked Leo.

"Nothing and no one. The only person who could make him listen was your great-grandmother Khalifa Hearth-Bringer. He stopped paying heed to anyone after she and your grandfather Kendall went to the Hearth-Bringers during the interclan exchange."

"What was the interclan exchange again?"

"It is the Veiled One custom of exchanging members of one clan to another if they exhibit powers of another clan. Your great-grandmother and her son Kendall were exchanged from the Renegaders to the Hearth-Bringers. Then she participated in the Battle of Behemoths from the Elemental side and died in it. If she was alive, she could convince him to fight on our side to save Areliam. However, since she is dead, we are doomed," answered Ethan.

"Not necessarily."

"What do you mean?" asked Des, who had stayed quiet until now. Even Lore stopped playing with her toy and looked at Leo.

"First, you tell me how you found out about me being related to Ivan Renegader?" Leo asked Des.

"I overheard your parents speaking and did my own research on the side." Replied Des.

"You mean you eavesdropped, poked your nose around, and failed to inform me what you found out." Leo corrected Des.

"However, you wanna take it." Said Des while shrugging her shoulders. "Now, how are we going to make your great-grandfather listen to us? I don't want to be stuck here forever. I miss home."

"I just thought of something that might work. Everyone, follow me!" said Leo.

Leo searched for Ivan throughout the cabin with the other children, but he wasn't there. So, they went outside. It was lovely out. The greenery, the mountain view, and the fresh air all added to the beauty of the place. As soon as they went out, though, a huge lioness came out from the nearby trees and ambushed them.

The lioness seemed to be extra fond of Leo and Ethan. She put each of them under one of her front paws and started licking them insistently while purring loudly. Ethan was barely able to pass Lore to Desdemona before that happened.

"Hey! Let me go! He is the Gainsworth. His clan loves cats. So, shower all your love on him instead!" said Leo as he wiggled to get out from under the lioness's paw.

"What are you talking about? Your name is Leon, which literally means lion, you idiot!" Ethan yelled at Leo as he too tried to get out of the clutches of the lioness.

"Stop fangirling and help us!" Leo snapped at Des and Lore, who were too busy admiring and petting the lioness.

"Oh, look! The cat caught two little mice!" said Ivan Renegader as he came out from behind the building.

"Hahaha, you have a great sense of humor, great-grandfather."

"You know what else I have? A sixth sense. Currently, it is warning me that my over-smart great-grandson is trying to fool me."

"Oh, great Anorea! What has the world come to? Innocent children like me are being accused of fooling others!"

No one said anything back to Leo, but all of them glared intensely at him for a while. Finally, Ivan said, "Let them go, Krayola," as he entered the cabin.

The breakfast table was set in the basement, right next to another home-built snake pit. Ivan had arranged some simple food items for the children. There was freshly made bread, bird meat, baked potatoes, a salad, orange juice, and refreshing cold mountain spring water. However, Ivan was still only eating snake meat. None of the children said anything out loud, but all of them were thinking the same thing: why does this man love eating snake meat so much?

Leo was the first one to speak. "Great-grandfather..."

"No."

"But I haven't said anything yet!"

"I know, and that no was to keep things that way."

"I was just going to say you look really young for someone who is one hundred and twenty-five!"

"No, you weren't, and I am only a hundred and twenty-three."

"Still, we thought you would be a hunchbacked, feeble and wrinkly old man by now. Yet you don't even have a single gray hair! Is it because of all the snake meat you eat? If that is it, can I have some, too?" Des butted in, putting her plate forward.

"Ok, enough! I can't stand this false flattery anymore. Let's just get this conversation over with."

"I was being genuine, though. I did want to eat more snake meat," said a dejected Des.

Leo took this opportunity to try and persuade Ivan to help them. "Great-grandfather, Areliam is dying. After the Elementals were defeated, no new elements were created to keep Areliam going. The Anons keep destroying what is left through their Amassings. In addition, they have enslaved our whole race. We must save both Areliam and the other Veiled Ones!"

"You want to save Areliam? You, who can't even use both your powers simultaneously?"

"Wait, how did you know that?"

"I wasn't born yesterday, kid. Even if I was, I would still be smarter than you. If you could portal out while healing yourself, then I wouldn't have needed to save you from the scorpion."

"Oh! I can't believe I didn't say it before, thank you for saving me! Thank you for saving all of us," interjected Des.

"You are welcome. Child, you are extremely powerful. Given enough time, you will be able to single-handedly defeat strong foes like that and much more. The powers of Destruction Elementals work similarly to Renegaders. So, I can teach you how to use your powers to the fullest if you like."

"Oh, that would be wonderful!" replied Des.

"The price of your teachings, however, will be a lifetime imprisonment on this planet for all of us, right?" asked Ethan.

"You should have thought of that before coming here, Gainsworth. This whole planet is full of Renegaders thirsty for your blood. If it weren't for me, they would've already killed you several times over."

"What Ethan is trying to say is that we don't need to be looked after. Even with our limited powers we have accomplished great feats! Like, we stole the Creation flames from the Volcano of Creation, right from under the noses of the Anons. Then used it to revitalize Ragonia! This proves that we can both take care of ourselves and others. So, you don't have to keep us locked up for our safety," said Leo to calm Ivan down.

"After reinvigorating Ragonia, you proceeded to bring it here, in the same star system as Kracten. Bringing along with it the attention and ire of the Anons," said, Ivan.

"What? Ragonia is already here? No wonder I am feeling its presence. I kept looking at the skies all night last night, not knowing I was searching for it!" Said Des.

"We knew Ragonia was close to Kracten but didn't know it would travel here so fast. Also, I admit I didn't know that the Anons will be able to track Ragonia!" said Leo.

"I didn't know that you barbarians could sense such things. If you are so afraid of the Anons, then let us go before my uncles catch you. You know, fall back on your isolationist policy, keep yourselves safe while the rest of the world burns," taunted Ethan.

Ivan remained quietly stoic and let the children say their fill. Once they calmed down, he just said one line: "The next one to interrupt me gets thrown into the snake pit." Desdemona immediately smacked her lips closed and put one hand on each of the boys'.

However, Lore picked this moment to speak up, "Gugugahgahgagaga?"

"Of course, that doesn't include you, little one," said Ivan as he smiled for the first time while looking at Lore.

Leo's first thought was, *Why does this man treat an Anon kid better than me, his own blood?* However, he remained silent in fear of being thrown to the snakes. Even Ethan didn't say anything more, but he was still giving Ivan the evil eye.

"Much better. Now to answer your question Desdemona, yes, Ragonia is already in the space surrounding Kracten. I'll show its position to you tonight. As for the abilities we possess, Gainsworth, remember that apart from Hearth-Bringers, Renegaders are the only ones unaffected by the curse. So, we are not afraid of the Anons, they are afraid of us. Lastly, Leo, seems like you don't know a lot of things. For example, you are not aware of how far the Veiled Ones have fallen. If you knew, then you would never hope to save them let alone try and save all of Areliam."

"What do you mean? Please explain in detail! All types of knowledge were withheld from us enslaved Veiled Ones. So, I didn't get to learn about much of anything. However, I have a right to know about my people. So please, great-grandfather, tell me what is going on!" Leo pleaded passionately.

"Out of the nine Veiled Ones Clans, three are completely out of commission. The Paradigms were wiped out, the Pathfinders lost their abilities long ago, and the Hearth-Bringer children are currently being brainwashed. Then the Warhammers, Craftmasters, and Keepers are used as slaves. Gainsworths are trying to save whatever little power they have left. The Renegaders are divided. Half of us want to live out the rest of our days in peace here. The other half is fighting a guerrilla war against the Anons and the Gainsworths. As for the Transenders, you already saw what happened to them."

"What do you mean? What happened to the Transenders?" asked a confused Leo.

"The abilities of the Transenders allow them to change their physical forms. The curse only works on Veiled Ones' physical forms. So, to escape the curse, they changed their forms. However, after remaining in their transcended forms for the past ten years, a lot of them have lost their former selves. They can no longer change back to Veiled Ones. The scorpion that attacked you and Krayola, and the giant lioness you met outside, were once Transenders."

CHAPTER TWENTY-SEVEN

A clearing was created in the middle of a forested area not too far from the mountain cabin. A massive death-link ritual was being held there. After hearing about the dire state of the Veiled Ones, Leo knew he had to do something quick. So, he lied and said Khalifa wanted Ivan to help the children restore Areliam and Veiled Ones. Of course, Ivan wanted proof. Leo and Ethan were traveling to the ancestral realm to bring Khalifa Hearth-Bringer's spirit to confirm Leo told the truth.

In addition to outlawing death-link ceremonies, the Gainsworths also cast spells blocking communication with the ancestors. As a result, no Veiled One, apart from the Gainsworths and Leo, has been able to commune with the ancestors. Leo knew this, and that is why he lied to Ivan. He wanted to use his connection to the ancestors to have Khalifa Hearth-Bringer convince Ivan to help them.

Ivan needed something more though. He wanted to make sure what happened to Khalifa and him wouldn't repeat with others. So, he made Leo promise that he'd get support from all the clans to abolish the interclan exchanges. He also asked that the clans put aside their politics and focus on the betterment of all Veiled Ones.

A circular rope hung from the nearby trees. On it were nine flags. Each flag had the symbol and animal of the clan it represented. Empty firepits were created underneath the flags. They would be lit automatically when the ancestors belonging to a particular clan showed up in their ghost forms. The black Pegasus and the infinity symbol represented the Paradigms. The wolf and the circle represented the Hearth-Bringers. The Gainsworths had cats as both their animal and their symbol. The Pathfinders had the phoenix as their animal and the nine-pointed star as their symbol. The snake was both the animal and the symbol that represented Renegaders. Continuing with the theme of an animal being both the symbol and the creature representing a clan, gorillas were representative of the Warhammers. Chameleons were representative of the Transenders. The craftsmasters were represented with butterflies as their animal and a diamond as their symbol. Lastly, the Keepers were represented with a turtle as their animal and books as their symbol.

Leo and Ethan were laid in the middle of the clearing. They were put to sleep with the help of Ivan's special powder. Their conscious minds being asleep will make their souls' journey to the ancestral realm easier. It was midday when the ritual began. Ivan gave them until the next midday to accomplish their task. Ivan, Krayola, Des, and Lore stayed behind to guard the boys while they were communing with the ancestors.

The first hour of the death-link ceremony went without problems. However, soon trouble came looking for them when a group of Renegaders confronted them. They surrounded Ivan, with one old man leading the charge.

"Ivan! How dare you side with the enemy?" asked the old man.

"Watch your tone, Husk. I'm still the leader of this clan."

"Some leader you are, harboring enemies in our midst."

"They are just children!"

"The children of the enemies are also enemies! Their parents were the ones who killed our children! Did you forget that?"

"I remember, but I can't hurt children. They have nothing to do with this. In fact, they are trying to fix things. My great-grandson is currently in the ancestral planes to unite all Veiled Ones and plan a counterattack against the Anons."

"Oh, I see what all of this is about. You found yourself a new great-grandchild and can't bring yourself to say no to him. What about all of us? Our lines ended fighting the same Gainsworths and Anons you are protecting right now!"

"No, you misunderstand! He has a plan to make things right. Khalifa sent him and he has the backing of all the ancestors. That is why he can still commune with them while none of us can."

Husk let out a long sigh and said, "Khalifa again? Your obsession with her is hurting the clan. Not just her. Your whole family has been a curse for us. It's time we nullify that curse."

"What do you mean, Husk?" Ivan asked curtly.

"Active immediately, you are no longer the leader of our clan. We take back the role of leadership from you. Now, stand down while we finish off the enemies," said Husk as he approached Lore and Ethan.

"Stop, if you disturb the death-link procedure, my great-grandson will be harmed. He is too young to survive the backlash of energy from an unfinished death-link ceremony. So please wait until the ritual is done."

"Why should I? Calico was the daughter of my daughter. When she died, all of my family went to avenge her. Then they all lost their lives in that Battle of Behemoths, as did almost all other younglings of our clan. Now we are mostly childless. So, why should you be the one of the few who gets to continue his lineage?" asked a vindictive Husk.

"Husk, stop! These are innocent children. They do not deserve this. Even the Anons didn't kill children. You who claim to be better than them have to act better than them, too."

"No, I'm done with all the civilities. Now it's time for justice to be served," said Husk as he took out his knife and walked menacingly towards Leo and Ethan.

Leo opened his eyes in the darkness of the ancestral realm. He looked around for the illuminated spot that usually appeared right away, signaling him where to go. However, nothing but darkness greeted him.

"This is strange," said Leo.

"Stranger than you lying to your great-grandfather?" asked Ethan who woke up beside Leo.

"Technically, it wasn't a lie. The ancestors did send me, and since Khalifa Hearth-Bringer is one of my direct ancestors, she wants great-grandfather to help out too," said Leo.

"That is not true," said Kendall Hearth-Bringer.

An illuminated spot finally did appear, and Kendall was sitting in it. However, a moving red spot of light rushed past him like a flash and headed directly for Leo. It collided with him with such force that Leo fell backward.

"Ancestor Dorian!" said a surprised Leo while being embraced by Dorian's wings.

"I'm so happy you are all right, boy!" said Dorian.

"Aww. I'm really happy to see both of you are all right as well! I was worried!" said Leo.

"Worried? Worried for what? Nothing could've happened to us because we were already dead. It's you all we were worried about. By the way, did that Des girl survive?" asked Dorian and was relieved when Leo nodded yes. Then he continued speaking, "After Ragonia we couldn't get a hold of you, though, and that made us nervous," said Dorian.

"Don't know why, but our connection seemed to have severed after the events in Ragonia. I just started feeling connected to you guys again a few hours ago. Anyways, thank you for everything you did for us in Ragonia. We would've never survived without your help," said a grateful Leo while happily hugging Dorian back.

"Anytime, my boy!" said Dorian.

Kendall slowly walked towards Leo and stopped to give a nod to Ethan before continuing. Once he reached Leo, he gave him a look around and said, "You seem healthy. A little while ago, we felt you using your Hearth-Bringer healing powers."

"Oh, that's because I was hurt by the acid of a giant scorpion, who was once a Transender. By the way, we have reached Kracten and..."

"We know," Dorian said, cutting Leo off. "We can feel the death-link ritual originated from Kracten. We also heard that you lied about Khalifa wanting Ivan to help you out. You shouldn't have done that."

"Why not?" asked Leo.

"My mother does not know what is going on. She and most of her coconspirators are being imprisoned in the hellish portion of the ancestral realm. Even mere mention of her name can get you punished," said Kendall.

Silence echoed within the ancestral realm. It reflected Leo's weariness of all the things that he didn't know yet. *Why do things keep getting more and more complicated?*

"Ok, so who'll tell me what crime great-grandmother is being punished for?" asked a dejected Leo.

"Khalifa Hearth-Bringer never forgot that she was a Renegader. She started an interclan war by unjustly aiding the Renegaders to gain a ruling position amongst the clans," said Ethan, who had been quiet for a while now.

"What is this about ruling positions now?"

"Paradigms, Hearth-Bringers, and Pathfinders were the most powerful clans of the Veiled Ones. Followed by Gainsworths, Renegaders, Transenders, Warhammers, Craftmasters, and Keepers. The top three clans had the utmost say about how Veiled Ones should live. When the Pathfinders lost their powers, a ruling position opened up that should have gone to the Gainsworths. However, your great-grandmother manipulated things so that it went to the Renegaders. This started an internal war that the Anons and Elementals took advantage of. All this eventually led to our collective downfall. So, I guess she is paying for that now," explained Ethan.

"Plus, she is extremely angry at Calaren for marrying June," blurted out Dorian.

"Now why is that?" asked Leo.

"June is a powerless Pathfinder. Mother wanted Calaren to marry Quintessa Transender to cement an alliance with the Transenders. However, he refused, so Calaren was cast out of the Hearth-Bringer family," Kendall answered.

"Fine. Let's go and recruit her to our cause then," said Leo.

"Hey, idiot, did you not hear anything we have said so far? She won't help us!" said Ethan.

"She will because I'll make her," replied Leo.

CHAPTER TWENTY-EIGHT

The ancestors guided Leo and Ethan through the ancestral plane. The Veiled Ones' ancestral realm was divided into twelve parts. Each of the nine clans had their portion and there was a common area shared by all. Then there was a hellish part of the realm where all evil Veiled Ones went to. Lastly, prime ancestor Lapis Lazuli Paradigm, along with the very first Veiled Ones, lived in a special zone. They lived on the mountain present in the middle of the ancestral realm.

Leo explained what he promised to do to get Ivan's help to Kendall and Dorian. During this conversation, four other ghost wolves approached the kids. "Ah, Leo. Let me introduce you to your grandmother and uncles. The black wolf is Leona, your grandmother. Calaren named you after her. The white wolf is Kazdin, Calaren's older brother. The two brown wolves are Camdin and Camren, twin younger brothers of your father," said Kendall.

"Which one is Camdin and which one is Camren?" Leo asked.

"The one with brown eyes is Camdin, and the one with green eyes is Camren," replied Kendall.

"Oh, hello everyone! It's nice to finally meet you! Don't get me wrong, I love grandfather and ancestor Dorian, but it got boring with just the two of them. So, I'm really glad to see some new faces!" said Leo.

"Hey, who are you calling boring?" asked Dorian.

"Probably the one who asked that question," Ethan said smugly.

"I don't remember asking you, Gainsworth. So, keep quiet," said a miffed Dorian.

"As you wish," replied Ethan.

"I said quiet!" yelled Dorian.

While Ethan and Dorian were squabbling, the brown wolves jumped at Leo and brought him down to the ground. Then they started to sniff and lick him. The black wolf helped Leo get up and chased the brown ones away.

"Give the boy some space!" said Leona.

"He smells like Cal!" said Camdin.

"Yeah, but he has June's features!" Camren chimed in.

"Of course, Uncles! I'm both of their son after all!" said Leo.

"Haha, we know. By the way, don't call us uncles. It makes us feel old. I go by Ren, Camdin goes by Din, and Kazdin goes by Kaz. So, call us by those nicknames," said Camren.

"Will do, Ren!" said Leo.

The white wolf, however, approached Ethan instead of Leo with a low growl. He encircled Ethan from afar, searching for the best angle of attack. Ethan in turn also readied himself to fight.

"No, Kaz! Stop! He is on our side," said Kendall.

"A Gainsworth can never be on our side! Especially this one. He is Edwin's son. We need to punish him for his father's sins," said Kaz.

"No, it's true! Ethan is a friend, and he is going to help us save both our people and Areliam." Leo hurriedly butted in to calm his uncle. He also went to Ethan and softly said, "Please don't say that I'm not a friend right now!" Ethan begrudgingly nodded in response.

"I don't trust him!" said Kaz.

"I don't either. However, we don't have a choice," Dorian said resentfully.

"Enough! We have to move on to our next steps. Honey, take Leo to my mother. He has to discuss something urgent with her," said Kendall.

"Is that wise?" asked a nervous Leona.

"Wise or not, it needs to be done. Leo has promised Father that he'll convince all the clans to work together, as well as make them agree to dissolve the interclan exchange. Mother needs to be a part of this as well," said Kendall.

"It won't work," said Kaz.

"Never give up before trying, son," said Kendall.

"Then at least you should accompany Leo. You know how mother-in-law gets. If there is anyone here who can somewhat handle her, it's you," said Leona.

"Oh, don't worry, honey. I think our grandson will be more than a match for her. Isn't that right, Leo?" Kendall asked Leo.

"Don't you worry, Grandfather. I'll take care of it!" replied Leo.

"Good. Then Dorian, go to the Keepers and convince them to join us. Ren, go to the Warhammers. Din, go to the Craftmasters. Kaz, go convince the Transenders. I'll go with Ethan to convince the Gainsworths. Once they are convinced, we can reach out to the Renegaders. After that, we'll all go to convince the Paradigms," said Kendall.

"Oh, and remember this is urgent. We only have a few hours to make this work. So, please make haste!" said Leo.

"Fine. We'll get to it then. Meet you back in the common area in a few hours," said Ren and Din before running off.

"I don't think it'll work, but I'll give it a try," said Kaz before leaving.

"I'll get going too," said Dorian as he spread his wings to fly off to meet the Keepers.

"We should get going too, honey," Kendall said to Leona.

"Please convince the Gainsworth ancestors. They must join us," Leo said to Ethan.

"I'll do my part. You just make sure to get that evil great-grandmother of yours on our side," Ethan retorted back.

"Don't worry, I'll get it done for sure!" said Leo excitedly.

"We'll see," Ethan replied. Then the children went their separate ways, unaware of the trials awaiting them.

The Gainsworths' area was protected with a sealing dome, similar to the one around Ragonia's First Fire Pit. After what the Gainsworths had done, all the other ancestors had turned against them. So, it was a defensive measure to protect the Gainsworth ancestors. However, it also imprisoned them and made them easy prey for power-draining by Emanuel.

Kendall and Ethan traversed silently until they reached the dome. Ethan was happy to finally have some peace and quiet.

However, a part of him missed Leo's undying optimism about everything turning out all right. Ethan looked at Kendall and they both nodded at each other.

Ethan approached the sealed dome and called out to his father. "Father! Father! Are you in there? I need to talk to you!"

A silhouette started to form inside the dome. Soon it took the ghostly shape of Edwin. "Ethan! Where have you been? You had us all worried! We couldn't get in touch with you at all. What happened? Wait, how are you in the ancestral realm? Don't tell me you are dead!" asked a nervous Edwin.

"He is not dead. He came here with my grandson via a death-link ritual," Kendall clarified.

"Your grandson... You mean that over-smart Leon Hearth-Bringer? How is he still alive?" asked Edwin.

"Luck, trickery, and the use of his Pathfinder powers kept him alive, and we should be really thankful for that," replied Ethan.

"Did he force you to say this?" asked Edwin suspiciously.

"No," said Ethan.

"Then did you hit your head hard or something?" Edwin asked.

"Father...please, I need to discuss something important with you," said Ethan as he tried to steer the conversation towards saving Areliam and the rest of the Veiled Ones.

"Ok, I'll hear you out. However, I would like some privacy," Edwin said while looking at Kendall.

Kendall understood and started to go away. However, Ethan stopped him.

"No. He needs to stay. What I'm about to say affects all of us," said Ethan.

"Ah, finally someone in my family understands the value of inclusion!" said the apparition of Edward, who now emerged by Edwin's side.

"Yes, he does. He even willingly helped us revive the First Fire Pit in Ragonia," said Kendall.

"Is that true?" asked a shocked Edwin.

"Yes, it is," Ethan said.

"Why?" Edwin asked.

"Did you know that Emanuel is draining all of you to boost his powers?" asked Ethan.

"I wasn't aware of it before I died. But I know that now." Edwin answered.

"Uncle Ran was aware of it though. Did he never say anything to you?" asked Ethan.

"No!" said a surprised Edwin.

"Let me get straight to the point. We Veiled Ones as a race are suffering and Areliam is dying. We need to support each other to get out of this crisis. That is why I teamed up with Leon Hearth-Bringer and need you to do the same," said Ethan.

"No! Never!" yelled Edwin

"I guess some people never change," said a female voice in the shadows.

"Who?" Kendall and Edward asked in unison.

"Calico!" Edwin said softly.

"Good to know you still remember my voice," said a beautiful black woman with honey-colored eyes and braided hair as she walked out of the shadow. "Let's see if your son can make sacrifices for the greater good that you never could." Calico grabbed Ethan, and both of them disappeared into the shadows.

Leo and Leona stood in front of the gates to the hellish lands within the ancestral realm. The path leading up to the gates was fantastic. Leo bonded more with his grandmother in this short while than he ever did with his grandfather. She told him how Calaren was her favorite son, and Leo told her how happy his family life was. However, that all stopped as they faced the frightening gates. If those doors were any indication of what was inside, then they were in for some turbulent times ahead.

The gates opened when Leona touched them with her snout, revealing the terrifying scenario inside. The hellish lands resembled the insides of an overactive volcano. Metal cases containing sinful Veiled Ones were hanging in the air. The inhabitants inside the cases were slowly roasting in the heat, experiencing never-ending excruciating pain.

Scorching hot air hit Leo in the face as they entered. Soon one of the flying metal cases flew down to meet them. Khalifa

Hearth-Bringer was in it. The case had a small, barred window that allowed the occupant to see the world outside. Khalifa's half-burnt face appeared in it.

"Hello, Mother-in-Law. This is your great-grandson, Leon. He came to talk about something important today," said Leona, stepping away from the case immediately after.

"There is only one traitorous grandson I had who could produce a child. So, this must be Calaren's son with that Pathfinder woman," said Khalifa grimly.

In front of Khalifa, Leo felt like a pickpocket facing a crime lord. He knew no matter what he did he would not be able to convince her of anything she didn't want to do. *Damn! I can see why everyone is scared of her. However, I can't back down now, I have to gain her cooperation for saving Areliam and rest of the Veiled Ones. So, let's act tough and make her see that working with me will be beneficial for her too. That is the only way to get her to help us,* thought Leo and said, "June Pathfinder Hearth-Bringer. That is her name. I know it's a long one, so why don't you just call her June instead," retorted Leo.

"Well, at least you have your mother's spirit," said Khalifa.

"I also have my father's wisdom that I'm here to share with you," said Leo.

Khalifa smirked and said, "Is that right."

"Yes! The first lesson in wisdom is to accept opportunities as they arise. So, accept the opportunity I bring you today."

"What is this opportunity you speak of?" asked Khalifa.

"The opportunity to aid in the rescue of Areliam and earn some good deeds," said Leo.

Khalifa didn't reply. She just raised the eyebrow on the side of her face that wasn't burned. So, Leo continued, "Areliam is dying. The Elementals are almost wiped out, the Veiled Ones are enslaved, and the Anons' Amassings are destroying whatever is left. So, we need to band together to save both our people and Areliam."

"Our people you say. These are the same people your father had forsaken to be with your mother."

"Actually, I'm speaking of Veiled Ones as a whole and not any one clan per se. Also, as far as I know, it was you that kicked him out," said Leo.

"He left me no choice!"

"That's not true. You thought he got in your way, so you brutally removed him. Yet you still didn't get what you wanted. How sad!"

"Insolent child! You know nothing!" yelled Khalifa while grasping the bars on the window firmly.

"I know you wanted to bring the clans under one rule so you could dissolve the interclan exchanges. As a first step, you wanted Pa to marry a Transcender. However, a person like you also loves power. So, you'd never be happy until you ruled over them completely. So, did you have anything to do with wiping out the Paradigms? Is that why you are here?" asked Leo.

"Smart child! How did you know?"

"A friend of mine suggested Calico Paradigm, formerly known as Calico Renegader, tried to turn Veiled Ones against the Anons. However, why would she do that? Seemed like she was instigated by someone. Someone like you. Also, isn't it convenient that only Aunt Calico survived to tell everyone of the Paradigms termination? All the Veiled Ones turned against the Anons and Gainsworths because of that, no? Not to mention, no matter how powerful the Anons are, taking down the Paradigms would've been nearly impossible. Unless, of course, they had some inside help. You must have had something to do with the Paradigms' demise so you could reign supreme. Last but not the least, Veiled Ones are sent to the hellish lands only because they have sinned greatly. So, I thought you must be being punished for your role in all of this."

Leona looked at Leo in awe. On the way over they had discussed several things. The characteristics of Khalifa Hearth-Bringer being chief among them. However, they never talked of the reasons Khalifa was sent to the hellish lands. So, she never could've guessed that Leo could've figured out so much with just that one conversation.

"Muhahhahhah!" Khalifa laughed manically. "It's good to see that someone in the family inherited my brilliance. I was quite disappointed with my sons, to be frank."

"Why thank you! I think you should reward me for being so brilliant," said Leo confidently.

"What can a caged bird like me even give you?" asked Khalifa.

"Drop the act. You and I both know you won't be here for long," said Leo.

"What do you mean?" asked a confused and nervous Leona.

"Somehow, she is still in touch with her other son, Isaac Renegader. Who will get her out of here soon. Isn't that right, Great-Grandmother?"

"You really are my great-grandson! Now, how did you figure this one out?"

"Easy. My friend mentioned Isaac Renegader still being alive and that he orchestrated the Mother's Womb mishap. However, Great-Grandfather Ivan described Isaac as an emotional being not capable of plotting all this. So, I concluded that someone else was pulling the strings, and you are ruthless and conniving enough to plan it. Also, the only upside of being in the hellish lands is retaining your body. You would've escaped from here long ago, if the Gainsworths hadn't cut off access to the ancestral realm, that is. Thus, I know you will use this period where the connection has opened up because of me to escape," said Leo.

"Oh, you are just perfect! I'd love to have you on my side. So, join me!" offered Khalifa.

"Let me make you a counteroffer instead. You have seen what happens when your plan for world domination fails. So, why don't you keep me as a backup plan?" asked Leo.

"Go on?" prompted Khalifa.

"Our goals are currently aligned. To rule the world, you must first have a world left to rule. So, we need to save Areliam first. Secondly, you'd need loyal subjects under you as well; the Veiled Ones can fulfill that need. The best way to win them over is to free them from the Anon curse. So, I propose we work together to achieve these two goals. I will follow nonviolent ways while you can continue your wicked practices. We can deal with each other after we have defeated the Anons. Until then, though, let's help each other. What do you say?" asked Leo.

"A good idea, but I have to make sure you are strong enough first. So, why don't we see if you have what it takes?" asked Khalifa. As she finished talking, the gates closed behind Leo and Leona. Then, all the other cases started coming down one by one, unleashing the evil within.

CHAPTER TWENTY-NINE

Daylight was ending. Dusk was creeping upon Kracten, yet Husk and Ivan were still at an impasse. Ivan stood tall in front of Husk, blocking his advance on Leo and Ethan. Other clan members tried to take Husk's side, citing Leo's Hearth-Bringer powers would save him if anything went wrong. However, Ivan would not budge. He didn't want to take any chances with Leo's life.

Husk finally had enough. "Ivan, the clan has decided that I'm to be the new leader. So, my first order as leader of the Renegaders is for you to step aside and let me end this death-link ceremony right now!"

"No! I'm still the leader because you have not been declared the official leader yet. So, follow my orders and leave the kids alone!" said Ivan.

"You stubborn old mule! Let's finish this once and for all. I, Husk Renegader, challenge you to a one-on-one duel. Whoever wins gets to be the leader of our clan permanently," said, Husk.

"I accept," replied Ivan.

Being longtime allies, both of them were well acquainted with each other's fighting styles. Ivan knew Husk played dirty. So, he went to the girls and took off their power-binding bracelets. "Hope you won't need to use your powers, but still, stay away from our fight and be on guard. The others might take advantage of me being occupied and attack you. Krayola, keep the children safe."

Husk in return gave out a warning of his own. "Everyone, be wary of this old buffoon. Seems like he'll go to any length to save the enemy. Keep at a distance and don't interfere unless I tell you to." Thus, everyone moved away and gave them ample space to fight.

So, the stage was set for a battle between two of the greatest living warriors of the Veiled Ones. The Renegaders were dark magicians. Poison, decay and death were their forte. Husk specialized in causing deterioration inside while keeping the outside intact. Ivan, on the other hand, could cause explosions out of nothing.

The two of them circled each other from afar first. Ivan took out some black powder and sprinkled it in his vicinity. Husk did the same with some brown powder. The powders they used had their energies, and they hung in the air around them. The black powder was imbued with Ivan's explosive powers and the brown powder had Husk's deteriorating ability. These powders created a defensive zone around the users. Anyone other than the users would be harmed if they came in contact with them.

Husk struck first, decaying the soil beneath Ivan's feet and causing him to sink into the ground. Then he used his energy already present in the soil to degenerate Ivan's body stuck inside. Ivan wasn't going to fall for it though. He exploded away the land around him, creating a hole in the ground. At the same time, Ivan created small explosions around Husk to distract him while he got out of the hole. He also used the explosions to blow away the shield of decaying powder around Husk. Then, he attacked.

Ivan used his supreme physical strength to dominate Husk. He ran up to Husk and punched him hard. Small explosions went off simultaneously on Husk's body as he came into contact with Ivan's protective powder. Husk flew away several feet as a result. Without giving Husk time to recover, Ivan grabbed him by the leg and twirled him around, smacking him on the ground. Again, Ivan's protective powder cloud caused several small explosions, damaging Husk immensely.

Husk, however, used this opportunity to inject his decaying power inside Ivan. So, Ivan's right hand that came in contact with Husk's body became unable to move. Next, Husk tried to paralyze Ivan by reorganizing the scattered decaying cloud and sending it after him.

It didn't work. Husk's decaying cloud exploded when it came in contact with Ivan's exploding powder. Then, Ivan exploded the ground beneath Husk, following it up with exploding the terrain around him, which caused a pile of dirt to bury Husk alive.

However, Husk used his decaying power to turn all the hard rock, gravel, and earth around him into a fine dust. Then he used the cover created by the dust to get closer to Ivan and strike him from behind. Ivan's explosive powder saved him though.

"Damn it. I thought you would be all out of exploding powder by now!" said Husk as he coughed blood.

"The former me would have run out of exploding powder by now. However, unlike you, I've improved my skills. The powder I created splits in half before exploding. So, it lingers, giving protection for longer. Give up, Husk. You can't defeat me!" said Ivan.

"You are right. I cannot defeat you alone. Unfortunately for you, though, I'm not alone. Everyone, attack!" ordered Husk.

The clansmen supporting Husk were waiting for his signal, and all of them rushed Ivan at once after it was given. However, Ivan successfully evaded the crowd of people coming at him by jumping high in the air then launched his counterattack. Ivan caused a series of explosions in the earth that created an impassable crater in front of his assailants. They couldn't get to him anymore. Or so he thought. Suddenly, something exploded against his protective powder barrier and more projectiles were inbound. Husk got on his feet and glanced towards the children.

Ivan forgot about his safety and sent the explosive powder toward the children. A big mistake. The clansmen supporting Husk had gone around the crater by this time and were now coming for Ivan. They almost cornered him too. However, Ivan sensed the danger and was able to move away at the last moment. But in all this, he couldn't avoid the array of poison darts thrown at him this time.

Uncountable poison darts penetrated Ivan's body. Anyone else would've died from the deadly poison in them. Ivan was strong enough to survive, but he could no longer fight. His knees gave in and he dropped to the ground, face down. Once Ivan fell, the children were next. Ivan watched helplessly as a barrage of poison darts collided with his leftover powder barrier protecting the children.

"Give it up, old friend. That Gainsworth kid and the Anon toddler with him need to die. We'll try our best to save your great-grandson and the Elemental girl, though. I promise. So, for now, just concentrate on healing yourself," said Husk as he and the clan members on his side surrounded Ivan.

"You monster! Them being Gainsworth or Anon doesn't matter; what matters is that you are killing defenseless children!" said Ivan as he used all of his energy in a last-ditch explosion to hurt Husk and all his goons. Now, if I can only muster enough energy to take out the hidden dart shooters!

Night had finally come to Kracten. In the darkness of night, it was hard to find the dart shooters who had hidden well. The last of the explosive powders evaporated, yet the onslaught of poison darts kept coming. Husk and his men were regaining their footing as Ivan lay unmoving. The children's deaths seemed certain. Yet, miracles often happen in the direst moments.

Suddenly, Ivan saw a huge ice dome forming around the area where the children were, and the poison darts couldn't penetrate its thick walls. Husk and his men stopped moving too, almost as if someone sucked out all their energy. Finally, he saw Krayola running at full speed towards him.

"No! Don't come, protect the children instead of me," said Ivan meekly as he tried to remain conscious. However, Krayola reached Ivan despite his protests. She grabbed him by the neck and ran back to the girls.

Lore closed all entrances to the ice dome as soon as Krayola reached them. "Oh no, Mr. Renegader, you are badly hurt!" said a panicked Des.

"Don't worry about me! Concentrate on keeping this dome secure!" replied Ivan.

"Lore here has the abilities of a first-generation Anon. She is extremely powerful. So, she can keep us safe within this ice dome," Des assured Ivan.

"Yes, but not for long. She is just a baby, and the attackers are full-grown warriors. I need to get back out there and fight!" said Ivan as he tried to get up, but his body didn't support him, so he slumped back down.

"You are in no condition to stand, let alone fight!" said Des as she helped him sit upright against the wall of the ice dome.

"Then what? Should we just sit around and wait to be taken down?" asked Ivan.

"No. Teach me how to fight them instead," said Des.

"Teach you? Now? In midst of battle?" asked a shocked Ivan.

"It's either that or be beaten by those people outside," said Des, pointing at Husk and his men, who were trying their best to get inside the dome. However, Lore was using her power to the fullest while channeling the powers of Mother Anorea. So, none of the enemies could get in, until she got exhausted, that is.

Ivan thought about the situation and realized he had no choice. "Fine. Let's make the most of this brief respite. I'll teach you whatever I can," said Ivan.

CHAPTER THIRTY

Darkness shrouded Ethan and everything around him. He was no longer within the Gainsworth part of the ancestral realm. He was taken to another place. A more ancient and secluded space, existing within the bounds of the ancestral realm. He wasn't alone though. There was another presence.

Calico Paradigm, his father's former lover, was holding Ethan hostage, or so it seemed. She had been awfully quiet ever since kidnapping him. She didn't try to harm him in any way, neither did she physically constrict his movement. In fact, she helped him get on his feet after he stumbled in the darkness. It was then that she illuminated the shadow, so that Ethan had better visibility and could easily move around.

Ethan looked around and saw it was only the two of them there. "Why did you bring me here? Do you plan to kill me to fulfill the curse you gave?" he asked.

"The curse given to the Anon royals and your father to become bereft of children, you mean?" asked Calico.

"Yes."

"Do you know why that curse was given?"

"To avenge the fall of the Paradigms."

"That is one part of it."

"The other is your jealously for my mother, who you thought took my father away from you."

"Is that what Edwin told you? Lies! Hear me now, child. I had nothing but respect for your mother, Princess Regal of the Anons. It is your father that I have problems with. We were madly in love with each other, until I made the decision to support my family, the Renegaders. It was a mistake, for my family was in the wrong. I apologized for it several times, but your father didn't care. He married your mother just to spite me."

"That may be how things started out but, in the end, no one loved my mother more than my father."

"May be, but he too sided with the wrong people, for Princess Regal was one of the only good ones in the Anon royal family. The rest of them are weak and broken men who pretend to be almighty. In their quest to reign supreme, they have brought Areliam to the brink of ruin. I'm sure you saw an example of the destruction they caused in Ragonia."

"I have," said Ethan while lowering his eyes. An indication of the immense guilt he felt for his family's role in destroying Areliam.

"So, what do you think about all this, and what will you do to fix it?" asked Calico.

"Obviously, it's wrong, and I'll do anything in my power to correct things," replied Ethan.

"What of the Veiled Ones? Will you do everything you can to free us and return us to our former glory?"

"Yes, absolutely!"

"Why? How can a person like you, who has only benefitted from the new status quo, help us? What is your motive behind this?" asked a suspicious Calico.

"I...I realized the truth that no one can be happy by hurting others. Sooner or later, we have to serve the greater good, or we'll lose what little we have. My father sided with the Anons against his own people. He got a lot of wealth, power, and stature in return. However, first he lost his wife, then most of the Gainsworths lost their powers, and now he lost his life. My uncles fulfilled the long held Anon desire to rule supreme, but they are annihilating the universe in the process. So, I just want to right all our wrongdoings and create a better world for all," said Ethan.

"What if I tell you that the only way to create a better life for all is for you to die?" asked Calico.

Ethan closed his eyes, then smiled and said, "Kill me. I'm ready to forfeit my life for the greater good."

Calico looked at Ethan with pity and said, "You have given up on life, bogged down by the sins of kin and father. Such a heavy burden on one so young! I'm convinced of your dedication towards fixing the things your family has broken. So, I'll remove the curse I placed on your family. Not only that, I'll even help you break the power-draining curse on the Gainsworths. However, you must save them first."

"Save them? What do you mean?" Ethan asked worriedly.

Calico materialized three mirrors in front of Ethan with a snap of her fingers. Each of them showed a different scenario. In one, Leo and Leona were surrounded by an army of dead, in a fiery landscape. In another, Lore, Desdemona, Krayola and Ivan Renegader were stuck inside an ice dome that was under siege. The last mirror showed a group assaulting the protective shield around the Gainsworth ancestors.

"What is going on?" asked a panicked Ethan.

"All your allies are under attack. My grandmother is testing Leon to see if he is worthy enough to keep alive. Some of the Renegaders are trying to kill you and your sister to avenge their lost family members. On the other hand, my father brought some of his best fighters and a few Transenders to take down your ancestors."

"Take down my ancestors! How is that even possible? You cannot kill people who are already dead. Not to mention, how did they get inside the Ancestral Realm in the first place? The connection was sealed off!" said Ethan.

"They are Renegaders, age old rivals to Gainsworths. There isn't a spell in the world made by a Gainsworth that can't be broken by a Renegader. Given enough time, of course. Also, Leo's constant journeys into this realm diminished the potency of the sealing spell," explained Calico.

"All right, but there are far more Gainsworths than the attackers. They can take the few Renegaders and Transenders who showed up, right?" Ethan asked nervously.

"No, they can't. Not when they all are extremely weak from Emanuel's power syphoning and fighting against powerful enemies," replied Calico.

"I want to help them. No, I *need* to help all of them! What can I do to help? Please tell me?" Ethan asked desperately.

"Decide who you want to help first. Then we can strategize about how to help them."

Des and Lore are the safest for the moment. The ice dome is not showing any signs of breaking even after being attacked so fiercely. Leo seems to be in the most trouble right now, but I know he'll figure out a way. He always does. However, if I don't help my ancestors right now, all of them will be wiped out!

"We should help the Gainsworths first," said Ethan after a lot of deliberation in his mind.

"You sure you don't want to help Leo first? He seems in dire need of backup."

Ethan smiled. "You don't know Leon Hearth-Bringer the way I do. He can survive anything. However, my weakened ancestors don't stand a chance. I need to make sure they survive!"

"Fine. Then you need to break the death-link connection of the Renegaders."

"How do I do that?"

"See, death-link connections are basically out of body experiences where the spirit leaves the body to commune with ancestors. So, there are three ways to break a death-link connection. One is to successfully complete the ritual, another is to harm the body while the ritual is in progress. The last and the most difficult is to hurt the spirit strongly, so it automatically retreats to its vessel to heal. You have to use the third method, as the other two are not possible to accomplish right now."

"Ok, let's do it! Then we can go help the others."

"Let me warn you, though; it won't be easy."

"I don't think it was ever meant to be."

Edwin kept looking at the cracking protective dome overhead. When he first opened his eyes inside the Ancestral Realm, he was furious! How dare Emanuel erect this barrier and syphon of energy from their ancestors without his knowledge!? He was the leader of the clan, it was his right to know. However, now he was glad it was here to protect them against the Renegaders and the Transenders.

Edwin casted a spell to illuminate the usually black areas outside the dome to pinpoint enemy locations. Isaac Renegader was out there leading a group of Renegaders and transformed Transenders. There were only four Transenders who appeared in their morphed forms. A dragon, a giant python, a huge bear, and a colossal spider. All of them were attacking the dome and breaking it apart bit by bit. However, the real problem was Isaac and the one hundred warriors standing behind him.

Isaac, a tall, lean black man with short hair and eyes that spewed venom, stood ready to strike. Thankfully, Edwin still had most of his powers. For reasons unknown to him Emanuel never syphoned his powers. The loss of power Edwin did have came from when he was alive. Out of all the Gainsworths, he had the best chance of surviving the enemy. So, he decided to fight them head on.

Edward too retained most of his powers. The rest, though, already had a lot of their powers syphoned. Beating the attackers in their weakened state was not possible. Luckily, Kendall was on his way to get help from the Hearth-Bringers. They just needed to hold on until backup from the Hearth-Bringers arrived.

"Father! I don't think the dome will stand till the Hearth-Bringers get here. So, we must prepare to defend ourselves. Everyone, line up in accordance with your power levels. Those with the most power stand in the front. Those with the least will be at the rear. Everyone else with mixed power levels will stand in between, with the more powerful being closer to the front. Cursebinders on the left, Spellcasters on the right," said Edwin.

Edward agreed with his son's plan and stood at the helm of the Cursebinders. "Cursebinders, start casting curses to slow down their advances! Spellcasters, be ready with your barrier spells. Edwin and I have the most power left, so we will fight them directly while you all provide support. Is that clear?" asked Edward.

"Yes, sir!" replied everyone in unison.

"I will take the Renegaders. You take the Transenders," said Edwin.

"Be careful! The Renegaders seem to have brought their most powerful fighters," warned Edward.

Edwin nodded in reply and said, "I can still hold them off until the Hearth-Bringers get here."

"Good to see you are finally trusting others!" remarked Edward.

"Say what you want about them, but at least the Hearth-Bringers stick to their word," said Edwin.

"Agreed!" was the last word Edward said before the dome cracked open and the enemy poured in.

The Cursebinders were able to stop the enemies in their tracks for a few moments. That is all the time it took for Edward to take on the Transenders. Edward channeled his powers into long energy vines that spread out from him and bound all the Transenders. The vines sucked out their spiritual energy and cut them down to size. Then he hurled their stolen energy back at them swiftly. The energy hit them with a forceful impact strong enough hurt their spirits.

Their death-link connection was broken, and their spirits were returning to their bodies. However, Isaac Renegader intervened before that could happen. He sucked the energies of the Transenders into himself with his spirit blade, Spiritus Clepta, a weapon especially made to transfer the opponent's powers to the wielder. Except, in this case, he used it on his allies.

"That was low, even for you. Could you have not spared your own followers?" asked Edward.

"Oh! That's rich, coming from you. All I did was put these beings out of their misery. After the curse was enacted, the Transenders shapeshifted into their transcended forms to escape it. It worked, but eventually, many lost their consciousness as they continued to remain in those forms. Now most of them are no longer capable of returning to their original Veiled One forms. So, all I did was kill an animal and not an ally. You and your clan are the real sinners here. You are the ones that helped Anons destroy your own race!" replied Isaac.

"No one can change the past, Isaac. However, we still have a chance at rescuing the future. Drop your desire for revenge and work with us to save Areliam," beseeched Edward.

"Now you want to cooperate when it's your turn to be annihilated! You bloody coward!" yelled Isaac venomously.

"I'll take responsibility as the former head of the Gainsworths. So, punish me all you want, but please allow your vengeance to end with me. Let the rest of the Gainsworths go, please," pleaded Edward.

"Never! Your ancestral line ends today. I'll devour the spiritual energies of every Gainsworth ancestor here, then use that to kill all the living Gainsworths. After that, I'll destroy the Anons as well. None of you will escape my wrath!" proclaimed Isaac.

CHAPTER THIRTY-ONE

U tter chaos reigned supreme in the Gainsworth zone of the Ancestral Realm. The Renegaders had broken through the protective barrier and were attacking the Gainsworth ancestors. They wanted to dissolve Gainsworth spirits into raw energy, which could be weaponized against the Anons later. Luckily, the limited connection to the Ancestral Realm only enabled a hundred Renegaders to get through. However, due to Emanuel's power syphoning, most Gainsworths were too weak to fight back properly.

As one of the few left with a lot of power, Edwin knew he had to do most of the fighting. So, he jumped in headfirst, attacking the enemy. He took his spiritual form of a tiger and started munching on the front-line attackers. The ones that got through were slowed down by the few Cursebinders still able to use their powers, while several of the Spellcasters, who had some powers left, made a weak barrier against the oncoming assault.

Edwin was powerful enough to cast spells with just his thoughts. So, he thought of a magnetic spell that pulled back all the assailants that got past him. Once those assaulters were in front of him again, he tore into them.

Edwin vanquished twenty Renegaders by himself. He ripped them apart with his teeth, crushed them under his paws and slashed them to pieces with his claws, harming their spirits so violently that they might never be able to return to their bodies. This served the purpose of thinning enemy numbers in the real world as well as in the spirit world. However, Edwin grew weaker and more exhausted with each kill. He knew he wouldn't be able to keep this up for long.

The Renegaders were not fearful. They seemed ready to lose their lives in pursuit of their revenge against the Gainsworths. Nevertheless, they realized that close-quarter combat was a losing gamble. So, they changed tactics. They stepped back many paces and spread apart. Then they bombarded the Gainsworths with arrows made of spiritual energy. Edwin created a strong gust of wind that threw the arrows back at the Renegaders.

During the fighting, Edwin caught a glimpse of his father easily taking down the Transenders and talking to Isaac afterwards. *Good. Keep him busy, Father. He is an extremely powerful enemy who'll be hard to defeat. I need to beat all his lackies before I deal with him.* Alas, Isaac didn't spend too much time with Edward before joining his men in attacking the Gainsworths.

Isaac redistributed the stolen energy from the four morphed Transenders evenly amongst his men. This, in turn, resulted in the Renegaders producing larger and more dangerous projectiles. Spears, cannon balls, along with numerous more arrows were fired against the Gainsworths now. Edwin tried to stop as many of them as he could with his wind gust spell, but it wasn't enough. A lot of the projectiles got through and broke the weak barrier created by the Spellcasters.

Edward tried to help his son. His vines reached out to capture the spirits of the Renegaders. Isaac thwarted him, though, countering Edward's energy sapping vines with the dark energy of his own sword.

Once the last barrier protecting the Gainsworths was gone, irreparable harm was done. The projectiles crushed the souls of many Gainsworths, turning them into pure energy. Then Isaac collected those energies and reallocated them to his soldiers. Isaac's men used that excess energy to renew their attack more powerfully.

Both Edwin and Edward went into the defensive, where Edward created a barrier of vines. Edwin, on the other hand, tried to share his powers to strengthen the weakened Gainsworths. However, the continuous bombardment of projectiles broke through Edward's barrier easily. Edwin again tried to stop them, but it was too much for him to handle. Meanwhile, Edward struggled to remake his vine barrier;

however, Isaac stabbed him with his sword before he could do so.

One by one the Gainsworths began to fall, their immortal spirits being reduced to raw energy used as fodder to hurt other Gainsworth ancestors. It was then, when all hope seemed lost, that the Hearth-Bringers arrived.

An army of spirit wolves appeared on the battlefield. All of them made quick work of the Renegaders. However, their leader Kendall specifically aimed at Isaac. Kendall's blue wolf bit off Isaac's hand holding the Spiritus Clepta, stopping him from stealing any more energy.

"How dare you! Whose side are you on, Kendall?" asked Isaac as he punched Kendall with his one good hand.

"The side of betterment of all," replied Kendall.

"How can helping these Gainsworths be for the good of all?" Isaac asked.

"We gave the Anons a chance to manipulate and use them against us. It was us and our policies that outcast them. However, it's no longer just about us. Our infighting is leading to the death of Areliam. At this moment, we need to put all our grievances aside and work together to save Areliam," answered Kendall.

"Oh, how things change! You fought against them and lost miserably. All the Hearth-Bringer adults are dead, and your children are being brainwashed as we speak! So, what exactly has brought about this change of heart? Why do you want to help them now?" asked Isaac. However, Kendall did not answer him, remaining silent instead.

Isaac looked around and saw all his soldiers fall and their spirits return to their bodies in the real world. Then he looked at Kendall and smirked. "Do you think I'm defenseless now that you have taken away my sword and my men?"

"Give up, brother. Let all the hatred go so the new generation can save Areliam," said Kendall.

"New generation... Ah, I see what all this is about. You had one son who you turned back at the Battle of Behemoth. Calaren, was it? He must have created a family by now. So, you have grandchildren who convinced you to help the Gainsworths! Too bad the Gainsworths killed my only child. Now they must pay, and since you are siding with them, you must suffer as well," Isaac said as he activated his powers.

A dark fog originated out of Isaac that engulfed the entire area. All the souls trapped inside stood frozen and slowly started to decay into nothingness. Isaac's Renegader ability was the power of rot; anything he touched with his power decayed. His infamous sword, Spiritus Clepta, was dangerous, but he did not need its strength to win.

It was at this moment that Calico brought Ethan back to the Gainsworths. "Oh, no! Father used his power already. It is too late!" said Calico.

"No! It can't be! I can still see my ancestors struggling to keep their souls alive. We have to help them. There must be something we can do!" Ethan begged.

"I can try to talk to him, but I don't think he will listen to me," Calico concluded.

"Please, at least try your best to make him listen! Please!" Ethan pleaded with Calico.

Calico looked at Ethan empathetically. She knew what it was like to lose a whole clan, and she wouldn't wish it on her worst enemy. "Alright, I'll try to convince him and even fight him if need be, but see that sword over there? Take it and hide it where my father cannot use it anymore. We can't have that sword boost his powers," said Calico while pointing at the sword on the ground still being held by Isaac's bitten off hand.

Ethan nodded in response. "Good, also make sure to stay out of sight. I can't protect you while fighting my father. Understood?" asked Calico.

"Yes," said Ethan.

Calico waited until Ethan hid within the darkness. Then she called out to her father, "Father, Father, please stop this! Stop all this torture at once!"

Isaac heard his daughter's voice and stopped wreaking havoc instantly. "Calico, my daughter, is that you?" he asked.

"Yes, Father, it's me. I'm here to implore you to stop all this violence and forgive the Gainsworths. Uncle Kendall is right. We all need to work together to save Areliam," said Calico.

"What is the point of saving Areliam now that you no longer live in it?" asked a saddened Isaac.

"I, as a Veiled One soul, will always be a part of it and want it to thrive no matter what!" replied Calico as she kept tabs on Ethan, who took advantage of the thinning fog and grabbed Isaac's sword.

"I'm sorry, my daughter. I'm not as big-hearted as you are. I will never forgive them. I will destroy them even if you don't want it," said Isaac as he resumed his attack.

"Then you leave me with no choice," said Calico as she activated her Paradigm powers.

Paradigms were the clan of the Mother. Founded by Lapis Lazuli Hearth-Bringer, the Paradigms had the ability to channel Mother Anorea's powers. Calico used her Paradigm abilities to rein Isaac in.

All of a sudden, Isaac's fog started to thin out as his spirit form started disappearing. Meanwhile, Emanuel's sealing dome was rebuilding itself. "What have you done?" asked Isaac.

"I channeled enough power to regenerate the protective dome, which in turn diminished your power to damage the Gainsworth region," answered Calico.

"Fine, daughter. If you don't want me to hurt all these Gainsworths, then I won't. But I will have my revenge against the one who killed you," said Isaac as before disappearing, he put all his power into one last attack. In a feat of rage, he created a chunk of decaying fog that rushed towards Edwin.

Ethan saw the decaying fog charging at his father, and his body moved on its own. He had already lost both parents, but if he could at least keep his father's soul intact, he would—whatever the cost. So, he stood in front of Edwin and let the fog hit him instead, saving his father by sacrificing himself.

CHAPTER THIRTY-TWO

T he boiling lava of the hellish lands was creating a scorching heat wave. Leo was only there in spirit, but even he could feel the heat burning his soul. The hotness only increased after Khalifa shut the gate behind them. That was before she brought down all the flying cases. All the beings in them were now out and coming straight for Leona and him.

The inhabitants of the cases were all criminals. They had harmed Veiled Ones at large, in one way or another. So, there was no way they would let them go on account of them being a woman and a child. Leona tried to open the closed entrances many times. However, it didn't even budge a single inch.

Finally, Leona gave up trying to open the doors and turned around to face the incoming adversaries. It was hard to believe the things that came out of the cases were ever normal. Steam came out of some of the melting bodies as they walked towards them. The only good thing was that they moved slower than snails. Being stuck inside the cases for a long time severely hindered their mobility, and it would take a while for them to reach Leona and Leo. Slowly but surely, though, they progressed towards them.

Leona growled at them as they came closer. Khalifa chuckled, seeing Leona act tough. By this time, she had come out of her case and was leisurely sitting in a corner and observing everything. For some reason, Khalifa suffered none of the restricted motion like the rest of her hellmates. Khalifa was the strongest of them and had them all under her control. Seemed like she was just bored while waiting for her time of release. So, Leona and Leo's struggle was nothing but entertainment for her. "One little wolf against an army of dead. Sometimes life is so unfair, no?" Khalifa asked Leo.

Leo ignored her as he tried to use his Pathfinder powers to open a portal to escape from there. "Ah, did you forget that our powers don't work in here?" asked Khalifa in an amusing tone.

This can't be true. Otherwise, she couldn't contact outside and puppeteer the whole Mother's Womb incident. Not to mention she did close the gates and opened all the cases. There must be some trick to it.

Leo searched the gates minutely, hoping to find clues as to what was going on. He found many small open spots on the solid metal doors that carried a familiar energy. Leo smiled as he figured out what was going on with just these couple of clues.

As he turned around to share the information with Leona, he found both of them were surrounded. Leona put herself in between the horde and Leo. She would protect her grandson even if she had to sacrifice her immortal soul in the process. Thankfully, Leo already figured out a plan to get them out of this situation unscathed. He jumped on Leona's back and said, "Quick, Grandma, jump over them and land on the cases." Leona followed Leo's instruction and jumped over the heads of their pursuers.

Under Leo's command, Leona hopped around until she reached the case farthest from the horde.

"Well done! Putting distance between yourself and the enemy until you can figure out a counterattack. I'm impressed! However, you need to come up with a solution soon. Otherwise, it'll be impossible for you to get out of here alive," taunted Khalifa.

"Well, I live to achieve the impossible, Great-grandmother! Also, I'm more worried about you right now," retorted Leo.

"Really now?" asked Khalifa mockingly.

Leo smiled mischievously before speaking. "My dear forsaken Veiled Ones, please hear what I have to say. I know that Khalifa Hearth-Bringer must have promised you freedom, but she lied. She will not be able to keep that promise. Renegaders bypassed the Gainsworths sealing spells on the Ancestral Realm and contacted her. She was depending on that Renegader presence to get out of here. However, there is only one problem. The amount of Renegader energy present is not enough to get all of you out.

There is only enough for one person. Did she not tell you that?"

Leo paused dramatically to let this information sink in. Meanwhile, the dead kept looking from Leo to Khalifa to figure out the truth. "I sensed the same Renegader energy I felt on Kracten pouring in here through the holes in the door. Only the amount was very miniscule. If you don't believe me, feel the energies coming from outside yourself." Said Leo.

After Leo said so, several of the dead sluggishly walked over to the gates. There they felt the quantity of Renegader energy. Indeed, it was very small. Then they slowly turned to the others and affirmed Leo was telling the truth by nodding their heads.

Taking advantage of the situation, Leo said, "Currently, only one person can take you out of here, and that's me. However, I need to get rid of her before I can do that." He pointed at Khalifa.

When Leo looked at Khalifa, he noticed she was frustrated for the first time since they met. *Got you!* The tables had turned. Instead of Leona and Leo, Khalifa was the target now, and she did not like this new development. "They'll get rid of me? Don't be ridiculous! I'll get rid of them instead," said Khalifa before attacking the half-dead sinners.

Unlike the rest of the dead, Khalifa was able to move quickly. She used her speed to smash into the others, tearing apart the few in the front right away. Then she grabbed the nearest living dead and twirled him around, hitting the rest.

Khalifa Hearth-Bringer was a total monster. She crushed the heads of the fallen. Punched holes through some of them. She tore some of them from limb from limb with her bare hands. Broke their skulls with headbutts and used someone's broken arm as a club to beat the others.

Leo closed the lid of one of the cases and comfortably sat on it to enjoy the show. Leona, however, was very worried. She didn't want Leo to witness all this violence, so she put one of her paws in front of Leo's eyes. "So much violence is not suited for a young one like you."

"Don't worry, I'm very smart. I can handle it! Really, Grandma, I'm a prodigy of the ages stuck in the body of a ten year old boy. So, let me just enjoy the views, please," said Leo, removing Leona's paw.

"Be careful. She'll come after us as soon as she is done with them," Leona said nervously.

"No, she won't. Trust me," said Leo as he watched Khalifa dispatch the last of her former allies.

Once Khalifa was done killing all the opponents, she looked at Leo with bloodshot eyes and said, "You're next."

"Hey, it's not my fault that all your underlings were useless. Who knew they would turn on you so easily? You need better henchmen. Don't you know incompetent minions are the number one reason for the downfall of their masters?" Leo replied jovially.

Leo's wit completely disarmed Khalifa. She let her anger go, then laughed and said, "What can I do? It's hard to find good help these days."

"Well, that is where I come in. I freely offer my honest cooperation, in return for you abiding by my conditions, of course," said Leo.

"Of course. So, you want a truce until all Veiled Ones are free and Areliam is safe. After that, we'll fight it out and whoever wins gets to rule Areliam according to his or her ideology. Is that correct?" asked Khalifa.

"Why do your thoughts automatically veer towards fighting? Afterwards, we'll talk about things in more detail. Also, I need you to help me recruit Mr. Ivan Renegader. Just tell him to help me out in every way possible, and I'll take care of everything else," said Leo.

Instead of answering Leo immediately, Khalifa went silent with a thoughtful look on her bloody face. "Calaren, your father was much like you. Smart, capable, but never responsible enough to follow things to the end. He threw away everything for your mother. How can I trust you won't repeat his mistakes?" asked Khalifa.

"I think you are distorting the truth a lot here. Grandma and others told me how it was you that kicked him out. He only stood by the woman he loved. There is nothing wrong with that!" Leo stated firmly.

"There you go, like father like son. I understand the feeling of love and want. I have loved the same man all my life, but I never let that get in the way of my duties," said Khalifa.

"In the way of your ambitions, you mean," Leo corrected Khalifa.

"Call it whatever you like. However, I need assurance that you won't forsake your mission for a woman," Khalifa said grimly.

"Fine! Tell me, what can I do to make you believe my commitment to freeing all Veiled Ones and saving Areliam is genuine?"

"Take a blood oath on the Mother that you won't pursue love, sex, or other distracting elements. At least until you achieve your goal," said Khalifa.

"No! That is too extreme. He is just a child. The penalty for breaking a blood oath is certain death! You cannot ask this of him!" Leona interjected loudly.

"It's ok, Grandma. If taking this oath makes Great-grandmother trust me, then I'll take it. However, in return you have to take an oath to not hinder me and convince Great-grandfather to help out. Agreed?" asked Leo.

"Agreed," said Khalifa.

Khalifa drew an ancient sigil on the ground with her and Leo's blood. Both of them stood in it. Then Leo said, "I, Leon Hearth-Bringer, promise on Mother Anorea that I will not pursue love or sex until all Veiled Ones are free and Areliam is saved."

Khalifa also took an oath. "I, Khalifa Hearth-Bringer, promise that I will not get in Leon Hearth-Bringer's way until all Veiled Ones are free and Areliam is saved."

Once the oath was done, Leona asked, "Now what?"

"Now we go our separate ways. Great-grandmother, please bust the door open so I can find a Pathfinder ancestor to teleport you out of here. Before leaving, though, please come with me to meet Great-grandfather and convince him to help me!" said Leo.

"No need for you to go anywhere," said Khalifa as she reached out to Ivan and told him what needed to be said. "It is done," she said before breaking down the door with one mighty kick. Once outside, she said, "I have my own way of getting out of here. See you soon in the outside world. One last thing, this is for making me fight all those losers." That was the last thing Khalifa said before punching Leo hard in the stomach.

Khalifa's punch was strong enough to make Leo fly through the air. It caused enough damage to send Leo's spirit back to the real world. The only thing that still kept Leo in the spirit realm was his desire to save the Gainsworths. As Leo's spirit was returning to his body, he heard Dorian's voice yelling about the Gainsworths being attacked by the Renegaders. Thus, Leo willed his spirit to stay. However, it took a toll on his body, which was lying in a pool of blood back on Kracten.

CHAPTER THIRTY-THREE

The night was on its last hour in Kracten. Husk and his men tried all night to break inside the dome made by Lore but failed miserably. They even tried to dig a tunnel underneath, but Lore had frozen the ground beneath them as well. So, Husk and his men couldn't get in. Finally, they retreated to get some much-needed rest. Thus, Lore kept Ivan, Des and Krayola safe all this time.

Ivan used one of his powders to light a floating fire to illuminate and warm the inside of the dome. He also figured out a game plan to defeat Husk. Under his instruction, Des was meditating to balance the Creation Elemental powers within her. Ivan was extremely tired, though. Husk had weakened him considerably. It would take days for him to recuperate properly. Ultimately, Ivan gave way to his exhaustion and asked Krayola to keep an eye on the girls as he fell asleep.

It was when Ivan drifted away to sleep that Khalifa appeared in his dreams. "Hello, my love. It's been a long time," said Khalifa.

"My love! Is it really you?" Ivan asked excitedly.

"Yes, it is," replied Khalifa.

"It has been so long! I love you and I miss you! I miss you so, so much!" said Ivan as he broke into tears.

"If you truly loved me, you would've aided me in my conquest," said Khalifa.

"You know I want nothing more than to be forever by your side, but I do not condone bloodshed."

"Well, you know our great-grandson doesn't condone violence, either. Actually, it's because of him that I'm here. You need to help that boy. He has potential. Out of all my descendants, he is the only one that inherited my intelligence.

He is also nonviolent like you, so you should be a great fit," said Khalifa.

"So, it's true! You really did want me to help him! I thought he was just lying," said a shocked Ivan.

"Oh no, he lied. It's just he has both the wit and the guts to make even his untruths into reality. It is what I like about him," said Khalifa.

"Yes, he inherited the Pathfinder conmanship for sure," said Ivan.

"My love, I can feel you are injured, but I can also sense danger near you. You need to wake up now. I promise to come find you soon," said Khalifa before disappearing from Ivan's dream.

"Come find me? How? You are dead!" mumbled Ivan as he woke up at Desdemona's screams.

"Ethan! Ethan! What happened?" yelled Desdemona as she saw Ethan's body going into a seizure. Blood was coming out of his mouth and other deep wounds that suddenly appeared on his body.

Ivan saw Ethan losing too much blood fast. He had already bled enough that both he and Leo were laying in a pool of blood. "Quick! Feed Ethan this powder. It'll stop the bleeding! His soul must have suffered a huge blow for his body to react this away. We can't heal his soul, but we can make sure his body is intact at least," said Ivan as he handed over the last of his healing powder.

"What about Leo? A wound just appeared on his stomach area, too," said Des.

"That's probably because Khalifa hit him to teach him a lesson. Don't worry, he'll be fine," said Ivan.

It was around this time that the dome started to crack. Lore was at her limit. She was a first-generation Anon with access to Anorea's power. However, there was only so much her little body could handle. Blood was flowing out of her nose and ears, and her body was shaking.

"Ok, this is it. That little baby has done all she can. The rest is up to us. Take the lead, Desdemona. I still can't move much, so I'll stay back and defend. And Krayola, you already know what you have to do," Ivan said and fed something to Krayola before handing her a pouch of powder and a letter.

Ivan took out a metallic colored powder from one of his many pouches and sprinkled it in the surrounding area. The powder hung in the air and solidified, creating a floating cage. This magical cage had the power to deflect any projectiles and most other attacks for a short period. Desdemona helped Ivan and the boys get inside it, then she went back and grabbed Lore. "You have done more than enough, little one. Now, it's my turn," said Des as she handed Lore to Ivan and closed the cage's door. Both Des and Krayola stood ready to face the enemy outside the weakening ice dome.

The dome broke apart at the first light of dawn. Lore finally succumbed to unconsciousness as she used up the last of her powers. Krayola swished away as soon as the ice crumbled down, with Ivan's powder pouch and letter hanging from her mouth. Husk and his men didn't even see where she went, and they didn't care either. They were exhausted and just wanted to kill Ethan and Lore. So, they also didn't notice Des not putting up a fight and quietly stepping aside.

A hurt and exhausted Husk stayed behind with a couple of guards while the rest of his men attacked Ivan. They threw everything they had in trying to break Ivan's metallic cage. The hidden shooters also attacked Ivan with various projectiles. It was then that Des made her move. She ran up to Husk and his men and blasted them with creation energy. Husk, like most Renegaders, had destructive abilities, susceptible to attacks utilizing creation energy. Also, his injured body was in no condition to handle the burst of creation energy. So, Husk and his men immediately fainted, leaving the rest of the attacking party without any instruction on what to do.

Ivan had sensed both creation and destruction energy inside Des. However, thought creation energy will be more apt to use against the Renegaders. Given the limited time, though, he could only teach her how to harness her creation energy for one outburst. So, both of them decided to use Desdemona's creation energy burst on Husk in a single surprise attack. For, like Ivan, Husk too was hurt and would not be able to handle the dose of creation energy. Once Husk was out of the picture, dealing with the rest would become easier.

Des turned to face the others. Isaac Renegader had taken most of the clan's younger members to fight the Anons. So, the Renegaders left in Kracten were mostly of the older generation. Their powers had dwindled over time. However, experience took the place of limitless strength, and with it they were still able to wreak havoc.

Only a few minutes had passed since the collapse of the ice dome. However, the protective cage Ivan and the boys were in was almost dissolved at this point. They assaulted Ivan on two fronts. The angry Renegaders continuously used their leftover power to decay the cage. Meanwhile, the constant barrage of projectiles decreased the protective capability of the cage with every single moment. Sweat poured down from Ivan's body as he used all his powers to keep fortifying the cage.

Desdemona took on the Renegaders surrounding the cage to alleviate some pressure off of Ivan. She drained a large portion of power from the Renegaders surrounding the cage, only to infuse it back into them. Before, she could only syphon energy, but now she could use that same energy to do further damage. It was second of the three tricks she learned from Ivan the night before. However, she was still too weak in the execution of this skill, which could prove dangerous for her.

Unable to bear their own destructive powers, several of the attacking Renegaders fell. Many of the ones still left standing became incredibly angry. A large portion of the attackers stopped attacking Ivan and turned their attention to Desdemona instead. "Why are you helping the people who destroyed your race?" asked one of them.

"Ethan and Lore had no part to play in it. Lore wasn't even born then!" replied Des.

"But by killing them, we can hurt their parents, the Anon Royals who were directly responsible for destroying the Elementals," said another.

Poor kind and innocent Desdemona didn't know how to respond to so much hate. So, she used her mother's words instead. "I don't want to be a cog in the wheel that propels injustice. We kill them and they kill us back, while all of Areliam suffers in the process. If you truly want justice, then go punish the ones who actually committed the crimes. But I know you won't do that because all of you are cowards! You know they are too powerful, so you are trying to kill their unconscious children to get back at them. Shame on you!" said an enraged Desdemona.

"What do you know of the suffering we went through? You too are nothing but a coward who survived by hiding, and now you are siding with the enemy! You are on their side, so you have no right to live! Everyone, get her!" yelled someone.

If only they knew! In a brief moment all the misery Desdemona witnessed throughout her life flashed in her mind. Her parents' numerous sacrifices, years of solitude, growing up in utter lack where she didn't even have enough food. If it wasn't for Leo bringing in more rations, they'd still be eating bugs to survive. Not to mention if Ethan and Lore didn't help, Ragonia would have no hope of recovering. Lastly, if it weren't for them, Desdemona would've never left Sanctuary. So, she had suffered more than enough. However, unlike other people, she didn't wallow in self-pity. Instead, she was fighting to make a positive difference in Areliam, and won't let anyone stop her!

"Fine! Bring it on, oldies. I'll show you the power of the new generation that believes in peace and prosperity for all!" said Desdemona, who materialized her new weapon while boiling with rage: a white sickle made of creation energy attached to a black destruction energy chain with a ball at the end. Making it was the last thing Ivan taught her. However, just like the rest of the skills, this one too wouldn't last for long. *Let's use this to the fullest for as long as I can before I run out of energy!*

Des jumped back to put some distance between her and the attacking horde of Renegaders in front. Then she whipped around the destruction chain with the metal ball at the end and hit the attackers' front line. The chain's destructive element collided with the Renegaders' own destructive energy, causing repulsive shocks. Anyone touched by the chain experienced electric shocks running through their bodies. The heavy weight of the metal ball ramming against Renegader bodies caused a lot of physical harm as well.

After seeing their frontal assault going wrong, the Renegaders decided to surround Des from all sides instead. Des slammed her sickle to the ground in response. White creation energy sprawled out and spread from the point of impact until it reached the assailants. Like Husk, most Renegaders fell unconscious, as they couldn't take the surge of creation energy. Then Des went around putting minor cuts with the sickle on the Renegaders still standing. Giving them a more potent dose of creation energy.

All the attention was on Des at this point. The Renegaders decided to take her down before continuing their attack on

Ivan and the boys, leaving only the hidden shooters to keep bearing down attacks on Ivan's cage. However, what they did not notice was that the shooters had stopped firing for a while now.

Good! Krayola must've achieved her first objective. Now I just have to hold on till she gets back with help.

The angry Renegaders came charging at Des all at once, leaving her no choice but to hurt them seriously. Des started madly wielding her chain and sickle, resulting in the Renegaders sustaining substantial bodily injuries. Soon her weapon ran out of energy and disappeared. So, she had to resort to hand to hand combat. Thankfully, she was fully trained in close range fighting by her father and was able to stand her ground.

Desdemona kept punching and kicking the enemies until she couldn't anymore. There were too many for her to handle on her own. Finally, one of them got the best of her and threw her hard on the ground, breaking her rib cage. Before Des had a chance to get back up, one of the Renegaders pushed his foot down on her back. An immense pain engulfed Des and blood started pouring out of her mouth as she lost consciousness.

She would have died if Krayola didn't come to her rescue. Krayola pounced on the man holding Des down. Then she let out a terrifying roar that froze the attackers in fear. After that Ivan's supporters came to take care of the rest.

Ivan had given Krayola his sleeping powder, which she used around the hidden shooters to bring them down. It didn't affect her because of the antidote he fed her. So, she was able to stay awake to run and get Ivan's supporters. As displeased as the Renegaders were with Ivan for harboring Ethan and Lore, they still couldn't let Husk hurt him this badly. Ivan still had a lot of supporters in the clan. They took his side upon reading his letter explaining the situation, which he had sent with Krayola. Then they came to aid Ivan and the kids, subduing Husk and his men on their behalf.

CHAPTER THIRTY-FOUR

L eona ran like the wind towards the Gainsworths with Leo on her back. Leo was still reeling from Khalifa's punch, but right now, he was more worried about Ethan. Dorian said that the Gainsworths were in utter disarray and Ethan was badly hurt. *Something must be very wrong.*

They saw the broken protective dome of the Gainsworths trying to unsuccessfully repair itself as they neared the Gainsworth area. Signs of a fierce battle were seen from afar as well. Wounded Gainsworths and Hearth-Bringers littered the space. Their souls emitted a much fainter light than usual while they withered in pain. *I didn't know souls could even get hurt so badly!*

Leo couldn't spot Ethan anywhere. However, most of the people who could still move around were gathered in one spot. So, they went there in hopes of finding Ethan, and they did—at the brink of oblivion. His already very faint spirit was deteriorating more and more with every second. Several people around him were trying to heal him, but it was of no use.

"No, no, son! You cannot leave me! Do something, Calico!" yelled Edwin.

"He took a direct hit, Edwin. I'm trying to slow down the decaying process while you heal him, but it's not working. Most of the damage was done on impact, so rebuilding his soul from what little is left is not possible," replied Calico.

"I don't care! This is Renegader powers, and you are a Renegader. Hell, you are a Paradigm! So, channel Anorea's power to save him. Undo what your father did. Now!" Edwin yelled even louder.

"Calm down and use all your energy to save your son!" said Edward as he too tried to pour all his energy into Ethan.

"If I could've healed him, I would've done so already! It's impossible with my power level. I won't be able to bring him back even if I sacrifice my spirit for his. Only prime elder Lapis Lazuli can save him now," said Calico.

"Well then, go get her!" Edwin yelled once again.

"I don't think she will come. Uncle Kendall already went to get her a while ago. If she wanted to come, she would be here already," Calico said softly.

"Why? Is it because of me? Please, don't punish my son for my sins! I admit I was wrong in enslaving Veiled Ones, and I'll take whatever punishment you deem fit. Just please save my son. I'm sorry! Please forgive me! Destroy my spirit if you want, but please revive my son's soul. Please, please...please," howled Edwin as tears poured from his eyes. However, even he knew it was too late. All their attempts to save Ethan were nothing more than the struggles of a dying fire.

Leo stood stunned, watching the scene before him. He usually had a plan to fix any situation, but even he didn't know what to do now. Ethan saw Leo standing quietly and beckoned him. Leo slowly walked towards him and sat down by Ethan's side.

"Hey, idiot. Looks like I won't be much help to you from now on. But don't worry, my father and grandfather will help you in my stead. That is my last wish," said Ethan as the final semblances of his spirit started to fade.

In that moment, Leo reacted instinctively and reached out to grab Ethan's disappearing spirit. A bright white light blasted out of Leo, that consumed both him and Ethan. That light was the indication that Leo had finally awakened his Hearth-Bringer powers to the fullest. So far, he had mostly been using the powers of prime ancestor Areon Hearth-Bringer, but now Leo used his own.

Leo's first use of his power was to rescue his friend from certain death. However, it was a tall order to fulfill. He almost depleted all his spiritual energy to save Ethan. As Ethan's spirit regained its form, Leo's soul started to lose its own until finally both of them retained weaker forms of their souls. Once the healing was done, an exhausted Leo lay down beside Ethan.

"It's a miracle! Ethan is healed! He is back!" exclaimed Edward while Edwin said nothing and only hugged Ethan.

"It's not over yet. Both of them need to return to their bodies immediately and take proper measures to heal. Otherwise, their souls will decay," cautioned Calico.

"Send Ethan back first, I'm not going anywhere until I get what I want," said Leo softly but firmly.

"I refuse to go back alone. I'll leave when he leaves," said Ethan.

"You stubborn little mules! This is no time to throw tantrums! Get back to your bodies now and come back when you are healed. We'll discuss everything then," Edwin scolded Ethan and Leo.

"Oh, no! I'm not falling for this age-old adult trick. You think just because we are young, you get to sideline our needs and desires to suit your timetable. No, no, no! I will not leave until I get the things I'm after," said Leo as he struggled to get on his feet.

"I'm staying with Leo as well!" Ethan reiterated as he too tried to get up.

"Ethan Gainsworth, I brought you up better than this. You will listen to me and return to your body right this second!" Harked a frustrated Edwin.

"No," said Ethan defiantly as Calico helped him up.

"Fine, if you won't return on your own, then I'll just have to force it on you," said Edwin as he readied a spell to return Ethan's soul to his body.

"Hey, you can't force Ethan this way. It's child abuse!" Leo protested on Ethan's behalf when he finally got up on his feet with Leona's support.

"If you want our help in freeing the Veiled Ones we will oblige, but we have conditions. However, we will discuss all of this — later. Now get back to your bodies, both of you!" commanded Edwin.

"No," said Leo and Ethan simultaneously.

"Hearth-Bringers, please make your kid return to his body so my son can go back as well," said Edwin through gritted teeth.

Edward interjected before things got out of hand. "Why don't we just hear them out? It would certainly be much faster than arguing with them. What was it that you want, little one?"

"You didn't tell them everything?" Leo asked Ethan.

"I didn't have the time because of all this." Ethan moved his hand, pointing at the chaos surrounding them.

"No problem! I'll do it now. So, I need two things. The first is your cooperation in taking down the Anons, freeing the Veiled Ones, and saving Areliam. The second is your support for the abolishment of clan transfers," said Leo.

"Wait, isn't that four things?" asked Calico.

"Don't go on the math, dead aunty, go on the feelings. That is more important!" replied Leo.

There he goes with the dead aunty thing again! Thought Ethan.

Leo ignored Ethan's crooked side glance and continued speaking. "So, who's with me?"

"No one, except the Pathfinders and Hearth-Bringers. All the other clans refused to work with the Gainsworths," replied Kazdin.

"Well, that can't be. Did you tell them how important it is?" asked a shocked Leo, who couldn't believe what he just heard.

"I told them that the eminent destruction of Areliam can only be diverted with us working together. However, they said they don't care since they are already dead," said Kazdin.

"The prime elders also refused to help further. They said their duty was fulfilled when prime ancestor Areon gave Leon his powers," said Kendall, who had returned from his unsuccessful meeting with the prime ancestors.

"These good for nothing dead people!" exclaimed Leo angrily. "Hey, can someone enhance my voice so it reaches every corner of the Ancestral Realm? I need to chat with these lazy spirits."

Edwin and the other Gainsworths who still had some power left volunteered to do so, but Ethan objected. "I will do it," said Ethan.

"No, you are still hurt! You didn't have a lot of power to begin with, so you definitely shouldn't use your powers now!" Edwin said while trying to stop Ethan.

"It must be me, Father! Let me do my part," said Ethan as he concentrated all his powers and looked at Leo. Edwin understood his son's feeling and let him cast the spell while remaining on standby to help if needed. "Enhance voice," commanded Ethan, and Leo's voice was amplified. Once it was done, Ethan nodded at Leo, telling him his voice could reach everyone now.

"All mighty ancestors, I am your descendant Leon Hearth-Bringer. I have something important to say, so please listen with open hearts and minds! For eons past, both old and new generations of Veiled Ones protected Areliam. However, as time went on, we forgot our true purpose and started infighting. Instead of safeguarding Areliam, we spent our energies on putting each other down. The Anons took advantage of this and used us against one another. They used the Gainsworths who felt shunned by the rest of the Veiled Ones to enslave us all.

"We, who taught Anons to use their powers, today are enslaved, tortured, and humiliated by them. Let me tell you how bad things have become. When I was just five years old, I accompanied my father to a private performance. A wealthy and powerful Anon nobleman invited us. Unfortunately, I somehow got something really sticky in my hair that couldn't be removed. So, my hair needed to be cut. My father took me out to the nobleman's estate in the countryside to cut my hair. He told me the creation story of Areliam and the Primordials to keep me calm while doing so. However, cruel reality set in as soon as the story ended.

"A few Anons overheard Father and started beating him to death. They said he broke the law of Veiled Ones not being allowed to discuss past information. I tried to stop them, but I was too small and weak to do anything. So, I asked for help from every Anon present there, including the nobleman who owned the estate. No one helped, though." Leo's hands started shaking at the memory of that traumatic event. Tears were threatening to overwhelm him, but he kept them at bay. "Everyone stood still and let the violence continue. Only one man stepped up, and that person was none other than Edwin Gainsworth. He was the only one who helped despite all the grievances he had against Father and the rest of us Veiled Ones," said Leo while pointing at Edwin.

Edwin lowered his eyes. He was shameful for the part he played in the downfall of the Veiled Ones. As much he wanted, though, he could no longer change things back to the way they were. Helping out people like Calaren in some instances was the only thing he could do. He took no pride in doing the right thing in those cases. For he was one of the main culprits that made such cases possible in the first place.

Leo took a brief pause to collect himself before he started to talk again. "It was only recently that I remembered about Mr. Edwin Gainsworth saving my father's life. In fact, I didn't recognize him at all the second time we met. Slowly but surely, though, I recalled that it was him and wanted to see if he would still help. However, he was dead by then, so I recruited his son instead."

Actually, what you did was not recruitment but kidnapping. However, I'll let it pass for now, thought Ethan as he saw his father's face give testament that Leo was telling the truth.

Leo's plea to the ancestors persisted. "That incident taught me that we need to unite to fight the Anons. So, I came to you, my ancestors, seeking your knowledge and strength. However, you won't help because instead of fixing the future, you are busy doling out punishment for past transgressions. You stay silent and watch Areliam burn in the name of penalizing the Gainsworths. However, the truth is that, you have become weak and cowardly!

"You are comfortable up here, away from all the torment and pain. You are afraid to lose your peaceful afterlife by engaging in our struggles. So, you're using your might and legendary intelligence in only preserving the Ancestral Realm while the rest of us suffer! Some of you might also be tired of watching us hurt others and ourselves with our endless infighting. Just think, though: if you are this fatigued from watching, then how exhausted are we from living through this hell? Nevertheless, we still hold on to hope. Yes, we have faltered. Yes, we have sinned, but unlike you, we haven't given up yet."

Leo's voice shook with rage as he continued speaking. "I will fight on even without your help, but let me ask you a few questions. What is the use of an intellect which only serves one? What use is that power which doesn't defend anyone else from harm? What is the point of having all the knowledge and wisdom in the world if you won't use them to help others in need?

"We Veiled Ones have always been shepherds of creation. We cannot shrug off that responsibility! Especially when all of Areliam is at risk. So, I call on you now to step up and fulfill your duty, both to your descendants and to Areliam! Answer the call, ancestors! Respond! Please help! Areliam needs you, all living Veiled Ones need you—I need you!" said Leo as he fell on his knees and broke into tears. A sense of abandonment seeped into the deepest part of his soul. Ethan too ran out of power and slumped down on the ground. He didn't raise his head to hide the silent tears flowing down his cheeks.

The Hearth-Bringers and Gainsworths looked on helplessly as Leo broke into inconsolable weeping. Dorian and the few other Pathfinders that joined him were also motionless. All of them were lamenting their own actions that had led to the current situation. All of them felt the children's agony, but there wasn't much they could do except cry with them. Uncountable hopeless tears were shed, as there wasn't a dry eye in the vicinity.

Suddenly, a voice echoed in the darkness. "We heard you, and we are here to help." Prime ancestor Lapis Lazuli and the other eight original clan leaders stepped out from the shadows. Lapis Lazuli, a plump black woman with poufy hair, walked up to Leo and gave him a tight hug. Leo stretched out his hand towards Ethan and he stumbled through till he got to Leo. Lapis Lazuli then embraced both the boys who had grown up too soon due to their circumstances.

"Don't worry, everything will be alright," said Lapis Lazuli as she patted the boys' heads.

"Now we just have to figure out a way to explain Lore's and my absence to my uncles," commented Ethan.

Leo immediately stopped crying and said, "Oh! I have a plan for that!"

Ethan smiled and asked, "Don't you always?"

CHAPTER THIRTY-FIVE

T he Anons were preparing for war. Inside the walls of the Anon palace, strategies were being made to re-invade Ragonia. Since finding out Ethan and Lore were there, Emanuel had spent every waking moment figuring out Ragonia's current position. Meanwhile, Ran and Orias were preparing special gear to allow their men to survive Ragonia's toxic environment. King Ran was going to personally head the search party. He was going to do everything in his power, even wage another war, to get his children back.

At the moment, Emanuel, Ran and Orias were cooped up inside the palace strategy room, having another discussion about how to proceed. "How can you still not know where Ragonia is? What happened to all the tracking devices we placed there?" asked Ran angrily as he slammed his fist on the table. His voice echoed through the silent room, amplifying the effect of his anger.

"You think I haven't tried hard enough? I tried everything, Ran! From searching the cosmos for Ragonia's energy imprints to acquiring data from the tracking devices. But nothing is working. All traces of Ragonia seemed to have disappeared, and the tracking devices have gone silent. The last data point communicated was when Ragonia started to move. We got nothing after that," Emanuel defended himself passionately.

"What about your ancestors? What did they say?" asked Orias, who, knowing things would get heated, smartly vacated the room of everyone but the three of them beforehand.

"Contact with the Ancestral Realm has been forcibly cut off as of yesterday," replied Emanuel.

"Not like they were of much help to begin with!" scoffed Ran.

Emanuel defended the ancestors by saying, "I talked to Edwin, Ran, and even he couldn't find Ethan and Lore. He said something was blocking the Gainsworth ancestors' attempts at locating them. Then, all of a sudden, I lost all communication with the ancestors. Whoever kidnapped the children also made sure we couldn't find them, no matter how hard we try."

"Enough games. It's time to make them pay. If we can't use the dead Veiled Ones, then we'll use the alive ones to figure out what's going on. So, Orias, torture all the living Veiled Ones until one of them spills something or the Veiled One ancestors start helping," King Ran commanded.

It was amongst this discussion that Ivan Renegader entered the palace strategy room through a teleportation mirror placed there. "That won't be necessary, Anon king," said Ivan as he pushed down a heavily injured Ethan on his knees in front of him.

"Ethan!" screamed Orias and Emanuel while King Ran used his water Anon power to materialize ice blades around Ivan.

"How dare you kidnap our children!" shouted Orias.

"Let Ethan go right now!" Emanuel demanded frantically.

King Ran was the only one who kept quiet amongst the chaos. Instead of him showing his emotions, the atmosphere reflected his silent rage. The room temperature dropped below freezing. Spiky ice blades grew out of every nook and cranny, all aiming at Ivan.

"Oh, stop with your overreaction. I'm just here to return your children," said Ivan, immediately exploding the ice blades around him.

"Well then, where is Lore and what did you do to Ethan for him to be like that?" asked an enraged Orias while getting ready to use his powers. Orias held amassing crystals that stored fire in his hands. He could crush them in moment's notice to release the fire within them on Ivan. Emanuel, standing by him, was ready to cast curses as well. He was making up curses in his mind.

"Now, now, is that any way to talk to someone who rescued your children?" asked Ivan.

"Rescued? From whom? Who are you talking about?" asked Emanuel.

"Think about things carefully. Do I look like the type who would go around stealing children? All my life I have kept to the Veiled One isolationist policy. I didn't participate in the war even though my wife and child died in it. I'm not the one who kidnapped your children. It was another from my bloodline. All I did was save them," said Ivan.

King Ran looked at Ivan's bloody clothes and haggard stance. *He seems to have fought a battle to free Ethan. But where is Lore? Is she ok?* Thought King Ran.

"What? From who?" asked a surprised Orias.

"It must be Isaac because he was the only one who escaped while Kendall Hearth-Bringer died in front of us! Calaren and his family also perished in the Mother's Womb incident. So, it has to be Isaac," Emanuel said aloud. "Is he also the one that caused the Mother's Womb incident? Also, what about moving Ragonia and cutting off connection to the Ancestral Realm?"

"Yes, you are right in your assumption. Isaac was involved in all of it. However, he is not alone in this. Khalifa is with him too," said Ivan.

"Wait, how? Khalifa Hearth-Bringer should be detained within the hellish lands of the Ancestral Realm!" said Orias.

"The Veiled One Ancestral Realm, *as you know it*, is no more!" exclaimed Ivan.

"What do you mean by that?" asked a shocked Emanuel.

"Doesn't matter what I say. You will double check anyways. So, you'll find out for yourselves very soon," replied Ivan.

Emanuel reeled from the revelation. Like all Veiled Ones, he too had a deep connection with the ancestors. For the first time, he was feeling what all the other Veiled Ones were feeling when their connection was cut off. He couldn't believe this actually happened and looked at Orias for reassurance. Orias felt Emanuel's discomfort and gave him a supportive look.

Ran, though, didn't care about much else except Lore and Ethan's safe return. "For the many times you have uttered the word, *children*, I only see one child. Where is my daughter, Renegader?" asked King Ran menacingly.

"She is unharmed. You will have her delivered to you upon my safe return," Ivan replied.

King Ran smirked. "Smart move. Now give my nephew back and name your price, or are you doing this from the goodness of your heart?"

"I can't waste my goodness on the likes of you. However, I have my own principles and I think Ethan has suffered enough," said Ivan.

"You monster! What have you done to him?" asked an enraged Emanuel.

"I have done nothing but protect him. Even put my own life on the line to keep him alive. However, I cannot continue to do so. So, you take him back now and give me what I want," said Ivan.

"What is it that you want for the safe return of both our children?" asked King Ran.

"I want the same thing I have always wanted. Peace. If you remember, I was the only impartial one during the Primordial Wars. I stayed out of things even when Khalifa and the rest of the Veiled Ones interfered. I want the same thing now. A new war has started, and I want nothing to do with it. Give me your word on the Mother that I, my clan, and all the inhabitants of Kracten won't be harmed by you during this war."

Orias wanted to give his word right away, but Ivan shook his head and pointed at King Ran, indicating the promise must come from Ran. King Ran stood quiet for a long time before drawing his sword and using it to spill his own blood. "Fine, Renegader. I'll give you what you want, but I want assurance from you that you will sit this war out as well," said King Ran.

"I give my word that no inhabitant of Kracten, including myself, will actively participate in this war," said Ivan as he stepped forward and gave Ethan to Orias, after which he spilled his own blood on the ground alongside King Ran's.

"Good, and when will I get my daughter?" asked King Ran.

"As soon as I return unscathed, she will be delivered to her room," replied Ivan.

Then Emanuel used the spilled blood to make a sigil on the ground upon which both King Ran and Ivan swore on the Mother. After which Ivan left through the mirror way, which broke apart as soon as Ivan used it to get back. Orias and Emanuel were already hovering over Ethan.

"Is Ethan alright?" asked King Ran.

"Physically, he is wounded, but that is not the problem. His spiritual and Veiled One energy is highly damaged," replied Emanuel.

"You two make sure he is taken care of. I'll go check on Lore," said Ran before running to reunite with his daughter.

***

Leo entered Lore's chamber through a portal with Lore in his arms and Desdemona right beside him. The room was elaborate. It was huge, much bigger than the place Leo shared with his parents in Solem. An extravagant crib was in the middle that had the softest white sheets and pillows in all of Areliam. Expensive and fancy toys lined the walls and lavish furniture adorned the space.

"Man, the rich and powerful sure know how to live it up! All of this just for a toddler! Can you imagine?" Leo asked Des.

"Mr. Renegader must have returned by now, so we should hurry and get back as well," said Des in return.

"You worry needlessly. This palace is so big that it'll take a few minutes even if they run at full speed to get here from the strategy room. Plus, we can portal out even at the last moment, and they'll never be able to follow us. You know, because I have full control of who gets to use my portals. So, we have more than enough time to enjoy the views," said Leo proudly.

"We need to return asap and disable all the tracking devices on Ragonia, so Anons can't trace us anymore. Also, our parents are worried sick by now. I'll handle my father, but what about you? Can you handle your parents, especially your mother?" asked Des.

"Ok, you and Ethan can't spend any more time together, because you are beginning to sound just like him. Anyways, you are right, those tracking devices need to be disabled. That and I cannot afford to anger my mother too much or she'll never let me out of her sight again." Leo sat Lore down on the crib. "The delivery of one Princess Lore of the Anons is now complete. Just as promised. Before we part ways, though, I want to thank you for all the times you saved us."

"Me too!" said Des.

"Kidnapping you was never part of my plan, but thank the Goddess that you were there. Otherwise, things would've been much more difficult. I know your brother doesn't want you being part of any future missions, but I have a feeling that it's inevitable. So, see you again soon, the youngest member of the free Veiled Ones and save Areliam movement! Until then, please trouble your brother a lot on my behalf, my little troublemaker!" said Leo.

"Gugugahgahgagaga," said Lore while nodding her head, indicating she'll do as Leo asked.

At that moment, Des heard running footsteps outside and alerted Leo. Leo immediately opened a portal to Ragonia and they left the Anon palace. Before leaving, though, Leo saw Lore smiling at him, assuring him that she will side with him in the upcoming war.

EPILOGUE

An atmosphere of celebration mixed with tension permeated throughout Sanctuary. Change was in the air, and everyone could feel it—they just didn't know how to react to it. The children rekindled the First Fire Pit. However, they have not come back yet. So, even though everyone was happy for Ragonia's revival, they feared losing Leon Hearth-Bringer, their primary resource bringer.

Politics was shifting inside the Ragonian underground city. The Hearth-Bringers, who were mostly ignored or scorned before, were now the main attraction. The Creation Elementals buttered up to June and Calaren, hoping to gain future favors from Leo. While the Destruction Elementals were acting friendly owing to Leo's role in relighting the First Fire Pit. Cal and June were even offered better accommodations, but June refused. Somehow, she, Cal and Leo became fond of Anorea's temple. It was where they spent most of their time in Ragonia. Plus, June always felt a sense of calm and strength whenever she was near Anorea's statue. So, she didn't want to leave its presence.

Besides certain hours when prayers were made, the temple stood empty. It was in those quiet times that June vocalized her worries to Cal. Currently, it was one of those times. "I'm going to ground that son of yours indefinitely once he returns," claimed June.

Calaren smiled and replied, "So you always say, but never do."

"Oh no, you watch. This time, I'll do it for sure!" June reiterated.

"Just make sure you let him out to get supplies. Otherwise, the rest of the Elementals will get angry," said Atlas, who walked into the temple at that moment.

"You're here again? Don't you have anything better to do than bug us continuously?" asked Cal.

"Well, Calaren I do not come here to see you. I keep coming here in hopes of seeing my Desdemona return safely," said Atlas as he sadly eyed a broken travel mirror tucked in a corner. It was the same mirror brought the Hearth-Bringers to Sanctuary, and ushered in the changing times.

Calaren saw where Atlas was looking, heaved a long sigh, and said, "Don't worry, they'll be back soon."

"You have been saying this ever since they left, but they haven't come back yet," said Atlas.

"Well, knowing my son, he should be appearing any minute now!" said Calaren confidently.

"Ma may love me most, but no one knows me better than you, ha Pa?" Leo asked jokingly as he, Des and Ivan stepped out of a portal at the exact moment Calaren finished speaking.

"DES!" yelled Atlas.

"LEO!" yelled June.

The children were ecstatic to meet their parents. Atlas broke into tears as he hugged Desdemona. Meanwhile, June lamented that Leo had lost too much weight, which he hadn't. After that, all was well, except Calaren became speechless after seeing Ivan.

Ivan walked up to Calaren and said, "So, you are the only adult Hearth-Bringer that survived. Who knew the runt of the litter would come this far?"

"Um... Hello, grandfather. Thank you for bringing the children home. Uh... It really is a pleasure meeting you again. But, um... I know how much you hate leaving Kracten. So, I'll have Leo open a portal to Kracten for your return trip right away," Calaren finished saying, while stammering throughout.

Ivan laughed and said, "You should wait on that. For if I were to leave, Leo would come with me too."

"Wait! What do you mean by that?" June asked.

"He means we need to evacuate to Kracten for safety. The Anon King promised not to harm the inhabitants of Kracten. So, all of us will become Kracten dwellers to remain protected from his wrath," Leo informed them all.

"Well, not all of us. Remember, you and I need to stay behind and remove all the Anon trackers. So, we can keep Ragonia out of Anon's clutches and all," Des reminded Leo.

"Ah yes! All this backend work is very important too!" exclaimed Leo.

"Don't worry. You will be leading the rebellion from the front by the time I'm done with you," Ivan said.

"Rebellion! What rebellion. You know what, don't tell me. I've already decided that no son of mine will partake in any rebellion, and that's final," interjected June.

"I agree! We are Hearth-Bringers, our forte is healing and artistic works. We don't do physical hard work like fighting very well. The last time we rode to war all the adults in our clan died!" said Calaren.

"Then what? Do you want your son to disarm his enemies with his wit alone, like he did with Khalifa?" asked Ivan.

"He did what!?" asked June and Calaren simultaneously.

"Ma, Pa, we obviously have a lot to discuss. Have no fear, though; I have planned for everything," said Leo, explaining his plans to his parents. It took a lot of convincing, but eventually, they gave in to Leo's persuasion. Thus, Leon Hearth-Bringer orchestrated the beginning of the counterattack against the Anons. Many hardships, obstacles, and sacrifices awaited him on this journey, but how he faced them is a story for another day.

ABOUT AUTHOR

Hi everyone! It's Diana. I also go by LegendofMystics on social media platforms like YouTube and Twitter. I'm a first-generation Bangladeshi immigrant currently living in the United States. I am an architect of dreams, an inventor of mythical worlds, and a pioneer of fantastical stories.

I write truthful, relevant, and entertaining stories in my spare time. Now you must be wondering, how does an author include real-world concepts like truth and relevancy in a fiction book? Well, my answer to that is even though my stories are fictional, the feelings and social messages in them are truthful and relevant. Now as for if they are entertaining or not, well, you just have to keep reading them to find out...hehe.

Also, fair warning: a lot of my stories reflect my political beliefs. I even wrote a book about how politics propels racism in America called THINK LIKE A DEMOCRAT FIGHT LIKE A REPUBLICAN: A Short Guide to Better Navigate America's Racist Environment. You can get a free digital copy of it by visiting my website, legendarymystics.com and signing up for my newsletter there. However, if you have a problem with the inclusion of politics in fantasy, then my books are not for you—I am not for you. That being said, I also plan to write in different genres like non-fiction, fiction, and romance. So, if you stick with me, I'm sure I can provide you with an enjoyable reading experience.

Lastly, I work as a full-time caregiver, which takes up most of my time. So, I plan on publishing only one book a year. Currently, I'm working on another epic fantasy book, called Gift of the Goddess (GOTG). It is about an end of the world scenario where a goddess offers to awaken divinity within humanity as the last chance for their survival. Please visit my website to find out more about it. GOTG should be done by the end of this year or the beginning of next year. I'll start working on the second book in the *Infinite* series after that. Thus, the second entry in the Infinite series is scheduled to be published in 2024.

So, that's it. Hope you enjoyed this book. If you liked it, please don't forget to leave a review! Also, connect with me on social media and sign up to my newsletter for updates on my future projects. Goodbye for now. I'll see you again soon on the plains of imagination, a.k.a. my next book.

ACKNOWLEDGMENTS

I would like to thank Lord Shiva, the God of destruction in Hinduism who destroys the unworthy. Thank you, God Shiva, for blessing me with the ability to write this book. Also, thanks a lot for helping me defeat all obstacles that came in the way of publishing it. Then I would like to thank my ancestors. The idea of the Ancestral Realm in this book came while I was doing various rituals of Hinduism dedicated to respecting the ancestors. Most importantly I want to thank my mother, without whose blessings my life is incomplete. Lastly, I would like to thank the wonderful people at Fiverr who made this book possible.

Book Cover Designer: Adeeba Sial (Fiverr ID: adeebasial0)
Editor: Cara Flannery (Fiverr ID: fluckyfiction)
Audiobook Narrator: Skye Alley (Fiver ID: aubergine07)
Formating done by Atticus